magic
&mayhem

Other titles by S. Usher Evans

The Razia Series
Double Life
Alliances
Conviction
Fusion

Empath

The Madion War Trilogy
The Island
The Chasm
The Union

The Demon Spring Trilogy
Resurgence
Redemption
Revival

magic & mayhem

The Lexie Carrigan Chronicles

S. Usher Evans

Sun's Golden Ray
Publishing

Pensacola, FL

Line Editing by Danielle Fine, By Definition Editing

Sun's Golden Ray Publishing
Pensacola, FL
www.sgr-pub.com

For ordering information, please visit
www.sgr-pub.com/orders

The Lexie Carrigan Chronicles

Spells and Sorcery
Magic and Mayhem
Dawn and Devilry
Illusion and Indemnity

Available in eBook, paperback,
hardcover, and audiobook

Contents

Dedication

To those who are broken,
May you come back stronger

One

I hit the ground hard, spraying sand everywhere and into every crack I had. But I couldn't linger long, not when a glowing ball of purple magic was flying straight for my head. I rolled out of the way and sprang to my feet, facing the glowing creature on the other side of the dark beach.

Creature wasn't really a good word for it but magical-representation-of-myself-I-used-when-I-wanted-to-spar was too long to say every time. I'd cleaved half my magic from myself, used a bit more to breathe some life into it, and then told it to come at me with everything it had.

Right now, it was kicking my ass.

Seeing as it was still my magic, I could've thrown in the towel and called it back. After all, I was starting my senior year of high school in the morning, and I didn't want to exhaust myself. But as a Warrior, a magical with the unique capability to use my magic in battle, quitting was anathema. The more I trained, the more I wanted to, until it was an itch that wouldn't stop. The only cure was to transport to this beach in the middle of nowhere and spar with myself until I couldn't move.

My muscles were already aching, but mostly because I'd been distracted and careless tonight. But if I was weak, so was my counterpart, and if I could land one good, hard attack spell, it would be over.

The problem was landing said attack spell. I was a habitual overthinker; my creature was not.

The creature moved, and so I did too. I feinted left then right, practicing short transport spells to stay one step ahead of the purple balls of magic flying toward me. She relied on magical memory, or the impression of spells I'd previously attempted, to fight, and I didn't imprint a memory until at least a few weeks of practice. This was a new technique I was trying, and I was fairly sure she couldn't keep up.

"Crap!" I cried as an attack spell smacked into my left shoulder, stopping me.

The creature came for me again, and I had to practice defense. I knocked away her attack spell with my own like two pool balls, sending them both across the ocean. It wasn't the best move because it drained me faster, but sometimes I had to stop worrying about efficiency and get the job done.

I fell to my knees and let a particularly harsh spell fly over my head. While she was recovering, I closed my eyes and let my magic do what it did best.

Although I felt I had nothing left to give, my magic knew better. It was good at finding the crumbs of power hidden in the tips of my fingers and toes. As magic gathered in my core, I formed an attack spell so powerful it could kill me. I made sure to leave a little behind, so it *wouldn't*. Then, remembering I had school tomorrow, I left behind a little more. The creature was already low on energy, so it wouldn't take too much.

I jumped out of the way just as a crackling ball of energy zoomed toward my head, and as I did, released the ball of magic I'd been holding.

The collision exploded so bright it blinded me. I didn't need to lift my head to know I'd won and was, yet again, alone on the beach. The sound of the waves lapping against the shore came back to me, lulling me into calm. I inhaled the salt air, dug my weak fingers into the soft sand beneath my body until my heartbeat came back to normal.

Deep down, I knew all my own moves, so victory was always hollow. This was simply a distraction, a way to keep my mind off the worries and fears that had plagued me for eighteen months, when a man from New Salem had killed my aunt and nearly killed me, too.

It had all started on the eve of my fifteenth birthday, when Aunt Jeanie informed me that I, and the rest of my family, had magic. She'd been pretty light on the details, which, at the time, had infuriated me. But then Gavon had shown up—and ruined everything.

First, he was kind. He mentored me, taught me how to use this new gift, and was the solid rock I'd counted on during those scary first weeks of magic. If that hadn't tipped me off that he was no good, I should've known when I found out he was from a gang of evil magicals who'd been banished to another world. But no, stupid me thought, "Oh, how interesting!" and continued to follow him like a lost puppy.

And that was how I'd ended up fighting for my life in a duel with Gavon's apprentice. And how Jeanie ended up dead.

I tried not to dwell on that last part.

I sucked in a breath and forced myself to sit up, letting the sand fall from my hair. It would take a few more minutes before I'd recovered enough to transport myself back home. Magic was a finite energy, and although I was much faster at healing than when I'd started sparring, it took a lot out of me to fight with myself.

Sadly, even though my sisters were a potion-maker and healer, neither one knew about my nightly activities. One because I didn't want her to worry. The other, well…

Thinking about Marie was enough to force me to stand. I brushed the sand off my arms and legs and found the small bit of my magic I'd kept in reserve. Then, knowing I would crash the moment I got home, I transported straight into my bed, feeling the cool pillow against my cheek before blackness overtook me.

I was back on the beach, standing beneath the moonlight. This time, I wasn't alone.

"Oh, don't cry, Lexie," he said, drawing up a deadly-looking spell. "You'll be back with her soon enough. Then your sisters will join you."

My magic throbbed beneath my skin, remembering what it was to fight with skill and practice, and I let go of control, deflecting and attacking with the grace of a practitioner much more advanced. My body danced as effortlessly as Gavon's had, and I drew up three spells of my own, not to kill, but to confuse.

"I do like a challenge," Cyrus said. "Unfortunately, I don't have time—"

I released a blast, if only to shut him up, and he blocked with a spell of his own, but the force had knocked him back a few feet. When I saw the confusion on his face, I knew he'd underestimated me, which meant I had him.

I exploded in purple and fury and power. The spell crashed into Cyrus, pummeling him mercilessly until he fell to his knees. Blood dripped from the corner of his mouth, and he panted, struggling to gather his magic. Somehow I knew, perhaps through the magical memory, that I was going to use the rest of my magic to destroy him, and I was going to die.

Goodbye Nicole. Goodbye Marie.

With a loud crack, I released my final magic—

I awoke suddenly, gasping for air and searching the room for the face that haunted my dreams. But the only sound was my own panicked breathing. Slowly, I sank back down into my pillows, tears mixing with the sweat coating my cheeks. I turned to muffle my cries in my pillow; our apartment was too small, and Nicole was in the next room over.

I still had no idea what really happened the night I almost lost my life in a duel with Cyrus, nor did I know why he hadn't come for us again. But I hadn't seen hide nor hair of him—or anyone else from New Salem.

Muscles aching, I rolled out of bed and wiped my face. I cracked open my door to the dark apartment and listened. Our apartment was small, so even from across the hall I heard my sister's soft snoring. It comforted me—but I wasn't quite satisfied.

I slid on my flip-flops and tiptoed out of the apartment, softly closing the door behind me. Ours was on the second floor of two, so I padded down the concrete and metal stairs as quietly as I could.

I kept to the shadows of the parking lot until I found a spot next to a tall oak tree. I gathered what was left of my magic and released it into the air, reaching toward the invisible barrier I'd erected. The magic responded in kind, lighting up before my eyes and confirming what I'd already known—nothing magical would get in or out unless I allowed it.

That was, of course, assuming I'd gotten the damned spell right.

As the light of the barrier faded and my magic returned, loneliness echoed in my chest. I needed help. Sparring only came naturally thanks to the magical memories I'd retained from before I was born. Everything else was always a question—was I doing it right? Did the charms and spells and enchantments do what they were supposed to, or was I just seeing what I wanted to?

As much as I hated to admit it, I missed Gavon. Or rather, I missed the Gavon I'd known before I found out who he really was. The man who'd taken me under his wing and answered every stupid question I had, even when I sounded like an idiot.

But even as I missed him, I couldn't ignore what he'd let happen—or that he'd been absent from my life since. I'd spent weeks parsing out if my feelings for him were because we were both Warriors, or because he'd intentionally made himself more appealing to me, or because he was my f—

I released a breath. I still had a hard time saying the word, even in my mind.

Nights like tonight, when my insecurity roared like a dragon, I wished he would appear out of nowhere again, offering a kind smile and a thoughtful response to whatever worry I had that night. But he was why I needed a barrier in the first place. I had to hope that this spell, which I'd enacted about three months after my near-death experience, was the reason why Cyrus hadn't come back for round two.

Because if I didn't, the fear would eat me alive.

A wave of exhaustion descended like a curtain, and I leaned into the oak tree. I was sure it was past midnight, and I was also sure that sparring with myself plus this late-night barrier checking meant that extra coffee would be required to get me out of bed in the morning.

But somehow it seemed fitting to continue to torture myself over the past. After all, had I just told someone about Gavon the first day I saw him, my family would've still been intact.

Two

My alarm blared at me what seemed like seconds after I'd put my head down on the pillow. In the darkness, I groped for my phone to mute the offending sound. Then, with a grunt, I threw it back down on the nightstand, hoping for a few more hours of sleep. The previous night's exercise hung heavily on my eyelids and behind my temples. But there were things to do, school to attend, volunteering to complete…

The list continued in the back of my mind as I pushed myself out of bed. Sand in my bedsheets scratched against my palms, and with a wave of my hand, I magically returned it to the beach. My sister might've had some questions about why I was tracking sand in when I'd said I was volunteering at the animal shelter last night.

My summer schedule had been jampacked with activities as I tried to fit every last extra-curricular onto my college applications. As long as I continued getting straight As, too, I *had* to get a scholarship and a spot at Georgetown. That had been my goal for about a year, and I was so close I could taste it.

But first I had to get myself out of bed.

With a loud whine, I stood and headed to the bathroom. My bones ached and protested the movement, and every part of me wished to go back to my soft pillows. Gavon once told me that Warriors don't whine, we just do. So I went, but I still whined.

Because screw him.

After I showered and dressed, I found Nicole in the kitchen, already hard at work cooking breakfast for the two of us. Of all the lives I'd ruined, hers had been the most affected by my stupidity. Just twenty-two, she'd dropped out of college to work full-time to pay the bills. She never told me much, but I knew things were tight financially. The only thing we had was the house, which we were able to sell to pay off Jeanie's debts. If Jeanie had left anything to us in her will, we didn't know about it, thanks to Gram…

At times, I had flashes of my grandmother, and I knew that something had happened to make me unbelievably angry at her. But when I stretched my memory for more, it went blank. I sensed there was magic at play, but all I knew for sure was we were completely on our own.

Nicole grinned when I shuffled into the kitchen. She and I looked a lot alike, with brown hair and pale complexions that burned rather than browned in the Florida sun.

"Good *morning*, senior!" she chirped loudly as she bounced around the kitchen, assembling my breakfast.

"You didn't have to go all out," I said, sliding onto a chair.

"Of course I did! You're a senior. It's such a fun year. Togas and homecoming and crowns and—"

"And if you think I'm going to do *any* of that nonsense…" I yawned as I pulled my phone to me, tapping at the screen to display my calendar for the week. "So I've got volunteer work this afternoon then I'm spending a few hours tutoring at the library. I won't be back until late, but I'll have my phone."

"Do you really have to keep volunteering?" Nicole asked, joining me at the table. "You should lighten your load a bit now that you're back in school."

I shook my head. "Georgetown's not going to see it that way."

Nicole pursed her lips. She wasn't exactly dissuading me from pursuing the college of my dreams, but she wasn't enthusiastic about it. "Georgetown is a lot of money, you know," she said, cleaning the pan in the sink. "It's not just tuition. It's books and fees, dorm and food—"

"I *know*," I said, shoveling the eggs into my mouth. "I've looked at all the fees and charges and I know how much I need every semester. And if they don't give me scholarships, I'll get loans."

"I don't want you saddled with thousands of dollars in debt, Lexie," Nicole said. "Why not try a local school here? You could save all your money and—"

"I'm *not* staying here." That was final. Too many memories in this town, none of which I wanted to bring with me. And even though I wanted to protect Nicole, I didn't want to be…*so close* to her. I couldn't even sneeze in my bedroom without her yelling "Bless you." I'd be lying if I didn't admit that part of my busy schedule was to get away from her, although I felt horrible about it.

"You're still a kid, Lexie," she said quietly, taking my now-empty plate from me. "I don't want you to have to grow up too soon."

"I'll take care of my dishes," I said, and, using a quick bit of magic, washed and dried my plate and returned it to the cabinet in the blink of an eye.

Nicole stared at her empty hands, but said nothing. Ever since…well, all *that* had happened, she'd been less enthused about the idea of magic. For her, it was simple to pretend she was a nonmagical. Potion-makers lacked the ability to transport, conjure, or even summon. Nicole's healing potions could replenish two-thirds of my magic with a single sip, but her cauldron had disappeared with the rest of our belongings when we'd sold the house. Now, the only thing she brewed was coffee.

As for me, I could ignore my magic as easily as I could stop breathing. The hum against my skin was ever-present, the urge to practice always there, even overpowering my guilt.

"I guess I should be going," I said, after a too-long pause.

"Have a good day at school," Nicole said, a little too brightly, the way she always did when we ventured into uncomfortable territory.

I walked out of the kitchen and summoned my bag. Then, making sure Nicole wasn't watching, I transported myself to school.

Transport spells were pretty routine now. The bathrooms in the arts wing were usually unpopulated this early in the morning, so I'd use my magic to find an empty stall and appear there. I'd wait a few breaths to make sure no one was in the bathroom with me then head to my locker.

Before I did, I checked my phone, just in case. Knowing what the outcome would be, I tapped out a short note to add to the long string of unanswered messages.

It's the first day of senior year. I wish you were here.

I waited.

Read 7:34am

Marie and Nicole had lasted two weeks in our apartment before their first blow-up fight. I'd come home to them screaming at each other with red faces, and had to play referee to calm them both down. Marie had stormed out—nothing new for my second oldest sister, who had the temper of a five-year-old.

It was new when she didn't come home.

At first, I'd been terrified Gavon or Cyrus had taken her. After being kidnapped myself (and being plagued by dreams of it for weeks afterward), I was almost certain she was being tortured—or worse. Nicole had seemed less concerned, but to calm me down, she'd sent Marie a text, which came back with a read receipt. That was enough for her; after all, it was doubtful Cyrus knew how to work a phone. And there was probably no cell reception in New Salem.

After three weeks and fifty more read-but-unanswered texts, I stopped trying. Whatever had set Marie off had been so bad that she didn't even want to communicate. And when an entire month passed without change, I realized this would be our new normal. Marie had always threatened to move out, but she hadn't even graduated high school. Though, knowing her, she'd probably used her magic to forge a diploma.

But because I'm a glutton for punishment, I still sent her texts on birthdays and holidays, along with the occasional photo, and got read receipts back. Eighteen months seemed like a long time to hold a grudge, but that was Marie. Even though we'd never gotten along, I missed her. We'd formed this strange unspoken bond when she'd healed me after sparring lessons, although I'd found out it was only because Gavon had agreed to give her money in exchange.

I glanced at my phone again. As far as I knew, Gavon had never made good on that promise, but Marie had to be getting money from somewhere. She was pretty, but she didn't like to work very hard. I tried not to think about all the other ways she could be supporting herself.

But there was nothing to be done about it, so I silenced my phone and magicked it back into my backpack, shifting mentally from Marie to the day ahead.

The first day of school always felt fresh and new, although today was bittersweet. Excited energy permeated the halls as I meandered toward the senior lockers. Doe-eyed freshmen greeted their friends and cast wary glances at seniors. Ragged juniors trudged like zombies, and I felt for them. My junior year had been jampacked with SATs, and college preparations, and every advanced and dual enrollment course I could fit into my schedule. This year seemed like a breeze comparatively, but I needed to keep my grades up all the way through to graduation. I had big plans, and I wasn't going to let *anything* derail them.

I stopped in the middle of the hallway, my gaze landing on a new face. That, in and of itself, was cause for surprise. My school was pretty small, and rarely did we get new kids enrolling. But add on to that the dark hair and thick, gorgeous lashes lining light eyes that could've been blue or green. Sharp cheekbones and full lips that complimented his soft, pale skin. My magic definitely saw something it liked as it squirmed and throbbed in my stomach. I couldn't tear my eyes away, caught by the *sexy* way the corners of his mouth turned up in amusement when he caught me staring.

At once, a thousand book-and-movie plots ran through my head and I hated myself for feeling so…smitten by a stranger. For all I knew, he could've been a serial killer—or worse, a distraction.

College, Lexie. Remember you need to get into college. You need lots of money to get into college. You are broke. You have no parents.

Well, I had a…

No. No parents.

I turned my flushed cheeks away, hoping it was just the shock of a new person that had caused such a reaction, and not that I was becoming, well, *twitterpated*. I'd had my share of crushes over the years, but my dating life was about as empty as my magic after I sparred. It was difficult to date in such a small school—most people were already paired off and would probably marry their significant other right out of school. Besides that, I'd always felt like an outsider, even before magic made the division clearer. I couldn't even count a best friend amongst my peers, let alone a boyfriend.

But this guy, wow. Handsome *and* new. He'd get snapped up quick.

By someone other than me. I had bigger things to focus on.

Still, when he followed me into my first period class, my

heart skipped a beat. His gaze lingered on me as he passed by to sit behind me, and my fluttering heart began to race. This couldn't be a coincidence. Was there actually a super cute guy who thought *I* was cute?

I struggled to keep it together, feeling his gaze on the back of my head and worrying if I'd brushed my hair this morning. Or if my shirt was crooked, or my underwear was showing over the tops of my jeans, or—

Get it together, Lexie.

This was why I didn't date. Not even ten minutes after meeting this guy, and I was already a mess. I retrieved my English notebook from my bag and wrote down my to-do list for the evening, if only to tear my brain away from Super Hot Guy.

Finally, the morning announcements were complete and the teacher, Ms. Grace, introduced herself and the expectations for the year. Then, she called attendance.

"Alexis Carrigan?"

I raised my hand. "I prefer Lexie."

The boy snorted behind me, reminding me of his presence. Well, at the very least, I'd find out his name. Then I could spend the rest of the year trying to forget it. Maybe Ms. Grace would put us in alphabetical order, and he'd be on the other side of the classroom.

"James Riley?"

"Right here."

The pen fell out of my hand.

Three

James Riley.

James Riley.

James *Gavon's fricking apprentice* Riley.

My pulse pounded in my ears and my fingertips glowed. How could I not have remembered the son of a bitch who tried to kill me in a dueling match two years before?

Oh yeah, I'd been too busy trying not get killed to decide if he was hot or not.

Well, he was definitely hot. And definitely a serial killer.

I glanced around the room, waiting for…something. Him to stand up and tell the class they were now under his…power? Something like that. But, except for the occasional sigh of boredom or scribble of his pencil, he caused no trouble. Ms. Grace was handing out the textbooks for the year, and when the stack came to me, I turned around and glared at him.

"What the ever-loving hell are you doing here?"

"Learning," he said, taking the stack from me with

infuriating normalcy.

"Learning *what*?"

"Lexie, is it? Please keep conversations to a minimum," Ms. Grace said, walking by.

The boy with the power to blow her to smithereens offered me nothing but a superior look, and I turned away from him.

I heard nothing of what Ms. Grace was saying. Hell, I'd even forgotten what the class was about. Two years, I'd been waiting for this moment. Waiting for Cyrus to reappear and finish the job he'd started in my aunt's kitchen—

"Careful, *Alexis*, you don't want the nonmagicals knowing your secret," came a deep voice in my ear.

I glanced at my fingertips, now sparking with purple magic. Ignoring the lingering warmth of his breath on my neck, I inhaled and exhaled, forcing myself to calm down until the magic receded into my body. But my pulse remained elevated, my gaze on the windows of the classroom, searching for the evil magicals from New Salem that I knew were going to appear at any second—

"I'm sorry, Lexie, am I boring you today?"

I jumped out of my chair. Ms. Grace peered down at me, her arms folded across her chest. Someone began to snicker as I stared at the teacher, unsure what I'd done wrong or what I needed to say.

"I asked if you would please read the first part of the syllabus to the class."

I quickly recited the first paragraph about tardies and expectations, and she moved on to someone else.

I heard his breathy chuckle behind me, and my anger

returned. What did I care if Ms. Grace thought I wasn't paying attention? I was going to single-handedly save the school from all the evil magicals.

Except, there was a severe lack of evil activity. There were no proclamations, no fireballs. None of the horrible things I'd lost countless hours of sleep over were happening.

So what the hell was going on?

I spent the class trying to keep my fingers from sparking and developing a strategy for engaging with James. All the carefully laid plans went out the window when class ended, and I spun around in my chair.

"Okay, *what* the hell are you doing here? What's your plan? Is Cyrus here? Is he ready for round two? Because I'm ready any —"

"If Cyrus were here, do you think *I* would be?" he drawled placing the book into his bag. "I already told you, *Alexis*, I'm here to study. Same as you."

"Bull fucking shit."

He chuckled and swung the bag over his shoulder. "I'll have to tell your father about your swearing."

Cold water doused my anger. *Your father.* He'd said it so casually, like it was a simple fact. And to him, it was. To me, it was an awful realization while sitting in a cold jail cell, being jeered at by a man who wanted me dead.

Of the many things I'd never forgive, Gavon not telling me himself after we'd spent six weeks together was pretty close to the top. Right after him allowing Cyrus to kill my mother and aunt.

James took my silence as a victory—the only one I swore he'd get—and left as if this was the most normal thing he'd ever done.

"Lexie?" Ms. Grace said. "You'll be late for your next class."

With a nod, I gathered my things and hurried off.

Where the son of a bitch was waiting for me. Although this time, he was having an easy conversation with Callista, a pretty girl who'd been in some of my advanced classes. She was as excited about James as I'd been before I knew who he was, and I couldn't blame her. There was nothing about him that wasn't handsome. But I felt it my duty, as her classmate, to warn her.

"I wouldn't if I were you," I said, walking to an empty seat nearby.

"W-what?" Callista said, glancing between the two of us.

I settled in my seat, unwilling to lose this war against him and glaring icy daggers at James. "He's not a good person. I'd avoid him."

James glanced over his shoulder, reminding me of a cat lounging in the sun. "That's not very welcoming, Alexis."

"My name is Lexie. And you aren't welcome here."

"The name your father gave you is *Alexis*."

My face must've betrayed the storm of emotions that f-word awoke in me, because James' grin widened.

"I thought your father was dead, Lexie?" Callista asked, looking between us. "Or gone? Do you know her father? Where did you say you came from again?"

James quirked a brow in my direction, and I dared him to say something. But the physics teacher called the class to take their seats to begin the period.

I barely paid attention to the introductions, taking my textbook from James with a glower as I passed the stack behind me. Whatever he was playing at, I would find out and put a stop to it. Like hell he was just here to *learn*.

But learn he did. From my vantage point behind him, he seemed for all the world like an earnest student. He wasn't called on to answer questions, nor did he offer any, but his pen was never far from the paper. If I hadn't known better, I would've thought he was just as studious as I was.

But I did know better. Which was why I didn't believe any of it.

When he showed up in my third period, I was now sure he'd be in every single one of my classes. Because why not? This was obviously an attempt to torture me into submission. Or to annoy me so much I'd make a mistake.

Or maybe I already had. Perhaps Cyrus *was* using James as a decoy, and had already gone after my sisters. It had been three hours since I'd last seen Nicole. Could she already be dead?

Panic blossomed in my chest, and I reached into my bag to search for my phone. Leaving it hidden in the bag, I hastily tapped out a message to Nicole.

Are you all right?

"Alexis, no phones in class," came the terse reply from the advanced vocabulary teacher.

I put the phone down, blushing as James caught my eye with a smirk. Was that because I'd gotten in trouble, or because he had my sisters on the brink of death? Again, he offered me that curious quirk of his brow, as if he knew something I didn't and was enjoying it very much.

My phone buzzed and I dove for it in my bag.

Fine. Why wouldn't I be?

"Lexie, if you don't put away your phone, I will have to take it."

My face grew hot again, and I stashed the phone back in my bag. Nicole was safe, but what about Marie? A read receipt could be forged very easily. Cyrus could figure it out. Gavon could *definitely* figure it out. What if Marie had really been dead all this time or *tortured* and I hadn't even gone to look for her and
—

My breaths grew shorter and spots danced in front of my eyes. Not *again*. The last thing I needed was another panic attack. I was supposed to be a Warrior. How could I possibly defend my sisters if I couldn't even breathe right—

Not helping.

Heart pounding in my chest, I glanced around the room. I counted five items I saw: my pen, my notebook, the desk, the carpet, the shoe of the boy sitting in front of me. I touched the pen, felt the paper and the wood of the desk, then grabbed the cloth of my jeans. I listened, pinpointing the sound of the teacher, the squeak of the dry erase marker, and the sound of the clock ticking on the wall. I breathed in the cool, AC-filled air of the classroom, and caught a whiff of the perfume of the girl in front of me. And I bit my pen, tasting the plastic in my mouth. I repeated the process until the pounding in my chest subsided, which took a good twenty minutes.

Then I exhaled, exhausted and embarrassed.

After Jeanie had died, I'd started getting panic attacks, normally when I thought I saw Cyrus or dreamed about him. It was odd how I'd faced death without fear, but when it came to living after it, I was a chicken. So I'd Googled a few tricks for how to deal with it, mostly so I wouldn't have to burden Nicole with *another* cost, and had been using them ever since.

But the attacks left me drained and miserable, not to mention ashamed that I couldn't control my own thoughts. Although at least this time, I had reason to be fearful.

The anxiety still burned my chest, but it wasn't careening out of control anymore. No one was the wiser, and I wanted to keep it that way. Carefully, I chanced a look behind me at James. Head down, scribbling quickly, focused on the teacher. He met my gaze and smiled cruelly.

I mustered what was left of my anger and glared back.

I'd never been so thankful for lunch. At the very least, I knew I could slip away for an hour and no one would notice I was gone. I wanted to check on my sister, and on the spells I'd cast around our house.

Nicole had worked at the local pharmacy even before Jeanie died. It honestly fit with her potion-making magic, not that she'd ever pick up a potion book again. Before things went to crap, she'd had aspirations of working as a chemical engineer at a pharmaceutical company. Now she stood at a cash register and dealt with crotchety old people all day. She swore she was happy, but it was a total lie.

"Lexie! What are you doing here?" she asked, concern evident on her face as soon as she saw me. "Are you all right? You look pale."

"Fine, fine, just..." The words died on my tongue. If I told

Nicole that James was at school with me, she'd worry. Scratch that, she'd flip out and never let me leave the house. But she couldn't protect us against him or anyone else. So what good would come from stressing her out? This was my problem to deal with, not hers.

"Lexie, are you sick?" She'd met me on the floor of the store and pressed a hand to my forehead. "You're sweating like crazy and you're clammy. Do I need to take you to the doctor?"

"No!" I said. "No, I mean. I'm fine. Just wanted to see you. Make sure you're okay."

She half-smiled. "I'm fine. What about you? Do you need to eat?"

"Yeah, that's all. Just hungry." I needed to leave before I aroused more suspicion.

"I told you you're working yourself too hard," Nicole said, pressing the back of her hand to my forehead to check again. "You're going to run yourself into the ground."

"Sorry for worrying you," I said, stepping back. "I just needed…tampons. That's all."

"I thought you wanted to make sure I was okay?" Nicole said, eyeing me. "Lexie, is there something you aren't telling me?"

And there it was, my opening to be honest with her. To just tell her James had shown up and I had no idea what it meant. To confess that I'd just had a panic attack when I thought of her and Marie dead and that I could probably use an anti-anxiety medication or maybe even a good therapist. To mention that I spent weekends sparring with a magical apparition of myself in case Cyrus came back and I had to protect the family.

But I couldn't burden her, not when I'd already ruined so much of her life. Ignorance was bliss, and I promised myself *this* time, I would deal with the problem before anyone got hurt.

"Lexie?" Nicole pressed.

"I'm on my period. Of course I'm emotional right now."

It was a boldfaced lie, but it worked. Nicole dropped her hands from my head and pursed her lips. "Okay…so what was that text earlier?"

"Just… wanted to make sure you were having a good day at work." I needed to leave, before I blurted out the truth and made things worse. "Bye!"

And with that, I darted out of the pharmacy.

Are you okay?
Read 12:52pm

A few days ago, that would've been enough to quell my fears, but today I needed more proof. Which was why I was back in the apartment, digging through my closet until I found it: the hairbrush Marie had left when she'd stormed out. It was the only thing I had with her DNA on it.

The spell book I needed appeared next to me, already flipped to the right page. This was one of the books Gavon had given me, and although he hadn't stuck around long enough to teach me how to use the spell, I'd figured it out eventually.

Health Charm

This charm can be applied to an object containing bodily material. When magic is

added, the object will reflect the health of
said person.

If the object glows,

White, then the person is healthy and
hale;

Yellow, then the person is sick or in
distress;

Red, then the person is losing blood;

Black, then the person has perished.

I held the brush in my hand and concentrated, releasing magic from my palms into the strands of hair. I felt the connection with Marie, the white glow of her healing magic that permeated her DNA, somewhere far away.

Gavon had once said that magic moves faster than light and in more ways than was explainable by nonmagical science. So it was no surprise that the hairbrush vibrated almost immediately, and then flashed a pure white.

I dropped the brush to the floor in relief. Marie was safe, but that didn't mean I could fully relax. The New Salem baddies weren't above playing a long game. I could see the strategy now —come declaring peace and a willingness to learn, befriend me, then, just when I trusted them, rip the carpet out from under me.

But now I knew my sisters were alive and well, and my house was secure. I finally released the last bit of tension from the bottom of my lungs. Exhaustion weighed on the back of my eyelids, but something else was growing. Anger.

My fingertips glowed and I let the feeling of control take over. I was a Warrior, damn it. And if James Riley thought he could come into my school and do…whatever evil thing he wanted to, well, he had another thing coming. I wasn't a gullible teenager anymore.

Four

I returned to school filled with fire and two shots of espresso. Between the panic attack, sparring with myself the night before, and flitting all over the city, my energy was waning, but black gold was all I'd needed to perk back up. As expected, James was already in my fifth period class, making small talk with two girls who'd zeroed in on him.

I leveled a challenging glare at him as I settled in an empty seat to observe. I would figure out his game, nip this distraction in the bud and send him packing back to New Salem before the week was out. Then I could refocus my efforts on college and reiterate to Gavon that I wasn't to be messed with.

"Tonight, you asshole," I said, cornering him as soon as the class let out. "Sparring beach. Let's settle this once and for all."

"You want to fight me?" James said. "Are you sure?"

"Are *you* sure?"

"Be there at seven," he said with a small shrug.

In hindsight, I wished I'd said *four* instead of seven. For one thing, the adrenaline disappeared around fifteen minutes after I left school, leaving me with a headache.

For another, my brain filled with scenarios and worries about what would happen if I failed. If James killed me—or worse, took me back to New Salem.

My panic came back with a vengeance as I wasted the hours pacing in my bedroom. I knew, intellectually, that ruminating over the past would simply weaken me and leave me less able to concentrate during my duel. But anxiety is a dragon-like bastard and doesn't listen to reason.

Instead of being productive and gathering my strength, I tortured myself by replaying the day Cyrus had killed Jeanie. I could recall with vivid clarity every second of that day, from the argument about Gavon to finding Cyrus in the park to waking up in the jail cell. The horrible, cold realization that I'd always known Gavon was my…f-word. On top of that, finding out he was the Guildmaster and apparently had big plans for me. The fear I'd carried as I walked into the sparring ring, the dashed hopes that Gavon would put a stop to it and let me go home. The relief when my Gram had appeared to rescue me—even after I'd done something to piss her off (the details remained vague). The false feeling of security when I'd gotten home.

The terror when Cyrus appeared in our kitchen. The horror when an attack spell ended Jeanie's life.

I shook my head to keep the images out, but they crowded in anyway. Her open eyes, staring back at me. The guilt of knowing it was my fault she was gone. Knowing I'd be next. The need to get my sisters away from him, to get them somewhere safe.

Hearing my mother's voice in my head as my magic recalled the day she'd died fighting him.

It was that magical memory that had given me such sparring prowess. My mother had used my magic when I was in the womb, and it had left an impression, allowing me to tap into the memory and fight Cyrus. That night had left me near death, but thanks to Marie's healing and Nicole's potions, I'd survived.

Unlike Jeanie.

Guilt pressed around my throat and I fought to keep the tears from falling as I did another lap in my bedroom. Could I have done more? Could I have knocked the attack spell out of the way? Even with my magical memories, though, I was still a novice. I didn't have the reaction times or skills Cyrus had.

Which was what had prompted me to seek out magical books to become better. I'd vowed that no one else would die because I couldn't protect them.

I finally sat down on the floor next to my bed and summoned my texts. Most of my library had come from Gavon, but I'd added to the collection recently, thanks to the discovery of a store in New Orleans. It had been serendipitous, really. A week after Marie had stormed out of the apartment, Nicole announced that we should take a road trip over to New Orleans and have a girls' day. The old bookshop had been crammed between two tourist trap shops, and Nicole, never one for reading, had left me to my devices. In the upstairs section, I happened across a magical book that had spells and charms for protection.

Every time I'd gone back to the store (magically), there was another book that had been almost exactly what I'd needed.

Three trips in, I found the book with the incantation to summon a magical form to spar with. Another trip, a book containing a look-away charm. It had been a nice substitute since…well, since my usual source of books had disappeared completely.

I chewed my lip, panic giving way to anger at Gavon. How terribly fitting: he didn't show his face for eighteen months then sent his apprentice instead.

"Lexie? You home?"

Crap. Nicole was early. I stood and wiped the remaining tears and worry from my face. If Nicole even suspected something was wrong, she wouldn't let me out of her sight.

I jumped up and bounded out of my room before she could happen across the pile of books on my bed. I met her in the hallway and closed the door behind me.

"Oh, you're here," Nicole said with a frown. "Don't you have tutoring today?"

"I…" *Crap again.* "Had to cancel." I needed to call my student and let him know something had come up.

"Are you sure you're feeling all right? You scared me today."

"Oh, sorry about that," I said with a fake smile. "First day jitters."

"You said you were on your period," Nicole replied, her eyes narrowing in scrutiny. "Lexie, what is going on with you?"

"I'm *fine.* Just being weird today."

"You're not this weird." She was in full-on Mother Mode, if the look on her face was any indication. "Lexie, you need to take a break. You don't need to worry so much about Georgetown. There are better schools that don't cost as much money—"

"Nicole, I promise you, I'm *fine*." At least hearing her talk about Georgetown had snapped my brain out of panic. Her dissuasion was like catnip to my stubborn side. "And stop telling me I'm not good enough to get into Georgetown."

She pursed her lips. "That's not what I'm saying. I'm trying to tell you that killing yourself to get into this one school isn't a smart decision."

"And I'm telling you this is what I want."

She crossed her arms over her chest. "At what cost, though? You'll be paying off student loans until you're ninety. Not only that, but you're turning into a basket case. You show up at work, sweaty and clammy, and you're sending me texts making sure I'm all right. Are…" Her eyes widened. "He's not back, is he?"

Shit. "No, Nicole."

"I'm serious, Lexie. If he's back, you have to tell me."

"He's not back, I promise you."

I hated myself for lying to Nicole, especially since that had caused everything to go to hell in the first place. But if everything went according to plan, James would be sent packing tonight. Once he was out of the picture, I might mention it to Nicole. Some day. In about fifty years.

"Fine," Nicole said with a face that said she still didn't believe me. "But promise me you'll take it easy this year."

Fat chance. "I will."

I arrived at the beach almost an hour early, more because I couldn't sit in the apartment with Nicole for much longer. She thought I was having some kind of mental break, so she was more suffocating than usual. I'd mastered the art of hiding my panic attacks and nightmares from her, but I was out of practice lying about New Salem. And to be honest, I didn't like betraying the one family member I had left.

The beach still bore the black skid marks of my sparring session the night before, and I rubbed the back of my neck nervously. I hadn't even noticed I was still about half-empty. Perhaps agreeing to duel tonight wasn't the smartest idea I'd ever had.

Also, perhaps lying to my potion-making sister wasn't too intelligent either. Although Nicole wouldn't have brewed me a healing potion as much as something to prevent me from leaving the house.

I plopped down on the beach and waited two seconds before getting up and pacing. I was on edge, waiting for the sound of an incoming transport spell, readying my magic.

When seven came and went, my panic went into overdrive.

Was this some kind of ploy? Some way to get me off guard? Oh, but if he thought he could fool me, he had another thing coming.

I was the only thing standing between my family and this bunch of lunatics, so if I failed… I didn't want to think about it. I wouldn't fail, I would—

"Alexis."

I froze, all fight draining from my body like water down a roof during a downpour. He wore dockers and a collared shirt— the same sort of clothes he used to wear when we'd sparred together. His dark hair—the same color as mine and Nicole's— had become a little grayer, but his eyes held the same kind, patient gaze that had sucked me in from the very first day.

To keep myself from falling for it a second time, I forced anger into my words. "Where's my dueling partner?"

"There will be no duel tonight," he said with a stern glance. "And I'll thank you not to request any more."

My heart thudded in my chest. I couldn't believe his mere presence affected me more than the duel I apparently wasn't going to have after all. Forced to choose between an explosion of questions, tears, hysteria, or anger, I chose the latter.

"Are you afraid your stupid apprentice will get what's coming to him?" I asked, balling my fists so tight my nails dug into my palms.

Gavon sighed, and it almost sounded impatient. Damn, but he looked so much like Nicole. "You know better than to agree to duel. It's a good thing you're both still under my purview and I could annul it."

"I'm *not* under your purview," I snapped.

"Since you don't belong to a clan, and you're my daughter, yes, actually, you are."

That word plucked something deep in my gut and zapped my anger, leaving a stunned, unsure numbness.

"In case you've forgotten," he continued at my silence, "agreeing to a duel means that you are magically bound to the outcome. Therefore, you and James would've had to fight to the death."

"I know," I forced out.

He quirked a brow. "Are you that eager to die?"

"Are you that sure I wouldn't kill him?"

Gavon pinched the bridge of his nose. "Alexis…this isn't what I wanted to happen."

"Then *why the hell is he here*?" I barked.

"To learn."

I kicked the sand beneath my feet, a bit of an attack spell going with it. "For once in your life, *Gavon*, don't lie to me."

"I'm not lying," he said, holding up his hands in surrender. "The truth is that James is arrogant, selfish, petulant, and most worrisome, incredibly powerful. He's the only Warrior born to our guild in almost half a century. He knows he's going to be next in line for the Guildmaster, and he's never had to work for it. I don't want someone like that taking over an already volatile group of magicals."

I couldn't argue with any of that, but, damn, I wanted to. The relief of seeing him again was threatening to overpower my better sense, so I dug my fingernails harder into my palms.

"And I thought there no better way to humble him than to enroll him in high school." Gavon smiled, a little smugly. "After this first day, he already seems taken down a few pegs. Turns out not everyone is as amenable to his charms as in New Salem."

I had my doubts about that. He seemed to be the apple of every girl's eye. "And you'd just let this egotistical, powerful magical loose in my school without any supervision?"

Gavon tilted his head to the side, a curious smile teasing the corner of his mouth. "In your anger, it appears you neglected to notice he is without magic."

My face grew hot. Knowing magicals from nonmagicals was something I hadn't yet figured out, another gaping hole in my magical education. And though part of me wanted him to tell me how, that ship had sailed.

"I promise, James is simply here to attend classes. He will

not cause you, nor your classmates, any trouble."

"Then why not ship him away to another school?"

"On the off chance he *does* cause trouble, I wanted someone around to set him straight." His gaze warmed a bit. "You've become incredibly powerful—"

"Save it." I was already halfway to forgiving him for the unforgivable and if he started pandering to that voice in my head that craved his approval, I'd be done for. So I stuffed my feelings with steel wool and leveled my gaze at him. "If he steps one *toe* out of line—"

"I trust you'll handle it."

"I will."

The son of a bitch actually smiled at me and my traitorous heart did a backflip. "I'd expect nothing less. Whether you want to hear it or not, you've become quite the force, Alexis."

"My name is Lexie."

"I prefer Alexis."

"You don't get to have a preference anymore," I snarled, finally finding the anger that had been set aside. "After you let my aunt die."

Something unreadable crossed his face. "I'm truly sorry—"

"No. You aren't. Because if you were, you wouldn't have let it happen. Like you let it happen to my mother. And you also wouldn't have disappeared for the past eighteen months and left me to deal with it on my own." My anger was speaking for me, and I was about to throw a spell or start bawling. Either way, I needed to leave. "You just make sure James knows I've got my eye on him."

Before Gavon could even respond, I transported back to my

room just in time for my emotions to barrel through my defenses. I collapsed onto my bed as my anger dissolved into thick hot tears that dripped down my face. I muffled my wails with my pillow, knowing I couldn't lie to Nicole about what had set me off.

It was easy to paint him as some nameless, faceless evil that had destroyed everything I loved when he was back on his side of reality. But hearing his voice, seeing his movements, all that conjured up visions of those beautiful weeks before he'd shown his true self, when all I'd wanted was his approval and guidance. He'd been everything I'd ever wanted until the bottom fell out.

After everything he'd done, and not done, I should've hated the very ground he walked on. And I did, but at the same time, I craved a few minutes in his presence. But really, all I wanted—all I'd wanted for two years—was an explanation.

Why hadn't he told me? Why had he trained me? Why didn't he stop Cyrus from killing Jeanie? Or trying to kill me? Why was my mother targeted all those years ago? Had he been really just using her, or was there more to the story?

I was afraid to hear it, though. I was afraid that what he'd say wouldn't make sense, that it would reveal some other, horrible truth. I was done digging for answers when people told me to leave it alone. And yet, I needed to know.

"Lexie? Is that you?"

I jumped at Nicole's voice on the other side of the door. Hastily wiping my eyes, I hoped I didn't look too blotchy. "Y-yeah, it's me."

She knocked then cracked open the door. "Where've you been? Have you been in here all this time?"

I licked my lips. "Yeah, got back a few hours ago. Been studying."

Nicole glanced at my bed, where the leftover magical books lay sprawled out on the bedsheets from this afternoon. There wasn't any time to glamour them into something different.

"Lexie, I thought you weren't reading magic anymore," Nicole said, leaning against the doorframe. "Don't you have tons and tons of homework?"

"Yeah, just had a question about something," I said lamely. "Got caught up in reading. You know how that goes."

Her expression was unreadable. "Yeah, I know how that goes. Just make sure you get your homework done."

I could've kicked myself as she closed the door behind her. I was still putting my foot in my mouth when it came to my sister's potion-making magic. But I needed to be more careful with hiding these new developments. Gavon may have promised peace, but I knew better than to trust him. I just needed to figure out his end game before anyone else got hurt—or worse.

Five

When I arrived at school for my second day, it hadn't burst into flames. Kids walked up and down the halls like normal. Nobody was screaming in terror. There was no sign of the apocalyptic scene I'd been dreading. In fact, James stood in front of his locker, considering his books like everyone else in the hallway. He glanced in my direction for a split second, but that was all the attention he paid me.

At first, I thought it was because Gavon had said something. But as the day wore on, I realized it was because I didn't matter to him, not when there were girls in every class giving the new guy the starry-eyed treatment. As expected, Super Hot plus New meant he was immediately popular. He certainly didn't seem eager to hurt any of them; quite the opposite in fact.

Which begged the question: How did a boy who'd grown up in a world stuck in 1692 fare in the modern world?

To my utter annoyance, better than me.

He remained quiet during classes, not offering answers to

any of the questions, except once in physics when he was called upon. In between, he was usually swamped by people, asking him questions about his likes and dislikes. Once I'd stopped glowering at him and actually listened, I realized he was giving a lot of non-answers and vague replies. To the normal ear, this was typical of a seventeen-year-old and probably added to his air of mystery.

To mine, though, it sounded like the same methods Gavon might've used when he'd first crossed over to this side. Had he taught James how to be a chameleon in an unfamiliar place? Or was James simply one of those people who could adapt?

The questions plagued me for most of the day, taking my attention away from class. Every time my mind wandered to the lecture, I would wrestle it back to James, watching him for signs of evil doing or anything that would give me a reason to blow his ass out of the school.

"You have to stop glaring at me," he said, standing in my path after lunch.

"I will when you leave my school," I retorted.

The corner of his mouth quirked up in an evil smile he apparently reserved just for me. "No."

"Then let's do this for real," I said, closing in on him. "Think you can get away from your *master*?"

There was a flash of something in his eyes—but whether it was challenge or fear, I couldn't tell. "You should be thanking your father for stepping in. Had we dueled, you most assuredly would've been killed."

"Is that so?" I said, brushing away the emotions that bubbled up. "As I recall, I kicked your ass two years ago with nothing but a few months of training—"

He scoffed. "You did no such thing. *I* was about to land the killing blow when your family interrupted."

"And that's why you fainted?" I taunted. My magic was humming now and, despite the dangers this conversation posed, I was ready to face them. "Tonight. For real this time. No Gavon. Just you and me—"

"I—" he started, and I saw it—uncertainty. It was quickly masked by indifference. "No. You aren't worth the effort. Just accept I'm the superior magical and quit bothering me."

My jaw fell to the floor. I didn't know James very well, but I knew him well enough to know he would never walk away from a fight. But it wasn't just his words that shocked me. He'd been ready to duel me, but something had stopped him. I doubted it was fear because it was clear he wasn't afraid of me.

Whatever it was had been stronger than his ego—and that was saying something.

Some of my worry eased as the second day of school wore on. James showed no signs of magic that I could see. Perhaps, for once, Gavon was telling the truth about James' purpose for being here. At least partially.

The other reason became clear halfway through world history, when I recalled a particular comment from my brief, horrific time with Cyrus. He'd said I was to be the next Guildmaster, a child born of both worlds that could help lead the takeover. Gavon, too, had mentioned that he'd spent the past thirty years learning everything he could. Perhaps this wasn't just about "knocking him down a few pegs," but about gathering intelligence on our world for their grand schemes. And while that didn't make me *completely* at ease, it did change my defensive strategy from active to observational. I would keep an eye on him, watch for signs that he was doing more than simply charming the pants off every girl in the school, and return to my studies.

And the mountain of other stresses I'd momentarily cast aside—including the three classes that had assigned homework I hadn't done.

Starting the semester with zeroes was enough to scare me into forgetting about James and focus on school. Georgetown wouldn't accept "saving the world from evil magicals" as an extra-curricular activity. I also had volunteer hours to worry about and tutoring this afternoon to make up for missing the day before. It would be a feat to accomplish everything, but this wasn't my first rodeo.

After school, I transported myself to the county animal shelter for my four hours of volunteer time. It wasn't that I was particularly fond of animals, but the volunteer work was done solo, allowing me to cheat a little. I signed in at the welcome desk, waving to Cindy, the manager. She was a bit weird, definitely overworked, but kind. And the best part: she never bothered me while I worked.

The dogs in the kennels began barking and jumping when I walked into the back room where we held them. I glanced at the recording camera then floated a little magic toward it. Magic and electronics didn't mix so well, but with a very light touch, I could play with it. In my mind's eye, I overlaid the image of me cleaning out each of the stalls for the next hour. Then, with a flick of my wrists, the kennels were clean, the water bowls replaced, and fresh water added.

To boot, I magically petted and scratched all the dogs behind the ears. The barking ceased as they relaxed. They'd stay this way for a while, and I figured it was the good that canceled out the bad of using magic for everything else.

Speaking of which, my phone vibrated, signaling it was time to head to my second job. I reset the alarm for an hour then transported myself out of the kennel to the nearby library. I arrived in the usual bathroom stall, listening for the sounds of anyone else in the room before walking out.

My shoulders drooped when I saw the kid sitting at my normal table.

"Hi Charles," I said, forcing a smile onto my face.

"Hullo," he said, glancing around nervously. Thirteen years old, he didn't want any of his friends knowing he was getting study help. Little did he know that I cast a charm around our table to keep them away. It was another addition to the "good powers" column that assuaged my guilt over using magic in every day situations.

I wished I could use magic to tutor Charles. He was a good kid, just easily distracted and seemingly impervious to my usual methods of helping. Most kids just needed someone to walk them through the steps slower than their teachers did. But Charles wasn't getting the concepts at all.

"This doesn't make any sense," he growled, throwing his pen down.

"Look," I said, growing frustrated myself. "It's simple. We're just solving for X. You need to—"

I pinched the bridge of my nose when my phone vibrated. It was too soon for the hour to be up, and my phone notifications were empty. That mean someone had tripped the charm around the kennel.

I popped to my feet. "Hang on, I need to grab this. Work on those problems, and I'll come back and check on them."

I ducked between two library stacks and transported myself back to the kennel before anyone saw me. I materialized just as the door was opening, and quickly forced an easy smile onto my face. "Hiya Cindy."

"Hi, Lexie. You sure finished quick today," she said, walking in a pair of prospective adopters. "Guess you can sign out early."

I hid the grimace—I'd only clocked twenty minutes instead of the full four hours of volunteer time. But I couldn't argue with her, so I dutifully went to sign out before returning to the library.

Where Charles was gone.

"Perfect."

In lieu of using magic, I scoured the library for him. Twenty minutes later, I found him climbing into his mother's car. She did not look pleased.

"What am I paying you for if you're taking personal calls instead of tutoring my child?" she barked. She was one of those mothers who wore her hair short, her makeup severe, and drove a minivan filled with sports equipment.

"My…sister was in the hospital," I lied, wishing I sounded more convincing. "I apologize, it won't happen again—"

"It won't. And you won't get your check today either."

I should've expected that. Charles gave me a forlorn look

from the backseat as they drove away, and I was left with the particular sense of failure that I'd screwed up not one but two jobs today. The money wasn't much—twenty bucks for two hours of tutoring—but if I lost Charles as a weekly check, that would be a problem. I prayed Mrs. Gilly wouldn't be too put out as I walked back to my bathroom to transport myself home.

I was exhausted, but two days' worth of homework welcomed me when I got to my bedroom. My head ached, but I dutifully summoned my physics textbook and began to read.

Well, I wouldn't call it *reading* per se, as I was scanning the pages with my magic, looking for the answers to my homework questions, which would be scribbled down with a magically-assisted pen.

"You can't use magic to do your homework." Jeanie's voice floated through the back of my mind and I put the book down. I didn't use my magic to cheat on tests, but I'd used it to help out on all the essays and research papers that had accumulated my junior year. It had reduced six hours' worth of homework to one, allowing me to pile on all the other things, like volunteering and tutoring.

But Jeanie was always there, in the back of my mind. The day she'd told me about my magic, she'd said it wasn't a big deal. Just another sense, that it wouldn't change anything about my life. I wished I could say she'd been right. Everything about my life was different.

Especially because she wasn't in it.

I'd never been as close to my aunt as I was with Nicole, but I noticed her absence unexpectedly. Sometimes, I'd catch myself waiting to hear her walk through the door. When Nicole and I would go out to eat at our favorite Mexican restaurant, I'd listen for the sound of her saying "margarita." I'd see a woman with short brown hair out on the town, and a flutter of hope would course through me. But my nightmares always ended with her dead, lifeless eyes staring back at me, and I knew she was truly gone. I felt no closure, though. There'd been no funeral for us to celebrate her life, to say our final goodbyes.

The familiar pang of loneliness threatened to bubble up, now combined with the newest memory of Gavon. It was so easy to fall into his trap—him saying how powerful I was, how proud he looked—but the truth was in his actions.

Scratching drew my attention; the pen had run out of paper and was writing on the wood of my desk. I waved my hand to stop the spell. Instead of my physics homework, the page was filled with the outpouring of all the emotions I'd just been feeling. I used my magic to lift the ink off the page and return it to the pen, leaving the homework page blank.

And with a heavy sigh, I picked up the pen and began to write.

<h1 style="text-align:center">Six</h1>

It had been two weeks since school started, and without any mishaps or evil happenings, I'd almost fully accepted my current theory that James was enrolled to gather intelligence. I kept a close eye on him (not hard, because he was in *every single class*) and I saw not one bit of magic from him. Well, magic-magic, that was. Somehow that bastard ingratiated himself with everyone who came into contact with him.

Gone was his eager notetaking from the first few days, replaced by a bored expression as he acted like he wanted to be anywhere else but in that classroom. He hadn't acknowledged my existence in several days, so I was convinced this lackadaisical attitude wasn't for my benefit. James actually *was* petulant and self-absorbed.

I was tempted to ask him if Gavon returned his power to him at night, but that would require asking about Gavon and New Salem, or talking to him at all, and I wasn't about to do that. But considering he barely took notes or paid attention, and yet was turning in homework every day, he had to be using it. He wasn't *that* smart.

At least, I hoped not.

Although my fears of impending disaster were gone, I still wanted to add some new tools to my defensive arsenal. So a trip to my favorite bookstore was required. I set aside some time on Saturday, and transported myself three hours west to New Orleans.

New Orleans never used to hold any appeal for me. We'd gone once or twice on a rare family vacation with Jeanie, but with three young girls on a tight budget, none of us ever had much fun. I always thought it too muggy, too touristy, too…not me. Now that it was the only source of magical knowledge, I was a bit more fond of it.

The first floor of the bookstore was dedicated to the new releases and bestsellers that presumably paid the rent. Upstairs, the merchandise was considerably older, the sort of books collectors sell on TV shows for millions of dollars. It was here where I found most of my magical books.

I waved to the young guy at the counter—very sure he didn't remember some kid who came in every few weeks—and climbed the creaky, dusty stairs to the second floor. I inhaled the musty scent, taking a moment to appreciate the knowledge and the age of the books around me. Hunting down magical books was the primary goal, but I couldn't argue that standing in a room of old books wasn't an awesome perk.

Slowly, I canvassed the room, my footsteps echoing with the groaning of the old floor. There wasn't really a rhyme or reason to how I found books, so I'd long stopped trying to force it. I passed over the titles on the spines, knowing that—

"Ah!"

Charms and Enchantments for the Un-Charmers jumped out at me almost instantly. Excitement and magic hummed in my skin as I pulled the book closer. It had been penned in 1637 by Richard Greentower, which was a bit disappointing. Most of the books I'd found were written before the Separation when New Salem was created. Now, I was curious about magicals *after* the Separation. I even tried a Google search on it, but I wasn't sure how much was real magic, and how much fake.

The book in my hands was *definitely* the real deal. I found my reading chair in the corner and carefully read through the first few pages. It was the same sort of too-wordy, too-up-its-own-butt kind of tone in all the other books. What was it about seventeenth century magical writers that made them so self-important?

I quickly scanned the appendix of spells, looking for the elusive locator spell I could use to find my sister. Unsurprisingly, it wasn't in there. But there was something that piqued my interest—a charm for a talisman to warn when someone was lying. That could come in handy with James—or Gavon, if I ever saw him again.

I closed the book and pressed it to my chest, glancing around the shelves to see if anything else caught my eye. But this would do for now.

I made my way downstairs, preparing for the story I'd tell the guy at the counter if he asked why I was buying a book on magic. Thus far, it hadn't come up. Most people just saw an old, worn book.

Counter-guy was kind of cute (or maybe he was cute for working in a bookstore). I approached the front desk and slid the book across it quietly.

"Is that it?" he asked, picking up the book and turning it over. "Don't see a price on it. Is it from upstairs?"

I nodded. "Yeah, I'm using it for an art project I saw on Pinterest."

He frowned. "You're going to destroy it?"

"Uh…no," I clarified hastily. "I'm going to…put it with a few other pieces I found on a shelf."

I wasn't sure he believed me, but he went to his computer anyway. He scratched his chin and typed on the keyboard then furrowed his brow and typed some more. "That's funny. We don't have a record of this book."

"O-oh?" I cursed myself. One of these days, I was going to transport myself and leave a twenty in the register. That would've been easier than trying to fake my way through the awkward purchase conversation.

"Look, how's five dollars sound?" he asked. "I mean, it's pretty beat up anyway."

To my eyes, it looked in near mint condition for a book written in 1637, but I wasn't sure what enchantments were on it. "Sure. Five is great." I fished the bill out of my wallet and smiled at him.

"You come in here a lot, don't you?" he asked. He couldn't have been older than twenty, now that I really looked at him. Soft brown hair cut short, dark eyes, a dimple on his left cheek.

"I do?" My face grew warm. "I mean, yeah, I do. I like this place."

"Promise me you aren't destroying these old books, though."

I had to laugh at the concerned tone in his voice. "No, I promise you. I'm keeping them in a dark place, away from light and dust."

"All right then." He handed me the book in a plastic bag and grinned. "See you next time."

"Bye!"

I dashed out of the store before he could ask me any more questions. I was nearly two blocks away before I realized that the cute boy at the bookstore had not only noticed me, but *remembered* me and had a conversation with me. It wasn't true love, but considering that most guys ignored my presence (or tried to kill me), it was a good start.

With a small giggle, I transported myself back home.

Doing magic at home was always risky, especially on the weekends when Nicole was around, so I transported myself to the sparring beach to attempt it. I was kind of rough with charms—they were different than the normal conjuring and summoning I'd learned with Gavon. Charms, as I understood them, used magic to bring forth the inherent properties of an object, either enhancing them or making them do stuff. The barrier outside my house was a charm based on the protective qualities of dirt and the air, but I'd nearly burned down the complex trying to figure it out.

I only had a few hours of sunlight left, so I passed all the interesting charms for never-melting candles and always-refilling ink wells until I found the one I was looking for.

Truth-Telling Charm

A truth-telling charm is placed upon a blue sapphire and worn by the Magical. When told a lie, the charm will cause the object to warm considerably. For this reason, the sapphire should be worn as a necklace or talisman.

To enact the charm, place the sapphire in the left hand. Use Magic to unlock the truth-telling properties within.

"Dammit."

Considering this book was called "Charms for the Un-Charmers," I'd hoped it would offer more insight into how charms actually worked. Unfortunately, most of what I'd read to date was the same: Find object, use magic. The barrier charms had at least had some more detail to them; I had to think long and hard about those I wanted to protect in order for the barrier to have the maximum impact.

First, I had to obtain a blue sapphire. A quick Google search on my phone showed their prices—way outside my budget. Which left me with the conundrum of either stealing from somewhere else or dropping it all together.

Ignoring my Aunt Jeanie's voice in my ear, I summoned one from the closest jewelry store. It was gorgeous, sparkling navy blue inset into a pendant. I promised myself I was just borrowing it until James disappeared again. Once that was over with, back it would go.

Cupping the pendant in my left hand, I closed my eyes and concentrated on my magic.

You're thinking too hard.

"Shut up, Gavon," I whispered to no one, but released the tension between my brows. My magic was a chainsaw and this required a scalpel. I tapped into the humming sensation under my skin, at once a separate entity and also part of me. And just as I'd been instructed all those months ago, I let go of the control and a zap of magic went to my left hand.

In my mind's eye, I saw the chemical construction, the way the molecules fastened together and formed the larger gem. They gave up their secrets to me, the magic within that was sensitive to liars and untruths. The pendant in my hand vibrated and grew warm, and I quickly opened my eyes to stop before I destroyed it.

I lifted the pendant and eyed it appreciatively. It seemed no different than when I'd summoned it, but at the same time, my magic whispered that I'd completed the charm. The best way to test it would be when I saw James next. Then, I could ask him all the questions I'd been holding onto, and find out whether he was a big, fat—

"That was an impressive display for an un-Charmer."

"*Shit!*" I screamed. Scrambling to my feet, I readied an attack spell in my free hand, preparing myself for battle.

James, however, held his hand up in surrender. "Before you strike, be aware I have no magic with which to defend myself."

"Yeah, and how am I supposed to know that?" I snarled, raising my fist higher.

"Check that pendant in your hand."

I started then glanced at the jewel. It remained cool against my skin. "Yeah, maybe the charm didn't work."

"I, James Riley, am completely in love with you."

Before I could ask what he meant by that, the jewel in my hand grew noticeably warm. In fact, uncomfortably so. I glanced between it and James for a long moment, unsure which to trust.

"See?" James said with a shrug. "Now you'll know when I'm lying. And I honestly don't have any magic, so please put yours away."

Cautiously, I lowered my hand and let the magic disappear. "What do you want, James?"

"I would like to spar with you."

I glanced at the stone again, and it was dormant. I wondered if the stone knew the difference between lying for real and skirting around the truth.

"So what, you want me to go back to New Salem with you?" I snorted. "As if I'm that stupid."

"I'm not trying to trick you. But I know from experience that a Warrior who doesn't spar becomes antsy. You haven't had another magical around in several months, and Gavon's been refusing to spar with me at all." He sighed. "And the rest of the Warriors are just so…exhausting."

Presumably, he was talking about Cyrus. Another reason I needed to excuse myself from this conversation before it got going. "I've seen this movie, I know how it ends. No, thank you."

He laughed, a throaty, jovial sound that reminded me how attractive he was. "Well, I'm a bit behind on seeing all the latest, so you'll have to enlighten me."

"It ends with you dragging me to New Salem and forcing me to fight for my life against my will," I said, folding my arms across my chest.

"Sparring is not a duel—"

"*I know that.*"

"You and I are almost evenly matched. I think if we trained together, we would find it immensely diverting." His gaze traveled up and down my body, as a smile curled onto his lips. I didn't want to know what else he found *diverting*.

Instead of arguing, he reached into his back pocket and produced a small book. Holding up his hands in surrender, he came closer and offered it to me.

"This is a book on magical pacts," he said. "All the different kinds, how they're used, who can agree to them. And, most importantly, how to word one so you don't end up agreeing to something you don't want to." He smiled. "I want you to write a pact stipulating that you and I will engage in a sparring match on a regular basis. And because it's a pact, you and I will be magically bound to adhere to whatever safeguards you wish to add to it."

I opened and closed my mouth, already thinking of a thousand ways this could blow up in my face. "Yeah, and you'll just find a loophole."

"Then you'd better make it ironclad." He pushed the book into my hand. "Think about it. The only thing I ask is that you and I can spar. The rest of it, including, I presume, that I not try to harm you or your sisters, is up to you."

I took a step back. Knowing James and the New Salem idiots, there had to be a trick here. But for some reason, I couldn't find one. He was giving me all the power. And sparring, as far as Gavon had explained it, didn't normally result in death.

"This is…this is just some… You're still trying to kill me, I know you are—"

He chuckled, and it made the hair on my arms stand up. "Why do you think I'm trying to kill you?"

"Uh, because you *tried to*?"

"That was two years ago. I'm a changed man."

I laughed. "I'm sure."

"Listen, Alexis—"

"*Lexie.*"

"Fine, whatever. *Lexie.*" He snorted, as if my name were stupid to him. "I am interested in one thing: a sparring partner who can keep up with me." He stopped and arched an eyebrow at me. "And based on the way you've been so eager to get into it with me, I'd wager you need the same thing."

I wanted to argue, but the words died on my tongue. He was right. Of course, I wanted to protect my sisters from all the crazies in New Salem, but…the promise of getting to fight with a real magical had set my blood on fire. Though the smarter part of my brain knew bargaining with James was bad news, the stupid half of my brain was ecstatic at the idea.

"I'll think about it," I said finally. That, to me, was a nice compromise between the warring factions in my brain. At the very least, it might force James to show his hand and I could find out what this new strategy was really about.

"See you at school," he said with a chuckle.

"Wait a minute," I said. "If you don't have magic, how did you get here?"

He pulled a small black vial from his pocket. "I know how to make potions." He threw the bottle to the ground and he was gone in a thick black cloud.

Seven

There was no way I was ever going to sign a pact with James Riley.

That was what I repeated to myself every time my thoughts grew too close to doing something moronic.

The magical pact book sat on the corner of my desk for the rest of the weekend, taunting me. I busied myself with work and volunteering and homework, and even tried reading the charms book I'd bought from the used bookstore. But I couldn't even focus on that—too curious what this pact book had to say.

There were a thousand and one reasons I should've just tossed the book in the trash and never thought of it again. But for the same reason I hadn't thrown out the magical primer, or anything else Gavon had given me, the pact-making manual remained on the corner of my desk. Regardless of who'd given it to me, it had information I needed.

Sunday night, I convinced myself there was no harm in just *reading* the book. After all, my knowledge of pacts was limited to what was in that old magical primer. Since it seemed to be a regular occurrence in the magical world, I decided it wouldn't hurt to know more about the practice. I wouldn't even have to tell James I'd read it, but I could be armed with the knowledge of how to deal with him.

So, with a mug of tea, I sat down in my bed and cracked it open.

Magical pacts are agreements between magicals, clans, guilds, and other entities. They use the combined power of the agreeing parties to enforce the agreements set within. A pact can only be broken when both parties agree to break it.

Caution must be taken when agreeing to a pact. Nefarious intentions have led many a-magical to be bound to outcomes they did not intend. A full and total understanding of the terms and conditions of such a pact should be attained before any signature or blood is passed.

None of this was new information to me. From what I'd known about magical pacts, they were incredibly powerful—and not easily broken. But I also knew that unless they were worded explicitly, they were open to interpretation. It had been such a loophole that had gotten me out of dueling to the death in New Salem. I'd already belonged to a clan, so I couldn't be inducted into Gavon's guild unless I renounced my membership.

That was the last time I'd sparred with a real person. Magic throbbed at my temples at the thought, whispering convincing arguments. If I did this right, James would be physically restricted from harming me, magically or otherwise. I could prevent him from ever screwing with my family. Or even the world. If he didn't agree to my terms, that just exposed his true intent, which was what I wanted anyway.

I summoned my notebook, along with a pen, and tapped the top of the pen on the paper. Writing down a few notes didn't mean I would make a pact. But I had some time to kill (and homework I was avoiding), and I was itching to complete this thought exercise.

So if I *were* to enter a pact with James (and I promised myself I would not), what would the ground rules be?

Things I don't want to happen:

1. To die

I snorted. That was obvious.

2. For Nicole or Marie to get hurt.

I glanced at my phone, wondering if I should text Marie to seek her advice. But that seemed like something better discussed face to face. And she still wasn't answering my texts.

3. To join Gavon's evil team

4. To be forced into doing something I don't want to do

I brought the pen tip to my mouth and chewed on it, deep in thought. There were a few obvious things I could put into the pact up front.

The undersigned, James Riley, agrees not to induct one, Alexis Carrigan, into the…

Evil Guild? Evil team?

I left that blank.

…in any way shape or form. The undersigned agrees not to harm, maim, harass, or otherwise be horrible to Nicole Carrigan or Marie Carrigan. The undersigned may only use an attack spell in

the context of a sparring match, which both have mutually agreed to entering into.

I sat back and read through what I'd written. It seemed woefully inadequate in my opinion, just a few lines. There were probably a million things I was missing in there. James would probably come up with some loophole that would permanently enslave me to the Guild—or worse.

I balled up the paper and threw it in the trash, ashamed I was even entertaining such a dangerous notion.

When I arrived at school the next day, I felt James behind me before I was two steps out of the girl's bathroom. For once, I didn't instinctively try to attack him, because I knew exactly what he wanted.

"Well?" he drawled when I didn't turn around.

"Well, what?" I hooked my hands into my backpack and walked briskly toward the door. If I could only make it to the main hall before he caught up with me—

"Nice try," James said, sprinting beside me. "You can't avoid me forever. Did you even look at the book?" I chewed on the inside of my cheek, and he smirked. "I knew it. You couldn't resist. Well, the book told you everything you needed to know —"

"Not exactly," I replied. "I still don't believe you're telling the truth about why you want to spar."

He reached his finger to my chest and hooked it around the silver chain, pulling out the sapphire I now wore every day. "If you don't trust me, trust your own magic."

I didn't like how close he was, or how my pulse beat against my temples. I released a breath when he let go of the chain.

"In any case, I'm not lying to you about this. I want to spar, and so do you. So let's just make this easy on ourselves and skip over the unnecessary hysterics. We'll sign a pact, spar once a week, and be done with it."

With a hearty roll of my eyes, I brushed past him into the main hall. But if I thought the conversation would end there, I was sorely mistaken. He leaned against the locker next to mine as I swapped out my books.

"C'mon, Ale…Lexie."

I shot him a dark look. "Calling me by my real name is a long way from buttering me up."

"Your real name is Alexis, but let's not split hairs."

I paused, counting to ten so I didn't blast him to the other side of the hall. "I'm not sparring with you. And I'm most assuredly not agreeing to a pact."

"So you wrote one then?"

The book I was holding fell out of my hand with a resounding *thunk*. "How did you know?"

The truth was, I'd retrieved the balled-up pact from the trash and added to it, only to throw it away again, at least five or six times. I was fairly sure I was losing my mind. After all, James was from New Salem. He'd learned everything from Gavon. I was sure they gave seminars on how to trick unsuspecting idiots into trusting them.

He quirked a brow. "You just told me. Let me see it."

"If I show it to you, you won't force me to sign it, will you?" I asked.

"One of these days, *Lexie*, you're going to have to trust me."

With a glare, I summoned the pact from inside my locker. James plucked it out of my hand and read it over, a crease appearing between his brows as he concentrated.

To ignore the awkward nervousness of him judging my pact-writing abilities, I turned to my locker to rearrange the books. "Tell me this: why are you so eager for me to sign a pact? Why not just meet me, and we'll spar then?"

To my surprise, a disgusted look flitted across his face. "I can't."

"Can't or won't?"

"Can't," he said. "Gavon has forbidden it."

That was curious. "Gavon is preventing you from sparring with me? Why?"

"Because you're his *precious daughter*." He spat the words as if they were poison. When I'd first gone to New Salem, I'd gleaned that James wasn't too pleased about my existence—or that Gavon was mentoring me. Whatever jealousy he'd been harboring obviously hadn't gone away completely.

"That doesn't mean anything," I said quietly before deciding to change the subject. "What would a pact do, then?"

"Get around the edict passed by the Guild."

"Edict? What edict?"

"No one is allowed to spar or duel with you unless you agree to it yourself. And your sisters are off limits too, as we don't want you coming after the Guild." He snorted. "At least, that's how Gavon worded it. It was signed a week after you were last in New Salem."

I stared at him, dumbfounded. "W-what?"

"There is a formal decree signed by the Guildmaster," James

began, as if he were talking to a child. "It forbids anyone in the guild from sparring or dueling with you."

"So that's why Cyrus hasn't come back for me?" I said, my dazed mind churning over this new information. "Because Gavon forbade it?"

"Yep."

"And why didn't he forbid it *before* Cyrus kidnapped me?"

"Probably because he couldn't get the agreement from the rest of the council to override Cyrus," James said, as if we were discussing the weather. "But once we saw that you're in a clan—well, *were*," he grinned meanly, "Gavon made a pretty compelling case, and the Council approved it."

I leaned against my locker, scrambling to recapture the breath that had escaped. Eighteen months I'd lived on the edge of my seat, waiting for another fight to the death with Cyrus. Eighteen months of panicked anticipation, of sleepless nights and tears of frustration. All for nothing. Gavon had dealt with it and, for some stupid reason, decided not to inform me.

That explained why Cyrus hadn't shown up again, but I couldn't find the relief in that thought. No, the only emotion coursing through my brain was pure, unadulterated rage at Gavon for letting me dangle for so long.

"And nobody thought to tell me about this particularly helpful bit of information?" I said through clenched teeth.

James shrugged. "I really can't keep track of what things he has and has not informed you of. And I don't very much care. So this pact—"

"Forget it," I snapped, knowing if I didn't get away from him, I might fling him into a wall.

But he blocked my path. "Don't make me beg."

"You? Beg?" I snorted and moved to the left, which he blocked too. "James, let me go."

"I know you want to do this. So why are you fighting it? It's right there in the pact: I can't induct you into the Guild. I can't harm you. There's no reason you shouldn't want to do this—"

"Other than Gavon betraying me?" I said.

He actually looked perplexed. "How? By teaching you magic?"

I glared at him. "You know what he did."

"Gavon didn't bring you to New Salem, Cyrus did," James said, matter-of-factly. "Cyrus was the one who forced you into the introduction match. Besides, Gavon and Cyrus have been at each other's throats for almost a quarter century. All of that was just an attempt to usurp Gavon's Guildmastership."

I couldn't believe my ears. "A-all of that? All of that included the *murder of my aunt!*"

The hallway went deathly silent as all eyes turned in our direction. My face warmed and, to my horror, my eyes grew wet. I'd be *damned* if I cried in front of James or anyone else, so I turned and headed back to the bathroom.

Unfortunately, James caught up with me. "Look, I'm—"

"Get away from me," I snarled. "Don't talk to me. I'm not sparring with you. You and that whole group can just...*go to hell.*"

I pushed him away and stormed into the bathroom, slamming the stall door behind me and transporting myself back to my bedroom.

In the silence of my room, I slumped onto my bed and

buried my head in my hands. My head was full of conflicts. Anger at Gavon that he'd let me suffer so long, but relief that he'd at least taken a step to protect us. Disgust at James for being so coldhearted, but that nagging feeling in the back of my mind that wanted to spar with him. The angrier I became, the more annoying the itch until my fingers were sparkling with unspent magic.

I looked down at my fingertips, grateful I could let my magic release without consequence. It made me feel better, like sucking poison from a wound. And left me feeling disgusted at myself for even entertaining the notion of spending time with the people responsible for Jeanie's death.

I heard a loud curse from outside. Wiping my face, I slowly approached my window and was surprised to see James standing there, wincing and rubbing his red face.

I opened my window and leaned against the sill. "What the hell are you doing here?"

"What is this, a barrier charm?" he said, wincing as his hand made contact with the invisible force. "A little warning would've been nice."

"Thank you for confirming my magic is working properly," I said. "Too bad it doesn't have a sound barrier too. Go away."

"Why are you so upset with me?" James asked. "I didn't do anything."

"Really?" I seethed, nearly flying out the window in anger. "You didn't do anything wrong?"

"Yes, Lexie, *I* haven't done a thing wrong since the moment I saw you in the hall on the first day of school. So why do you persist in making me out to be a villain?"

"Because you're an insensitive prick who also wants to kill me!" I said, clinging to my anger for dear life. He was making a little too much sense, and if I wasn't careful, I'd start agreeing with him.

"For the love of…I'm *not* trying to kill you! Isn't that why you have that truth-telling charm?"

"Fine," I said, retrieving the stone from under my shirt. Annoyingly, it hadn't changed in temperature. "You're just an insensitive prick then. I don't know why I'm even having this conversation with you. I learned my lesson the first time."

And with that, I shut the window and crawled onto my bed.

That was, until I heard rocks against my window. Groaning, I walked up to the window just as one came sailing by my head.

"Oops." James snickered. "Good. Now come down here and let's have a conversation about your grievances against me."

"No."

"Lexie. Don't be a child."

"I am a child."

"You can't hide in there forever," James called as I slammed the window shut again. "You won't be able to get into college if you never leave your house. Georgetown, right?"

I glowered at the ceiling and rolled out of bed, slamming the window open magically this time. "Don't you dare talk to me about Georgetown. How do you even know that anyway?"

"I listen," James said, simply. "A courtesy I would ask you to extend to me."

I stared at him for a good minute, unsure what to do. Then with a growl, I slammed the window shut. The rocks began hitting my window again, so I turned and walked into the kitchen. But even there, I couldn't escape the *ping-ping-ping* against the glass.

"Damn it all," I muttered, standing from the table. I left the apartment with a scowl on my face, stomping down the staircase so loudly that I knew he'd hear me. He stood next to the tall oak tree, a satisfied smirk on his face.

"You have one minute."

James cleared his throat. "I'm sorry I offended you. It was not my intention."

"Not good enough."

The corner of his lip twitched. "I am sorry for insinuating that your aunt's death wasn't as grave as it was. I know she must have meant a lot to you, and losing her must've been very hard."

Damn, but he was good when he wanted to be. "Not good enough."

"Fine," James said, annoyance seeping into his voice. "I am also incredibly sorry for my behavior two years ago when we dueled."

"Oh? Well, thank you so much for your apology. That makes it all better."

"Sarcasm isn't an attractive quality," he replied evenly. "I was manipulated into thinking Gavon had different plans than he did. Cyrus had done a good job of exploiting my insecurities." To his credit, his gaze hadn't wavered once. "Fortunately, they're no longer an issue."

"Meaning?"

"Meaning you have nothing to fear from me."

I opened my mouth to argue, but no sound came out. He was telling the truth about that, at least, because my pendant was still cold.

"I understand you have issues with Cyrus, but I will ask you not to form an opinion of all New Salem based on one unhinged individual," James said.

"It's not just him," I spat. "Gavon trained me for six weeks and then sat there and did nothing during our duel—"

"He couldn't," James said. "Magically, he was prevented from interfering. And..." He cleared his throat. "I had instructions to be gentle. Instructions I ignored in favor of a childish vendetta championed by Cyrus. He is the one who wishes you dead."

"Then why train me for six weeks?" I said, my anger slowly dissolving into curiosity. "Why even show up at all?"

"You really spent six weeks with Gavon and still question his motives?" James laughed. "If there's one thing I know about Gavon, it's that he's soft. Especially where you're concerned. That's why you made such an enticing target for Cyrus."

"That's because he—"

"Because he's your father," James said, and this time, I couldn't hide the flinch. "You're going to have to accept it sooner or later. Whether you want his affections is up to you, but they've been true."

"I don't have to if I don't want to," I said, knowing I sounded like a child. None of this new information changed the fact that he'd disappeared afterward. Or that he hadn't told me he was my f...word.

"Have I assuaged your fears enough to agree to a pact?" James said.

The warning bells sounded in my head, and I glared at him.

"You'd like that, wouldn't you? Sway me with platitudes about Gavon and how he really feels, and the next thing I know, I'm back in New Salem, or worse."

"I'm not—"

"Save it," I snapped. I liked James better when he was being the womanizing, carefree senior, but this was his true personality. He wanted me around because it suited him, and his apologies were nothing more than mandatory kindness so I would do as he wanted.

Which made the surprise knee to his solar plexus so damned delicious.

He lay flat on the ground, coughing in pain and shock. "Wh—"

"Get away from my house and leave me the hell alone," I snarled. "No deal."

Eight

I stewed in my room for the rest of the afternoon. My homework remained untouched, as my brain was too scattered. I wasn't sure which train of thought to focus on first, so they all jumbled together in a mishmash of emotions that dully pounded in the back of my head.

For all my resistance, James' efforts hadn't been completely in vain. I did want to spar with him, if only to have access to a magical who knew what he was talking about. No doubt, James would instruct me with more than a little superiority, but at this point, I would've taken just about anything. Which was the problem: my desperation to learn and use magic was clouding my judgment. Again.

My emotions must've been written on my face, because Nicole was barely through the door when she asked if I wanted Mexican for dinner. The tired look in her eyes said she'd also had a trying day, so we piled into her car and drove the short distance to our favorite place.

The familiar pang of nostalgia echoed in my chest, especially as Nicole ordered herself a margarita. I glanced at the door and imagined Jeanie and Marie walking in, arguing about whatever irresponsible thing Marie had done. A wave of sadness threatened to overtake me, and I wrenched my eyes away from the entrance to keep my tears from falling.

"You're quiet tonight," Nicole said, playing with the straw in her giant glass. "What's up?"

I shrugged, wishing I had the words to talk to her. I should've told her about Gavon's edict, and how we were no longer in the crosshairs of his guild. But that might've invited questions about how I knew this, which would've brought up James and just made things more difficult.

At first, I hadn't told Nicole because I thought James would be gone after that first day. When I finally came to terms with him being around, I kept coming up with excuses as to why I wasn't telling Nicole. The current rationale was James wasn't harming anyone, and I was keeping an eye on him, so why worry her?

Still, I hated that we had another big secret between us. But more than that, I needed guidance and had no idea where to find it.

"You know you can tell me anything," Nicole said.

"I know," I said, scrounging for an excuse. "There's just a lot of stuff happening at school. I'm worried about my applications." Applications I hadn't even started yet…

Nicole smiled. "Want to talk about it?"

"Are you going to try to convince me that Florida Coastal is a better school than Georgetown?"

"Better, no. Cheaper, yes." She grinned, and my own smile widened. "I just hate seeing you so bent out of shape about this. I don't want you to be disappointed if it doesn't happen."

I sat up. "It will happen."

The pitying look on her face burned my stomach more than the salsa. "I know you think that, but it's a really competitive school. A really expensive, competitive school. Just keep your options open, that's all."

I nodded and played with my straw. I understood where she was coming from, but I also really didn't appreciate her lack of faith in me. Before Jeanie died, Nicole had always made me feel like I could do anything. Now, she was almost too realistic.

"Are you going to go back to school when I move out?" I asked, a little hopefully.

She blinked for a moment, obviously not expecting the question. "Let's cross that bridge when we get to it. I mean, you could stay—"

"But if I don't…would you go back?"

"M…maybe." She shook her head. "Don't worry about that. Tell me about school. Do you like your classes? Everything going okay? Any boys I should know about?"

"N…not really," I said.

Nicole's grin widened. "You hesitated."

"I mean…" I sighed, glancing at the ceiling. "There is someone—"

"Ooh, *Lexie!*" Nicole squealed so loudly that the couple behind us turned to look at her.

"Not *that* kind of guy," I said quickly. "He's…a fellow volunteer. Tutor. And he wants me to do this…thing with him.

But he's a complete asshole."

"Uh-huh…"

"Get that smile off your face," I said, throwing a chip at her. "It's not that kind of a project."

"I dunno, Lexie. Guys don't just ask—"

"He's gay," I said, if only to stop the conversation from going off track. "Look, the point is—I don't really trust him. He's burned me in the past. And now he wants us to work together."

"Why would you work with someone who's burned you?"

Good question. Was I actually still entertaining this idea? I'd made it clear to James that I didn't want to spar with him. But at the same time, part of me knew he wouldn't give up that easily. And that same part of me didn't want him to.

"I guess…if we worked together, it would be a lot of fun. Maybe increase my chances of getting more scholarship money." Scholarship money, defending our lives from evil magicals, same difference.

"I dunno, Lexie. Maya Angelou says—"

"Yeah, when someone shows you who they are, believe them." I chomped down on another chip. All the signs were telling me not to trust James, and yet, the pit of my stomach was for the idea. Or maybe it was just the salsa.

"Look, I'm not an expert in people," Nicole said. "But maybe you can find someone else to work with? If you're having this much conflict about working with him, then you already know the answer. And if worst comes to worst, you can always do it by yourself."

But that was the rub. I'd been sparring by myself and James

was right; it was a cheap imitation of the real thing.

"I'm fine, by the way," James said, appearing next to my locker the next day as I switched out my books. If he'd been put out by my surprise attack, he didn't show it. In fact, he almost looked too eager.

"I'm sure I don't care," I replied without looking at him. "Isn't that what you said yesterday?"

"Well, perhaps you should care about this. I took your pathetic excuse of a pact to Gavon for him to look over. He made a few additions, and if you would like to spar, he will allow us to sign it."

Allow. What kind of cosmic kick in the pants was it that Gavon had parental control over me when he hadn't earned it?

"Stop clenching your jaw," James said. "And your magic is showing."

I glanced down at my glowing fingers and counted to ten to calm down. "I didn't ask you to take it to Gavon to approve."

"I would've had to anyway, so I saved us a step," James said, following on my heels as I closed my locker and walked away. "You can't tell me you don't want to spar with me. I can see it on your face."

"Stop looking at my face then." How I wished James were in a different class. Was it too late to call out sick for the rest of the year?

"Lexie, wait—" James grabbed my arm and pulled me out of the hallway traffic.

"Let me go."

"Not until you listen to me without that chip on your

shoulder." His grip was firm but not painful, and his eyes, for better or worse, looked sincere. "It is an absolute travesty that you've been without a true sparring partner all this time. You've got an immense amount of power and it's wasted in this world's easy nonmagical solutions. You deserve someone who can keep up with you and put you through your paces. If not for me, do it for yourself."

"You'll forgive me for not believing you," I said but it lacked the conviction I needed. His earnest declaration spoke to the part of me yearning to be proud of my accomplishments instead of hiding them on empty beaches and in my bedroom.

"And you should stop blaming yourself for what happened to your aunt," he said, releasing me. "You aren't the one who killed her."

My jaw fell open, and I took a step back, feeling his blow land in the pit of my soul. "I...I don't..."

"Like I said, I can see it on your face," he replied with an uncharacteristic softness. "Just look at the pact, okay? If you still think I'm here to trick you...then fine, I'll leave it. But just look at it."

He pushed the paper into my hand and walked away, shifting into the easy demeanor he wore when not trying to convince me to do something idiotic. I leaned against the wall, my heart thudding in my chest and my focus on the absence of warmth from my pendant.

I unfolded the paper. The crinkles and tears looked familiar, as did the stroke of my pen on the page and the scratches. But my heart skipped a beat when I saw the additions in his handwriting, the scratching out of one word and adding of another. His handwriting was fluid and crisp, especially compared to my rounded strokes.

I pictured him sitting in that giant library, reading over my words. What did he think of my work? Was it silly to him, or was he impressed? I found the note about an "evil gang" and flushed with embarrassment, although Gavon had very smartly added "New Salem Warrior's Guild" in its place. He'd also changed "induct" to "induct, introduce, or otherwise admit," which was a good catch. He extended the same protections to my sisters as well. Everything, to my eyes, seemed to be geared toward protecting me from the Guild. My gut was telling me this was all on the up and up.

But my gut had fallen for his schemes before, and I didn't trust it.

I balled up the paper and headed to class, hoping to put this mess out of my mind. But James' attention was on me when I walked through the classroom door.

You shouldn't blame yourself.

But I did, because the guilt kept me on track. It forced me to put aside my own happiness to serve others, to work myself into the ground because it was better than ruminating on all the terrible decisions I'd made. Even if sparring with James was completely innocent, it was something good, and I didn't feel like I deserved anything good after what I'd let happen.

But if you sparred with him, you could protect Nicole better.

That was true, and also a bit of mental gymnastics. I read the pact again, searching for loopholes and additions that could trip me up, and again, found nothing but the clear intent to keep me away from the New Salem Warrior's Guild.

You could learn new tricks if Cyrus came back.

The promise of having a trained magical nearby was so tempting and so terrifying. Desperation was a bad look, but…

James glanced over his shoulder. I recognized the expression —it was the same one I'd worn when Gavon and I had started sparring. It was the look of a Warrior with too much magic and not enough space to use it. It was someone desperate for companionship. Just like me.

Heart pounding, I slowly nodded.

"Okay, so how do we do this?" I said, already regretting what I hadn't done. We'd agreed to meet at my sparring beach after school to complete the pact, although I remained on the fence as to whether I'd go through with it. I figured I had up until I put pen to paper…or whatever it was I had to do.

"We need this particular pact to be strong enough to get around the edict, which is pretty formidable," James said, and in puffs of green smoke, a cauldron and table appeared, along with a set of ingredients.

"It's a…potion?" I said.

"Why are you surprised?"

"Because…" Because this was the second time I'd seen James use a potion, and that flew in the face of what I knew about New Salem magicals. Weren't they the ones who massacred two hundred potion-makers in the seventeenth century?

"Potions are damned useful. In this particular case, we can include the will of the Guildmaster without his presence being necessary." He picked up a small vial of red liquid and poured it into the cauldron.

"And why…" The concoction puffed with a familiar purple color. "…doesn't the Guildmaster want to be here?"

"You'll have to ask him," James muttered, adding two white flowers to the pot. "This shouldn't take very long. It's not a very complex potion, but it does need the pact."

I was too busy watching the bubbling mixture in the cauldron to realize he was talking to me. When he pressed again, I procured the sheet of notebook paper and handed it to him. He balled it up and tossed it in the potion, which released a puff of greenish-purple smoke.

"Now, the last thing we need, as is customary with a pact, is a bit of blood."

A dagger appeared in his hand, and I took three steps back. "Hang on a second!"

"You're too excitable," he said, turning the knife in his hand and pricking his palm. Three drops of blood fell into the liquid, and it turned a brilliant forest green. Then he wiped the knife on his shirt and handed it to me.

I didn't take it. "That's how you get diseases, you know."

"I don't have any diseases," he said with a frown.

"I'll conjure my own knife, thank you," I said, retrieving a knife from our kitchen cabinet. I held the blade close to my palm and asked myself once more if this was the right decision.

"I can do it if you're scared."

"I'm not *scared*," I said, before dragging the edge along my palm. The pain was slight at first then sharp. Blood pooled in my palm as I held it over the cauldron.

One, two, three drops into the potion.

The mixture turned bright purple—my magic's color—then

a brilliant white. Something tingled in the base of my stomach, and I knew it was done. We were both bound to the pact I'd written, that Gavon had tweaked.

Oh shit, what had I done?

"Now," James said, clapping his hands. "Let's get started, shall we?"

But I was staring at the cauldron, holding onto the feeling that I'd just made a grave mistake. "I'm such an idiot," I whispered.

There was no time to worry, because before I knew it, a bright green attack spell was headed straight for me. I had one second to react, diving out of the way. Curses spilled out of my mouth faster than I could think them. But James didn't give me an inch, firing three more, which had me scrambling across the sand as fast as I could.

"God, Alexis, make it a *challenge,* why don't you?" he drawled. "I asked you to *spar* with me, not play games."

I couldn't even get out the words to argue that he wasn't letting me breathe, but the more I dashed away, the more this became familiar. The tension in my chest, the anticipation of his next move. The pooling of magic in my hands. James was right —sparring with myself was no substitution for the thrill of having someone else hurling magic at me. He moved in ways I couldn't even fathom, his mastery of magic apparent from even my own amateur observations.

But he had a weakness—his own ego. He considered himself so above me that he'd left himself open to attack on his left side.

He saw the spell a second too late, and he flew backward, tumbling toward the shoreline. When he came to a stop, he looked dazed, sand dripping from his hair.

Despite myself, I grinned. Sparring with Gavon had always felt like I was playing catch-up; he'd held back for my benefit. But with James there would be no mercy. I'd either have to step up and fight back or get creamed.

I finally took a breath, gathering another attack spell in my hand. "You were saying?"

"Cockiness doesn't suit you, Alexis," he replied.

"Winning looks absolutely beautiful."

"Little early to be declaring yourself the victor."

"Yeah, I—" The force of magic hit hard, but harder still was the impact on the sand dune behind me. No, James would most assuredly not take it easy on me. He gave me just a moment to rest before another volley came like bright green cannonballs. I projected a wall of protective spells and watched the green balls bounce harmlessly off it. But that wouldn't hold for long.

Sure enough, the next volley tore right through my magical barrier. Just before it slammed into me, I transported to a safer spot on the beach. James' back was still turned, so I took advantage—

But my spells bounced harmlessly off his back. He glanced at me over his shoulder, wearing that cocky, smug smile.

"You never leave your back unprotected. Didn't you learn anything from Gavon?"

I glared at him. "You'll have to show me that trick."

"And give you an advantage? Not a chance."

"Like teaching me how to protect my back is an advantage," I said with a healthy roll of my eyes. "Unless..." I quirked a brow. "Are you saying we're evenly matched?"

The faintest hint of a blush appeared on his cheeks. "I'm saying that you're not a complete waste of my time. But I've also been taking it easy on you. Let's see how you fare when I come at you with all I've got."

I grinned wider. "Bring it on."

Nine

The sky was pink when I opened my eyes, and the sound of the waves lapping against the shore almost lulled me back to sleep. I couldn't remember how I'd gotten here except...

Awareness returned like a freight train and the memory of sparring with James came with it. I couldn't remember how or when I'd passed out, but the dull ache behind my eyes told me it was due to lack of magic. And the pink light above my head said I'd been asleep for hours.

Turning my head slowly, I spotted a dark form against the white sand. Gently, I gathered my strength to stand, each movement taking longer than usual from pain and exhaustion. Once I was upright, I stumbled over to the dark figure, ready for whatever he might throw at me.

His eyes were open as he stared at the stars, his face pale. He didn't acknowledge my presence except to blink twice. For a moment, I wondered if he was screwing with me. Perhaps he was trying to knock me off my guard. But at the same time, I doubted he could fake such lethargy. Besides, why wait until I was awake to hurt me when I'd been out cold for hours?

My body gave out, and I tumbled to my knees, before collapsing beside him.

"What happened?" I asked the sand.

"What do you think?" he replied hoarsely. "I can't move."

I was so weak I couldn't smile, but I could manage a snort. "I thought you were taking it easy on me."

"I was. Just you wait until next week."

"As far as I can tell, Riley, you're on the ground with me."

He released a loud breath. "True. I must be rusty. I was quite stupid not to bring a healing potion. I'm sure I'm going to hear all about it when I return home. Right after Gavon kills me."

I turned my head to watch him consider his unpleasant fate. "Why?"

"I've stayed out way past midnight." He groaned and rubbed his face. "This is going to be unpleasant."

"You…have a curfew?" It seemed so horribly mundane. James, the supposed leader of the evil gang that would take over the world…had to be home by midnight. "What, is Gavon going to ground you?"

"Ground?"

"You know, take away your magic."

He released a soft breath. "And a lecture, I'm sure. Gavon loves his lectures. I swear I've heard the same one ten times this year. Usually while I've got a rag in hand, cleaning that damned library of his. I *hate* that library."

My lack of magic had made me loopy, because that sounded hilarious. "Gavon makes you clean when you're in trouble?"

"That's his favorite method of punishment. Take away my magic, force me to clean until he's satisfied, then I get it back." James finally sat up, white sand falling from his hair. He mumbled something unintelligible while rubbing his pale face. Then, a bit of his charm returned as he smirked. "Next time, tell your sister to make us a healing potion."

"Sure, I'll just tell her you and I are having a rousing sparring match and she'll get right on it."

James shook his head. "Was that sarcasm?"

"*Duh*," I said. At his confused expression, I rolled my eyes as I pushed myself to sit. "*Obviously* she doesn't know about you. That would just freak her out."

"Then bring your other sister."

I blinked. "But she's… Gavon doesn't know about Marie?"

"What about her?"

I clamped my jaw shut. "Nothing. She's horrible. Doesn't heal me. That's all."

If Gavon didn't know that Marie had been gone the past year and a half, that meant he hadn't been…well, around. And although I hadn't seen him, I'd always had this vision of him hiding in the bushes or watching me in some crystal ball and making sure I was all right. Maybe I just wanted to believe that I was still wrong about him.

But it was too early to stress about Gavon, not when my eyes wanted to close and fall back into a deep, dark sleep.

"Well, then I suppose the next time we spar, we should take more care not to exhaust ourselves," James said. "Unlike you, I don't have a healer and a potion-maker waiting around at home for me." He pushed himself to stand and swayed for a moment before steadying himself. "I suppose I might as well get it over with."

"Warriors don't whine, we just do," I said, playing with the sand.

"Yeah." He made a face. "I *hate* when Gavon says that."

I smiled. "Good luck."

I transported myself back home, feeling like I could sleep for a thousand years. I'd never missed Marie more. I was tempted to text her and beg her to heal me, but I was pretty sure she'd ignore it. Which meant it was up to me to hide my exhaustion from Nicole.

Face pressed against the pillow, I waited for sleep to come. But there was an excited undercurrent swimming amongst the lethargy. Sparring with myself was tiring, but this? This was exhaustion mixed in with the supreme satisfaction of accomplishing something great. This was like working for days on a project and turning it in to receive an A. This was…

Probably what James had been talking about.

I'd been too new at sparring when I was fifteen to understand the difference. Then, sparring had been something I wanted—more like needed—to do, but I'd always assumed it was because I wanted to be closer to Gavon. Now, even though I hated James, I couldn't wait to get into the sparring ring with him.

But to be honest, it wasn't just about the fighting. James represented an entire existence that could have been mine, had things gone differently. Jeanie had always been a hands-off sort of guardian, leaving the three of us to our own devices most of the time. And with me, Gavon seemed to be okay with me failing miserably before he offered up some wisdom. James, however, seemed to have a much different opinion of him.

But I was Gavon's… (I shuddered) and James was…well, I didn't know who James was really. He was a Riley, which meant he'd probably descended from the James Riley who'd led the Separation. Gavon had said that Warriors usually take apprentices from other families, in order to keep to a strict training schedule without emotion.

Maybe that explained the difference between his approach with James and me.

Still, it didn't really matter. His actions spoke clearly: he'd let Cyrus come after me and my sisters. He'd let Cyrus kill my aunt, the same way he'd let my mother die.

Her memory floated back to me, another part of the magical memory I'd obtained because she'd used my magic to defend her family. Along with my almost innate ability to fight, the memory also gave me the blessing and curse of hearing my dead mother's last words. With them I felt the brunt of her fear, her bravery, and the resolution that she would die before she let anything happen to her family.

It was that emotional hurricane that I'd poured into the barrier spell around the house, and that had been driving me to spar, to be better, to learn everything I could. And even though I was still worried I'd made a terrible mistake with James, I could at least convince myself that it was in pursuit of making myself a more powerful protector.

I must've fallen asleep because a soft rapping jerked me

awake. "Lexie? Are you still asleep?"

"Yah," I said as she opened the door. The sun was brighter than I remembered, so I must've slept in. "Late night."

"You were out of it," she said with a suspicious glance. "Do you even remember me coming in this morning?"

I shook my head. Thank God I'd come back from the sparring beach before she'd noticed I was missing.

"My car's acting up again, so I had to take it to the shop," she said, leaning against the doorframe. "Five hundred bucks."

"Ow," I said. "Do you need some money?"

"No," Nicole said. "It's my car, my problem."

"I can use some of my tutoring money. I've got a bunch now."

"I can't ask that of you," she said before cracking a smile. "When you're still living here during college, then you can pay some rent."

I huffed. "I'm not staying here."

Her smile faltered for a moment then returned. "In any case, I appreciate the offer, but I don't need help. I've picked up a few shifts at the pharmacy."

The stone pressing against my chest grew warm and I quirked a brow. "Really?"

"Yeah," Nicole said. Even if the stone hadn't alerted me to her lie, I would've known by the way she glanced everywhere but me. Nicole had always been a terrible liar.

But now, she was looking at the clock on the wall. "Aren't you supposed to be tutoring right now?"

I seized, panic coursing through me. It was 2:20—and my tutoring with Charles started twenty minutes ago.

"Ah *shit!*"

I appeared in the bathroom of the library, bracing myself against the sides of the stall as the room swayed around me. I'd not only used magic to transport here, but also to do a quick costume change and tie my hair up. It would've been better to stay home and cancel, but I was already on one strike with Mrs. Gilly and if I flaked again, I'd lose my customer.

Once the world stopped moving, I hurried out of the bathroom, praying Charles hadn't left yet. I really needed the money, and Mrs. Gilly seemed like the kind of person who would blackball me if I crossed her.

"And then when you want to solve for X—"

I stopped short. James sat next to my young charge, who was looking up at the older teen with a wide-eyed admiration. The older guy had a pen in hand, hunched over a piece of paper while walking Charles through whatever he was talking about. As I came closer, I saw algebra. James was teaching Charles how to do algebra.

Well, wasn't that surprising.

"Um," I said, loud enough to get their attention.

"Oh good, you're here," James said, standing up. *He* didn't look tired at all, and considering how lethargic he'd been earlier, he must've found some kind of potion. His gaze traveled up and down my body. "Sleep late?"

I glared at him. "What are you doing here?"

"At the moment, helping Charles with his algebra since his tutor was twenty minutes late." The son of a bitch looked like he was trying not to smile, and that just made me angrier.

"I got waylaid," I snapped, brushing by him. "Sorry, Charles, I can stay later if you want—"

"No, I'm going to tell my mom that I want James to tutor me," he announced with his nose in the air. "At least he makes sense."

I turned back to James and placed a hand on my hip. "*You*? A good teacher?"

He simply smiled. "Sorry, I'm not available for tutoring. I'm sure *Lexie* will figure it out eventually. And as for why I'm here, I wanted to give you something."

I glanced at the kid then told him to wait while I followed James around a bookshelf. "What?"

He grinned. "Don't be so mean, Lexie, or I won't give you this healing potion."

My mouth watered at the idea, even though every healing potion I'd ever had tasted like feet. "What do you want in return?"

"A fully rested partner for Friday," he said, placing a small vial in my hand. "You look like the dead."

I closed my hand around the vial, but didn't move to drink it. "There's no poison in this is there? Or mind control or—"

"No, Lexie," he said, and my sapphire remained cool against my skin. "And one of these days, you're *going* to have to trust me. After all, we spent all night passed out on a beach together and not a hair on your head was harmed."

I blushed, although I wasn't sure why. Neither was I sure why I asked, "So did you get grounded?"

He shrugged, but not before his upper lip curled briefly. "I got a lecture about sparring without healing potions while he forced me to make one."

I looked down at the vial in my hand, suddenly curious if James was here because he wanted me fully rested or because Gavon had forced him to. Or maybe both.

"See you at school on Monday." And with that, he transported away.

I was so surprised to see his display of magic that it took me a moment to realize what it meant. Gavon had loosened the leash a bit, allowing James to have magic on this side. Or perhaps it was only so he could deliver the potion.

I opened the vial and sniffed. It certainly smelled like a healing potion. I pressed the glass to my lips and took a sip. The taste was immediate, as was the need to chase it with something better-tasting. But the dull ache behind my eyes lessened. It was a healing potion, all right.

Bracing myself for the disgusting taste, I tossed back the rest of it. Although it was just a few tablespoons, it filled me up from my head to my toes, like a cup of coffee without the jittery caffeine. My eyes opened a bit wider, my brain cleared, and my bones didn't hurt so much.

"Are you done back here?" came Charles' annoyed voice. "Where did James go?"

"Back home," I said, pocketing the vial so he wouldn't see it. "Come on, let's get to work."

But as we sat down and got started, a question entered my mind. "James wasn't really *that* good a teacher, was he? I mean, sure he's cool, but—"

"No, he showed me this cool trick with solving for X," Charles said, sliding over his paper to show me.

"Huh..." That seemed awfully...out of character for him. James was no idiot, and Gavon had made sure he was educated on all the important things. But to offer a kid some help, even if he was just passing the time until I showed up, was new.

I decided it was probably because he'd gotten some hero worship out of it.

"All right, show me what he taught you, and we'll work on that."

Ten

James and I sparred every Friday night for three weeks straight and I was starting to enjoy it. Not because I found his company pleasurable, but because I was able to see it for what it really was. A chance to make myself stronger, to become a better Warrior. This was an opportunity I'd probably never have again, so I wasn't going to squander it.

James constantly changed his tactics, keeping me on my toes, and making me feel like an idiot and a genius at the same time. I was always learning something new—either from myself or from him. Although we tried not to overdo it, inevitably, we always did. Luckily, James started bringing healing potions so we could at least make it back home afterward. Even with the potion, Saturday mornings were rough—especially when Nicole barged into my room, asking why I was so tired. I finally told her that I was going out with friends. After she stopped screaming from shock, she gave me a free pass to spend as much time with these "friends" as possible.

In reality, there'd been little change to my social life. My schedule was still overflowing with homework, volunteering, and tutoring, and James preferred to ignore me completely at school. He was now gathering his own group of friends—most of whom were pretty and popular like him. The only time he deigned to speak with me was the brief discussions after school about when we would spar next, and the occasional random question about popular culture.

"So basically, I'm just taking pictures of myself?" James said, showing me the new phone he'd acquired over the past week. He'd approached me as soon as I reached my locker, thrusting the device into my hand and peppering me with questions about it.

I took the phone from him, annoyed that it was much nicer than mine, and drew little devil horns on the photo he'd taken of himself. "Basically."

"Gavon didn't prepare me for all this… Thanks," he said with a dry look. He snatched the photo out of my hand and deleted it. "And what is this football thing everyone keeps talking about?"

"It's a game. Our team sucks though," I replied, envisioning the conversation between Gavon and James about the internet and cell phones. "The first game is this Friday."

"Huh. Callista wants me to go with her," James said with a frown as the girl in question walked down the other end of the hall. "Is this footsie thing just on Friday?"

"Yeah, but we're going to be sparring, remember?" I said, hoping the hint was enough.

But it went unnoticed. "Be right back." He stood and

walked over to Callista, conferring with her quietly. From the happy look on her face, I guessed he was asking her to the football game. He walked back to my locker, looking pleased with himself.

"Can we move our sparring match to tonight?" he asked, nonchalantly.

A surge of anger coursed through me. "Right, because I'm just going to rearrange my schedule so you can get laid on Friday night."

He squinted at me for a moment. "That means…"

"Ugh. Having sex."

"You say that like it's a bad thing," James said. "If the sparring partners in New Salem are woefully underwhelming, the women are terrible. Half the girls are empaths and enchanters, not even worth my time."

I had to laugh and glanced at the emptying hallway around us. "You realize these girls are nonmagical, right?"

"Yes, but they're nicer to look at and smell better." He cleared his throat. "To your point, I respect that you've got a lot on your plate and my intention was not to make your schedule for you. I was simply *asking* if we could reschedule so I could go out on Friday—"

"Oh, I'm sorry," I said unapologetically. "Maybe next time you shouldn't cancel on people because you've got a better offer."

"I'm not asking to cancel, simply move it." He smiled, turning on the charm. "And perhaps if Gavon were to ask where I was on Friday…"

I slammed my locker shut. "You've *got* to be kidding. Now

you're asking me to cover for you?"

The charm disappeared. "You don't understand. I can't even *breathe* without asking for permission. *Please* help me. If I don't get out from under Gavon's thumb soon, I might explode. The only time I get to myself is when I'm here, and even *then*, he won't even let me have my magic except when we spar."

My gaze held all the little care I had.

"I'm sorry I made you upset," James said, although he sounded more like I was the one in the wrong. "Please, can we spar tonight?"

"I've made other plans tonight."

He made a noise.

I rolled my eyes. "In case you were unaware, I'm *trying* to get enough money to go to college. And that means tutoring on Tuesdays and Thursdays, volunteering Wednesdays and Fridays, and spending all weekend studying and trying to keep my grades up. None of which, I'm sure, you care about—"

"I do care," he said, stepping in front of me while I tried to get around him. "I just happened to see an opportunity to do both things."

I glared at him. "Move."

"You really do make an amazing opponent." He smiled warmly and, despite my disgust at him, my heart fluttered. Especially when he grazed the skin of my collarbone to lift my pendant from beneath my shirt. "See? Telling the truth."

I stepped back from him, and the chain fell from his finger.

"And I'm also telling the truth about Gavon. He's been relentless lately about keeping me in New Salem when I'm not at school. What good is me learning the culture if I'm not free to experience it?"

I steadied my glare at him.

"Fine," he said, loudly. "In exchange for doing this for me, I'll do one favor for you."

"No."

"Come on. There has to be something I can do for you. A spell you haven't mastered? A potion I can brew you?"

"No… Wait." A thought came to mind. "Yes, there is something. I want a spell I can use to find someone."

"A locator spell?" James said, scratching the back of his head. "I guess. Why do you want one?"

"None of your business," I said. "So do we have a deal?"

"The terms of the deal are that you and I will spar tonight, you'll cover for me on Friday should Gavon ask, and I will find you one locator spell," James said, tapping the items on his fingers.

"Is this a magical pact?" I said, taking one step back.

"No. I mean, yes, but not nearly as binding." He held out his hand. "Deal?"

"Deal."

I had to come up with an excuse for getting out of tutoring early, and I had to completely cancel my volunteering, so I just hoped it would be worth it. The only thing that kept me from not showing up was the promise of a locator spell to find Marie.

James arrived in a puff of green smoke, a disgruntled look on his face. "Let's just get on with this. I have to be back before ten."

"Where's my spell?"

"Here." He pulled a scrap of paper out of his pants pocket and shoved it at me. "Best I could do."

I balked. "Did you *tear this out of a book*?"

"Yeah?"

I cradled the paper gently in my hands. "You're a monster."

"Yes, well, Gavon started asking questions when I was in the library. He was very suspicious of me when I asked him if we could spar more than once a week."

"Wait...you want to permanently change our sparring night?" I asked, still cradling the poor ripped page.

"You said that this ballfoot thing happens every Friday," James said with a wave of his hand. "I assume things will go well this Friday with Callista, so I also assume we'll be seeing more of each other. She apparently has a party at her parents' condo on the beach, so I was planning on going to that too."

I couldn't keep the anger off my face. "Great. You've been here for one month and you've already got more action than I do."

He actually laughed. "I'm popular in New Salem, too. Things aren't that different over here."

"I think they're a *lot* different."

"I meant people aren't that different," he said. "They like mystery. They like someone who listens to them and makes them feel important."

"That's...astute," I said. "Shockingly so."

"You wound me. I'm not as blind as you might think." He cocked his head in my direction. "Although I'm confused why you're angry at me right now."

"Because...because..." Why *was* I angry? I was a little

annoyed that he was forcing me to change my schedule, but I was also a little hurt. Hurt at my classmates for never including me, and hurt that James was abandoning me for them. Not that I liked him, of course, but he was my evil magical. Not theirs.

"I mean, *maybe* I want to go to the party too," I said, finally.

James blinked at me. "You want me to ask you out?"

My face flamed, and I kicked the sand. "Not like *that*, but I never get invited to parties. If you're going to say you're hanging out with me, you might actually *hang* out with me."

"Fine, would you like to go out to a party at Callista's on Friday?"

"Well, not if you're *obligated* to ask me—"

"Make up your damned mind!"

"Fine! Yes!" I barked. "I'd like to go to the party."

"Good, but in return, you have to tell Callista there's nothing going on between us," James said.

I was ready to vehemently deny any proposed changed to our ad hoc agreement; instead I could scarcely believe what I'd just heard. "I'm sorry, what?"

"She thinks that because you and I know each other, there's something going on between us."

"Yeah…no…" I laughed nervously, though not quite sure why the thought made me squirm. "Fine. If the topic comes up, I will tell her."

"And don't talk to me so much at school."

I glared at him. "You're the one always coming to me with questions."

"I'm glad we're on the same page. Now can we please get on with sparring? This conversation is exhausting."

We sparred for about half an hour, but it was clear neither of us wanted to be in each other's presence, so we called it a night. James didn't even bother to say goodbye before disappearing in his puff of green smoke.

I plopped down on a sand dune and pulled the torn paper out of my pocket. Once I completed the spell, I would force James to return the page to the book from whence he'd torn it. Damn him and his stupidity. He could've used magic if he'd wanted to hide the book.

Regardless, I finally had my locator spell, and I was finally going to get hold of Marie.

Locator Charm

To locate an individual, use magic to locate their aura then transport to that location.

"So, so helpful, James."

He couldn't have found a different kind of magic than another damned charm? Or maybe stuck around long enough to show me how to use it? But that was James. Egotistical, selfish James, who did nothing for others unless it benefitted him first.

Ugh. Good luck with that, Callista.

I placed the paper on the sand in front of me and took a few calming breaths, wiping James and his idiocy from my mind. Concentrating on the sound of the waves against the shore, I felt the breeze against my skin, signaling that fall wasn't too far off. After a few minutes of quiet meditation, I felt ready to attempt the spell.

This aura thing was something that had long perplexed me. I guessed it was the colored mist that surrounded magicals sometimes, like mine was purple and James' was green.

Marie's magic was white, so I closed my eyes and focused on the way it had looked, the way it felt mixing with my magic as she healed me. The particular knowing in my gut that it was Marie, and Marie's magic.

Flashes of light and indistinguishable objects crept by my mind's eye, but I couldn't grab any of them long enough to see them clearly. I felt Marie's presence—or rather, the particular signature of her healing magic somewhere among the energies, but it was like screaming in a crowded football stadium. After a few feeble attempts, I pulled the magic back to myself, defeated.

Yet another perfect example of how completely lost I was without a true magical tutor. This should've been easy, but there I was, fumbling my way through something I had no idea about.

I picked up the scrap of paper and searched the words for any other meaning, but they stared back at me with infuriating simplicity. Tears gathered in my eyes out of frustration and loneliness.

I'd been stupid to think James would be anything like Gavon. Then again, Gavon hadn't shown his face once since the first day of school, not even to oversee the pact. So maybe they were exactly the same.

Either way, it was clear I was still on my own.

Eleven

James didn't ask whether the locator spell worked; in fact, he ignored me for the rest of the week. Dutifully, when Callista asked me what was going on between us, I explained that we were old friends from childhood and that he was a pain in the ass.

"But if you like him, Godspeed," I said, knowing that whatever negatives I offered would go in one ear and out the other.

She was a little surprised when I'd also mentioned that James had invited me to the party, but was gracious enough not to veto it. Maybe James had offered some sob story about how awkward and lonely I was. At least, that's how I played it in my head.

I'd known my classmates had been drinking and partying for the past three years, but I'd never gotten an invite. Marie made sure of that during my freshman year. But after Jeanie died, I'd lost all interest in the concept, mostly because I couldn't see a reason for distracting myself when I had bigger things to worry about.

But I was a senior, my grades were decent, my volunteer schedule packed, and my checking account filling up. I could take a breather. Even so, the guilt of doing something fun instead of focusing on college was at an all-time high on Friday afternoon, so I did another round on my admissions essay and application for Georgetown, if only to distract myself before the party.

After an hour of unfocused effort where nothing I wrote seemed right, I went to my closet to figure out how to be a normal teenager for once. All my clothes suddenly looked ridiculous and underwhelming, and everything I tried on seemed to make me look weird. What I wouldn't have given for Marie right then…

I glanced at my phone then picked it up.

I'm going to my first party tonight. I need help figuring out what to wear.

A moment passed.

Read 6:45pm

I sighed, tossing my phone on the bed and frowning. I'd gotten my hopes up just a fraction—

My phone buzzed.

I scrambled across the room, grabbing it and holding my breath.

Jeans and t-shirt. Don't overthink it.

I sat on the bed, and relieved tears fell down my face. It wasn't much—it wasn't anything, really. But at this point, I'd take even the smallest inkling that Marie might consider coming home, especially after my disastrous locator spell had failed. This was proof that she wasn't unreachable.

"What are you—Lexie!" Nicole opened the door fully and rushed into the room. "Lexie, what is it?"

I held my phone out to show Nicole the text message. "She finally answered."

Nicole took the phone from me and scrolled through, her frown deepening. "You've been texting Marie all this time?"

I nodded and wiped my cheeks. "I needed to know she was okay and not—"

Nicole stopped scrolling and sat on the bed next to me. "Lexie, you don't need to worry about Marie. She made her own decision to leave—"

"It's not that," I said, wiping my face. "It's that… What if…" I wasn't sure I wanted to say the words 'Cyrus' or 'New Salem' to Nicole. "I just don't like not having you guys here."

Nicole pulled me into a hug and stroked my hair. "Marie needed space. So that's what she got."

My gem warmed—not hot, but enough to inform me that Nicole was skirting the truth. Then again, their fight had been epic, and I guessed she still wasn't over it.

I pulled away from Nicole and wiped the wetness off my cheeks. "I didn't mean to make you worry."

"I came in to see if you wanted dinner," she said, glancing around at my disaster of a room. "But it looks like you've already got plans…"

"Yeah," I said. Lying about going to a party seemed so mundane compared to the big, giant lie about James attending my school. "I got invited to a party."

"Really?" Nicole nodded approvingly. "That's great."

"Yeah…" Only I would have a guardian actively promoting my partying and socializing.

"I mean it," she said with a small laugh. "I worry that you're too focused on school. This is your senior year. If you don't slow down, you might miss your entire childhood. And next year, you won't be able to play around like this. Not while working."

I bit my tongue instead of arguing that I was going to get a scholarship. In any case, I knew myself well enough to know I'd work regardless. I didn't do well with downtime.

"I suppose I should lay down some ground rules," Nicole said. "No drinking and driving, no drinking and using magic. If you're going to be out later than midnight, text me and let me know."

"I will," I said.

"And I love you."

I stared at her for a moment before shaking the surprise out of my head. "What was that for?"

She brushed a stray piece of hair out of my face. "Just wanted to make sure you knew. Things haven't been easy since…well, for a while. And I know you miss Marie, and…and Jeanie. But I'm really proud of how you've handled everything."

I swallowed the words *Gavon's apprentice is going to school with me and we're sparring every week* and smiled at her. "Thanks, I guess."

"Marie's right, by the way. T-shirt and jeans. Don't overthink it."

I skipped the football game entirely, as sitting outside in the sweltering September humidity wasn't my idea of a good time. I kept popping over to Callista's condo on the beach, waiting for signs that the game was over, before returning home to pace my room and watch TV. Finally, around eleven, I saw shadows in the windows and lights on.

Taking a deep breath, I climbed the stairs, wondering why I was fearful of the kids I'd grown up with. It was ridiculous to be nervous, especially after all the other things I'd been through, but there it was. My hand shook as I opened the door, and the sounds of conversation filled my ears.

Nobody seemed to notice me walking in, which was nice. I felt a little better knowing everyone in the room, and was even greeted by a couple of girls from my classes. They helped me find a drink, and we stood in the living room making small talk.

"So, Lexie, where are you going to college?" asked Arpita, one of the girls who'd taken graphic design with me.

"Uh… Georgetown, I hope," I answered quietly.

"Wow, that's awesome."

"Far, though," said another girl, Emily. "Aren't you worried about leaving home?"

I chewed my lip, unsure how to answer that. Although I planned to be living far away, I could pop home whenever I wanted. I was taking too damned long to answer the question, so I spat out, "I mean, there's a lot here that I would rather forget."

"Oh, that's right," Tamara said. "Your aunt died a few years ago, right?"

I clicked my tongue at her flippant tone. "Yes. I've been living with my sister."

"Bummer."

"Yeah…bummer…"

"So," asked Gee, the editor of our yearbook, "what's the deal with James?"

"Um." I searched for the rehearsed words I'd been using all this time, but I couldn't find them. "He's an ass."

"Really? He seems so nice."

"He fakes it well," I said with a snort. "I mean, he—"

"He's coming over here now," Tamara said, brushing her hair behind her ears.

James said hello to everyone except me, drawing blushes and nervous giggles from all the girls. I pursed my lips at him, waiting for him to acknowledge me.

"Lexie, come get a drink with me," he said, taking my arm and dragging me into the mostly empty kitchen.

"Well, hello to you too," I said, ripping my arm out of his. "What do you want? I was socializing."

"Hardly. That was painfully awkward, even across the room. I could practically see you sweating," James said in a hurried whisper. "Explain this college application process, because everyone keeps asking me where I'm going and I don't know what to tell them."

"You can't just enroll in college in most places. You have to apply see if they'll accept you. Just say you're going to one of the state schools and be done with it."

"No, I want something that sounds impressive." A beat. "I should say I'm going to Georgetown with you."

"*Don't you dare!*" I hissed.

James chuckled, and I was sure my face was bright red. "Why not?"

"Because!"

"Because why?"

I dismissed the magic prickling at my fingertips. "Because it's a hard school to get into, and I don't want them thinking that you can get in because…because…"

He chuckled. "Because I could just snap my fingers and be enrolled?"

"*Yes.* That's cheating."

"How?" he asked with that damned smirk.

"Because you can't use magic to get whatever you want. You have to *work* for it—"

"I'm just telling them I'm going. I have no plans to, *obviously.*" He crossed his arms over his chest. "But do tell me more about this fascinating philosophy of not using magic to get what you want."

Instead of taking the bait, I swiped the glass out of his hand and marched out onto the balcony, both to calm my angry heart and to keep my magic from blasting him until next Tuesday. I leaned over the weathered wood and listened to the distant sound of the gulf against the sand until the tingling disappeared.

I wasn't sure what James had said that set me off. Maybe I was jealous he didn't carry with him a bucketload of guilt and angst about using magic. Maybe I couldn't stand him lying about the college of my dreams, especially with as hard as I'd worked over the past few years. Maybe I was just hurt and lonely, even in this party full of people I knew.

Inside, James was leaning against the marble countertops like he'd been doing it for decades. Callista sidled up next to him and offered him a drink, not knowing she was offering it to a boy whose ancestors had been banished to an alternate universe, and that he had the power to blow her to bits. No, to Callista, James was just the new, hot thing.

And...I *was* jealous. Not of the girl James was with, but of James himself. In less than a month, he'd managed to become more popular and more well-liked than I had in my entire thirteen years with these kids. When he wasn't being an asshole, he had an easygoing way about him, a confidence that made him just plain likable. He was quick to laugh and even quicker to smile, and those around him were obviously at ease.

How much of this came from his own natural inclinations, and how much from Gavon?

After all, Gavon had been the first to cross the tear, to ingratiate himself with the local magicals. He'd made my mother fall in love with him. He'd fooled me into thinking he cared, although that could've been because of my own naivete.

Perhaps it was because, for the first time, I'd found someone who really got me. It had been heartbreaking when he left, not just because I'd lost Jeanie, but I'd also lost my confidant and mentor. My friend.

And now I had another magical who—despite his flaws— understood me on a deeper level. But he was abandoning me as well, this time for the more interesting people in my class.

The longer I sulked, the clearer it became that coming to the party had been a bad idea. I opened the sliding glass door and headed for the exit.

"Whoa, wait, where are you going?" James said, leaving Callista in the kitchen and meeting me by the door. "You aren't leaving, are you?"

"Yeah," I said, glancing at Callista, whose expression had

darkened considerably. "This isn't fun. I'm going home."

"Okay, but..." James followed my gaze, frowned, then turned back to me. "You aren't still angry at me, are you? We can spar, and you'll cover for me if Gavon—"

"Sure," I said with a wave of my hand. "Whatever you want."

James seemed placated, because he returned to Callista, who was shooting questioning looks at him. I almost wanted to know what he'd say—friend? Convenient person he blasted magic at? Definitely not someone for Callista to be jealous of.

But as I looked behind me at the party of people, I decided maybe James was just one of them.

And I was not.

The moment I arrived home, I magicked myself out of my clothes and into my pajamas, letting out a loud sigh when my bra disappeared. Let James have his parties and girls. I had my bed, and that was all right with me.

But first, my stomach growled. I hadn't had more than a handful of chips at the party, so I meandered out of my bedroom and into the kitchen.

My rummaging must've woken Nicole up, because she opened her bedroom door and called for me.

"You're home early?" she said, walking into the kitchen in her pajamas. "Everything okay?"

"Turns out I'm not a partier," I said with a half-shrug. "Really not my scene."

"Is hanging out with me and watching Netflix your scene?" Nicole asked. "I decided to start Buffy tonight. I think there's a couple pints of ice cream in the freezer."

At that, I had to smile. "Yeah, actually, that sounds awesome."

It had been ages since Nicole and I had spent a night curled up on the couch watching TV. After Jeanie had died, it was our go-to evening routine so we wouldn't have to talk about our feelings. But when my schedule became busier, and Nicole's presence a bit overbearing, we'd let the practice fall to the wayside.

"So what happened?" she asked, handing me a pint and a spoon.

"I'm apparently not..." I sighed. "Cool. I guess. I don't know. I just feel like I don't fit in here. Or anywhere."

"This is a hard town to fit into," Nicole said thoughtfully. "I don't know why Jeanie picked it. Maybe because there wasn't another magical for miles."

"You did okay, though," I said, picking at the fabric of the couch. "I mean, you had friends. You had a social life."

Nicole half-smiled. "Did I, though? Sure I had a couple girlfriends, but I never really felt like this place fit me."

"So why did you stay?"

"Because you needed me," she replied. "Marie, too, whether she knew it or not."

I glanced at an empty chair on the other side of the room and imagined Marie sitting in it. "I'm glad she texted me. I was getting worried that she might never..." I chewed my lip. "I tried to find her the other day. Magically."

Nicole turned sharply. "How?"

"I found it in a book...one of my books," I said, looking at my hands. "But it didn't work."

"Wherever Marie is, she's probably using magic to hide herself," she said quietly. "Don't blame yourself."

"You think?" I asked, but it did make me feel a little better. If I couldn't find her, perhaps others couldn't either. "Do you think she'll ever come home?"

Nicole was quiet for a while. "She might not, Lexie. Marie's…well, she's Marie. And she can hold a grudge."

"I know she can, but it's been a really long time. At some point, you have to bury the hatchet and be a family." I paused. "Don't you?"

Nicole shrugged and took another bite of ice cream.

"Not to salt the wound, but what exactly happened between you two?" I asked cautiously.

She chewed on the spoon for a second then shook her head. "It really doesn't matter. She overreacted. I assume she's found some rich hot guy to take care of her, because I know she doesn't have any real world skills."

"That's not nice, Nicole."

"It's the truth. She thinks she can do anything because she has magic." Nicole snorted. "Let me tell you, magic isn't all it's cracked up to be. More trouble than it's worth."

"Is it, though?" I said, knowing we were veering into uncomfortable territory. "I mean, you don't even make potions, so—"

"Let's watch the show," Nicole said, reaching for the remote and turning up the volume.

That, in effect, killed our conversation.

Twelve

The calendar turned to October, and with it, came the dread of my seventeenth birthday. I doubted it would be as exciting as my fifteenth—no more nightstands being blown up—but if it was anything like the year before, it would kick off a chain reaction of depression that would last through the New Year. I was already steeling myself for the inevitable downward spiral.

James was now dating Callista, or something like that. We didn't discuss the specifics when we sparred on Wednesday nights. At school, he barely spoke to me, which was fine, especially as my birthday crept closer.

The morning of, I managed to get out of the apartment with only the minimal amount of singing from Nicole. If last year was any indication, she'd try to make this year the best birthday ever, regardless of whether I wanted to celebrate it or not. I told her I had tutoring and volunteering at night, so at least that would keep me out of the house until late. And if I transported myself into my room, I might not see her at all.

Blessedly, no one at school mentioned it was my birthday either, so I figured I might get away with having a nice, normal day with no reminders of what I was trying to avoid.

That was, until a giant spell book landed on my desk.

Thunk.

"Happy birthday."

"*James!*" I hissed, glancing around the room. He couldn't just bring spell books into the classroom!

"Relax, it's spelled, like all the others," James said. "Look-away charm."

"Well, okay, but…" I frowned. History seemed destined to repeat itself. Another birthday and another magical giving me a spell book. "I don't want this."

"Tough, you're taking it." He glanced around the room before leaning over the aisle. "Because *I'm* not going to be saddled with making potions every week."

"P-potions?" My stomach rose into my throat as memories of a particularly poor decision came back. I rubbed the back of my hand, wondering if I could still see the purple spots. "I don't want to make potions. G—" I swallowed, warmth creeping up my neck. "I'm not allowed to make them."

"Says who? Gavon?" James snorted. "Why? Did you mix a potion wrong once?"

So Gavon hadn't shared that particularly embarrassing episode with his apprentice, thankfully. "I'm not a potion-maker."

"This book is for the un-makers, meaning you and me." A sly grin grew on his face. "What, did you use one of your sister's books or something?" My traitorous blush deepened, and James cackled. "Oh, I would've loved to have seen that! What happened? Did you grow fur? Scales?"

"*Shut up!*" I barked, drawing Callista's attention. She glowered at me, probably wondering why I was talking to her boyfriend. She'd become awfully possessive of him of late, and it was apparently starting to grate on James. The power couple might not be long for this world, especially with how James freely offered his flirting.

"You're too easy," James said, his laughter resolving to a smug grin.

"Why do I have to make potions?" I said, careful to keep my voice down. "You're the one with all the resources—"

"I'll bring a cauldron to the beach tonight and show you how to summon the ingredients. Pretty simple."

"Tonight?" I blanched. Not as if I wanted to spend my birthday making potions, but… "Do we have to do it tonight?"

"If you want to spar on Wednesday, yes. It takes two sunrises to complete." He sighed like he'd rather be doing anything else. "I will show you *once,* then you'll have to figure it out yourself. And if you give me scales, there will be *hell* to pay."

I glanced behind him at Callista, eyeing us curiously. "Your girlfriend would be pissed off, then?"

James turned pink. "She's not my girlfriend."

"You'd better tell her that."

James looked behind me at Callista then walked over to her. Their conversation wasn't friendly, with several pointed glares to me. James took the seat behind her, his head bowed as he tried to sweet talk the frown off her face, so I decided to throw him a bone and ignore them. For I had yet another magical spell book at my fingertips, and a potion-making one to boot.

Ever since that catastrophic disaster with the healing potion, I'd avoided potions like the plague. But if what James said was true, and this book was for the—what did he call it, the un-makers?—then yet another avenue of my magic had opened up. From what James had said, potions could be used in place of actual magical spells.

Which begged the question: if Nicole could use potions to transport and conjure, why didn't she? The obvious answer was that the time and effort potions take outweighed their usefulness. Jeanie seemed to live by the philosophy that magic shouldn't replace hard work, and that probably played into it too.

Something cold slipped into my stomach. James was an adept potion-maker, which flew in the face of his ancestor's beliefs that potions were useless and those who made them should be put to death. Gavon must've taught him, which meant that Gavon had also researched potions and potion-making.

For Nicole.

And the books she had in the attic, including the one I'd stolen to make my potion, none of those would've come from New Salem. Gavon had gone looking for books to help Nicole use her magic. And, presumably, Gavon then passed that knowledge down to James.

I ran my finger along the cover, the same way I'd done with the magical primer that Gavon had given me on my fifteenth birthday. I still had no idea whether to love or hate the man, and every new bit of information I found out about him just left me more confused.

What time are you coming home?

"Crap."

The sun was setting, painting the sky a pretty purple and pink. I'd finished tutoring and volunteering early, so I gave myself a birthday present of enjoying a few moments of peace on the gulf before James showed up. It had been quite relaxing—until the reminder that my sister was waiting for me at home.

I'll be home just as soon as I finish making this potion with Gavon's apprentice. As if that text would go over well. Instead I told her I was staying late to help meet with a pair of potential adopters at the kennel, and I'd be home after a while.

I wasn't even sure why I was waiting for him. All my smarter instincts told me I shouldn't be making potions. After all, despite everything that had happened in New Salem, Gavon had been pretty spot-on in his advice about potions: Don't drink anything unless I was sure I'd done it right.

But the more that I'd skimmed my book, the more eager I'd become to learn all I could about the practice. There were tons of varieties: healing potions, of course, but potions for growing plants, potions for wards, potions for changing the color of your shirt. Potions for cleaning scum off cauldrons. Potions for sleep and potions for wakefulness. Potions for transport and summoning.

"Good, you're here," was all the welcome James gave me before he dumped a burlap bag and cauldron onto the sand in front of me. The pot was old and worn, and I wondered how many magicals had used it, and how many potions they'd brewed. I touched the outside and my fingers grew cold.

"Iron," James said, dumping out the contents of the sack onto the sand. "Contains the magic in the potion so it can congeal correctly."

"Ah." I picked up a purple, leafy branch and sniffed. "Lavender?"

"My favorite healing potion is this one," James said, summoning the book to his hands and flipping through the pages. He handed the book back to me, and I read aloud.

Healing Potion #12

1 gallon apple cider vinegar
1 aloe leaf - Add 2 additional aloe
2 echinacea 4 Marigold
3 bundles lavender
7 spider legs from 5 spiders Add the 2 pair of legs between the third and fourth

Assemble under moonlight. Boil two days with magic fire. Medium temperature

Drink in good health.

The handwriting wasn't James' though. "Who made all these markings?"

"Different people," James said, conjuring a fire under the cauldron. "Potion books are passed down from master to apprentice in New Salem."

"So this was…Gavon's?" I asked, examining the print again. It didn't look like his scrawl.

"At one point. But it's been mine since I was a boy." He cleared his throat. "So the first thing you need to know about potions is that you shouldn't drink them unless you know what you're doing."

I had to smile at that. "Noted."

"Potions begin with a liquid, usually vinegar, wine, or even water in some cases," he said, handing me a bottle.

I took a whiff of the pungent odor. "Vinegar, I take it?"

He dumped the whole bottle into the cauldron. "Next, you'll want to add the base herbs. Echinacea, lavender, aloe—most healing potions have a variation of some or all of these."

I squinted at the book, where I was following along with his directions. There was a note in the margins, written in a different hand than the others. "This book says to use marigolds."

"Yeah, I tried that once," James said, tossing the lavender bundle into the cauldron. "Didn't work as well as Echinacea. But that was Alexandra's note. She had a lot of weird additions that didn't do much for me."

"Who's Alexandra?" I asked, as he tossed in the Echinacea flowers.

"Your grandmother, Alexandra. Gavon's mother." James plucked off small buds from the lavender plant. "She was Guildmaster before him."

All potion-making thoughts flew out the window. "Hang on. *Hang on*. Gavon's mother's name is Alexandra? And she was the *Guildmaster* before him?"

"And his master, toward the end of his tutelage." He waved his hand around the cauldron, and the bright pink mixture began to swirl.

"But I thought… Gavon said Warrior parents don't really have relationships with their children?"

James glanced at me for a moment then returned his attention to the cauldron. "Normally, they don't. But there haven't been a lot of warriors born in New Salem in the past hundred years. Are you paying attention or not? I'm not going over this again."

But I was too intrigued. "So Gavon's mother was his master?"

"Gavon's original master died when Gavon was about fifteen," James said, putting down the lavender. "So he finished his training with Alexandra alongside Cyrus—"

Okay, *that* got me to my feet. "*Cyrus* was my grandmother's apprentice?"

James snorted. "Who else would've trained him? He was going to be the next Guildmaster."

I wasn't sure why that shocked me so much. "So you're telling me that my grandmother trained Cyrus because he was going to be the next Guildmaster?"

"Are we going to talk about New Salem politics or are we going to make a healing potion?" James asked with a heavy sigh.

"You can't just tell me something like that and not explain yourself," I said with a dismissive wave of the hand. "If Cyrus was going to be the next Guildmaster, how did Gavon get the job instead?"

"There were rumblings that Alexandra was going to step

down," James said. "I think Cyrus wasn't sure he could defeat Alexandra in a duel, or else he would've done it sooner. But then the conversation changed when Gavon announced he'd made the tear."

I nodded. "They all wanted Gavon to take over instead."

"Yeah, and they wanted him to lead the grand return to the world, though he felt differently," James said with a smirk. "By my calculations, Gavon was about thirty when he told the Guild about the tear."

"What does that mean?"

"Means he's forty-seven now…"

I calculated in my head. If he was forty-seven now, that meant he was thirty when I was born. And that meant… "He'd been keeping the tear a secret for five years. At least. My oldest sister is twenty-two, so…"

"Exactly," James said. "Now exactly why he decided to announce it—"

"Because my mom was pregnant with me," I said suddenly. "And that meant he had his…"

"His what?"

"His new Guildmaster," I finished lamely.

"No, Gavon never wanted you to be Guildmaster," James said definitively. "Since I was a small child, he was very clear that *I* was to be the next Guildmaster, even though he would often talk about you. When I was about eleven, he explained that he doubted you'd be in any shape to run a Guild, considering you'd been ignorant to magic your entire life."

I furrowed my brow. "But Cyrus told me…"

"Cyrus is a liar," James said. "And he's been out to get

revenge on Gavon ever since Gavon challenged him for Guildmaster and won."

"Wait a minute, I thought you said Alexandra was Guildmaster?"

James sighed as if I were a child asking stupid questions. "Alexandra was Guildmaster. Cyrus was to be her successor until Gavon made the tear. Then Gavon was to be her successor. So before that could happen, Cyrus challenged Alexandra for the Guildmastership and won."

"Wait, Cyrus *won*?" I gasped. "That means he…"

"Yeah, he killed Alexandra in the duel. Apparently it was an incredible match—went on for hours. But then *Gavon* challenged *Cyrus* for the Guildmastership."

My brows rose. "Really? Why?"

"Who knows. Maybe he wanted revenge for his mother's death?" James said with a shrug. "Three weeks after Cyrus defeated Alexandra, Gavon defeated Cyrus."

"But, wait a minute, if Gavon defeated Cyrus in a duel, why is Cyrus still alive?"

"Gavon didn't kill him," James said.

"*Why the hell not?*"

"Because at the time, it was just Gavon and Cyrus, a few very old Warriors, and, well, me, but I was only a few months old. Gavon apparently felt that killing two Warriors was too many, so he let Cyrus live."

I closed my eyes, Cyrus' voice unwelcome in my brain as I recalled the night my mother died. "And so Cyrus wanted revenge? Why not just challenge Gavon again?"

"Can't. Once he accepted Gavon's win in the duel, there was

no going back. And since dueling is outlawed except in ascension and induction matches…"

I buried my head in my hands, processing all of this new information. Gavon had never wanted to be Guildmaster, he'd waited years to tell the Guild about my mother and family. He'd named me after his own mother, but why, if, as James said, Gavon had always considered James his successor? There was too much for me to think about, too many unanswered questions.

"Are we going to make this potion or what?" James barked after my silence had gone on for a few minutes.

"Fine," I said, wrenching my thoughts away from Gavon and back to the bubbling cauldron. "So why don't Alexandra's notes work for your magic?"

"Healing potions vary from magical to magical. Some combinations work better with certain magic and some require a bit more tinkering. Knowing the color of your magic, you might be able to use some of the additions in here written by your grandmother. At least, those are the ones Gavon uses."

I ran my finger along the delicate strokes on the page, imagining the woman who wrote them and feeling an odd kinship, even though I knew nothing about her.

"Now what?" I asked.

"We wait two sunrises. Then, if it's silver, we drink it after our sparring match."

"What if it's not silver?" I asked.

"Then we'll try again and have a terrible week." He smiled. "I think we did all right." He stood and brushed the sand off his pants. "Oh, and happy birthday."

Just like that, all the air left my lungs. I'd almost forgotten.

"Sorry I mentioned it," James said.

"No, it's just..." I debated whether I should tell him about my complicated feelings surrounding my birthday. But luckily, my smarter half won over. "I've got to get back home. See ya at school tomorrow."

Thirteen

Truth be told, I hadn't paid any attention to James' instructions on making potions. But the next week, when I found myself hunched over the cauldron, my grandmother's notes proved to be all the help I needed. The potion that came out still tasted like the inside of a trashcan, but it replenished my magic almost completely—even better than James' potion had.

I chewed on the new information James had told me about Gavon and the political minefield that was the Guildmastership. There was so much I still didn't know, and so many questions I had about him, my grandmother, and Cyrus, but after a while, I tried to forget about them. There was no point in digging into Gavon's past any more than I had—after all, it wouldn't change anything. Gavon wasn't around, my mother was still dead, and Cyrus was still alive. At least now I knew why he'd been so intent on ruining Gavon, whatever small comfort that provided.

October turned to November, and although I survived my birthday unscathed, the winter holidays brought on a resurgence of guilt. Thanksgiving, in particular, arrived with a hazy memory of my Gram. I had memories of a library and a room overlooking a gray ocean. If I concentrated hard, I could almost remember Gram's face.

As I lay in bed, already smelling turkey and stuffing cooking in the oven, I grasped at what I could of my memory, although it was like running my hands through water.

"Gobble gobble!" Nicole said when I walked into the kitchen sometime later. She was already going overboard on the turkey day festivities—with enough food to feed an army and enough false cheer to make my stomach queasy.

"You know, for a woman in her twenties, you're entirely too corny," I said with a grimace.

Her bright smile faltered for just a moment then reappeared. "Oh, don't be a grumpy goose. Or grumpy turkey." She cackled to herself and went to check on the oven. "I figure we can eat around four. Does that sound okay?"

"Yeah." I cleared my throat. "Hey, did you get a chance to submit your tax information to Georgetown?" Nicole had been embarrassed when I asked for her tax returns, and told me she'd submit them herself.

"Mm," she said with a nod. "I don't understand why they need it already."

"I want to submit my application sooner rather than later, and they'll make a decision on scholarships and need-based aid then." I chewed my lip. "You're sure you—"

"Lexie, I told you I did it." Nicole handed me a plate of toast and a warning glare that signaled the end of it.

"Thanks," I said, biting off a piece of the hard toast. Still unsettled by my patchy memories, I decided to ask, "So…you haven't heard from Gram, have you?"

"Gram?" Nicole blinked for a moment, wracking her brain. She frowned. "Who's Gram?"

My mouth fell open in shock. Nicole didn't even *remember* Gram? "Our grandmother?"

"I don't… That's funny," Nicole said, turning to the gravy on the stove and stirring it. "I don't remember anything about Mom's parents. You'd think Jeanie would've said something."

"Yeah, you'd think," I said with a harsh breath. So…Gram had completely wiped herself from Nicole's memory, but apparently, not completely from mine. Or perhaps she'd wanted to, but I was too powerful.

I stared at Nicole for a moment, and more flashes came back to me—a photo of my mother and sisters in front of a house, an older woman with a mischievous smile tossing me out of the house, the ache in my chest when I'd realized my own grandmother didn't want me.

I stood up as the memories pulsed through me. Calls every birthday, the sight of her in our living room talking to me like I was beneath her. Sitting in her library while she informed me I was nothing to her. Watching her in the dueling ring in New Salem as she saved my ass from certain death.

"Lexie, are you okay?" Nicole asked.

"Yeah," I said, rubbing my face. "Yeah, just haven't had breakfast."

"Well, eat something," Nicole said, handing me a banana. "But don't eat too much because dinner is—"

"At four, you told me," I said, taking the fruit, but not eating it. "So you really don't remember Gram at all?"

"Gram?" Nicole squinted as she thought. "Maybe a little? She must've died when we were very young."

"And you don't remember living with Mom and Gavon—"

The spoon slipped out of her hand. "Lexie, please don't talk about him."

"Sorry," I said, but I was too furious to really care. "But you don't remember living in Salem?"

"I've never lived in Salem," Nicole said. "And I'd prefer *not* to remember that period of my life. It was nothing but a lie anyway."

"I'm sorry. I didn't mean to make you upset."

"It's all right," she said. "I just don't want you thinking of him as…well, as anything more than a stranger."

I didn't see how that was possible, but I nodded. "I don't, but I was just curious about…well, nothing, really. I'm sorry."

Nicole smiled brightly and went back to cooking, but I had a new idea. Perhaps it was time I paid my Gram a visit.

Transporting to Salem proved a little more difficult than I'd first anticipated. I was still shaky on transporting to new places (or, in this case, places I couldn't remember ever visiting), but even so, there was some powerful magic keeping me from finding a place to land in the city.

Instead, I transported myself to the tear. I hadn't been back in almost two years. I'd almost forgotten the ferocity of it. Gavon had explained it once as a rip between worlds that my ancestor, John Chase, had created to hold the gang of evil magicals who'd wanted to enslave humanity. It appeared as a slash in the air, moving and crackling with energy and lightning.

I narrowed my eyes as I watched the writhing line of energy, my memories now crystal clear. The first time I'd crossed over was after a particularly bad argument with my Gram. I'd thrown a tantrum and released too much magic. Gavon had taken me to his stately manor in New Salem, given me a healing potion, and then taken me back home through this tear. I'd been skeptical that it was safe, but he'd said, *It's how you got here.* Then, I'd thought he was referring to how I'd arrived in New Salem. Now, I realized he might've been speaking in more general terms.

Ass.

The longer I stared at the tear, the more I began to remember that fateful Thanksgiving and all the things that had gone wrong. If I'd just kept my head down and mouth shut, I wouldn't have pissed off Gram. I wouldn't have lost my temper. Perhaps Gavon would never have taken me to New Salem.

On the flip side, I also knew I wasn't completely in the wrong. Irene had been completely and unfairly aloof toward me —and if memory served, hadn't officially included me in Clan Carrigan, not until I'd been kidnapped and almost killed.

But then again, she'd come through for me when I'd most needed it. I'd never gotten the chance to thank her for coming to rescue me, because she'd turned around and excommunicated us.

So we both had things to apologize for.

Regardless, I felt her magic pressing in around me the closer I came to the small downtown. There were powerful barrier spells around the compound, the same ones I probably had around my apartment in Florida. But I thought it a little strange that she was protecting the entire city, and not just her property.

I wrapped my jacket tighter and cast a warming spell. And then, without any other plan, I found a coffee shop, bought myself the last pumpkin spice of the season, and waited. For whom, I had no idea. My hazy memory told me I had a ton of relatives that descended on this town during the Thanksgiving holidays, so perhaps one of them would stumble upon me.

Sipping the sweet, spicy latte, I scanned the other patrons in the cafe for signs of recognition. I still hadn't figured out that aura thing, but maybe in a town full of magicals, I could try. I set down my paper cup and closed my eyes. Maybe if I just released my magic into the universe, it would bring back the person I wanted.

I found something powerful that shot my magic back into my body. My eyes flew open, ready to search, but I didn't need to. An old woman stood in front of my table. I'd never seen her before, but at the same time, she looked…like Jeanie.

"Gram?" I said, blinking at her.

She sniffed and took the seat across from me. "It appears I need to strengthen my spells. What are you doing here, Alexis?"

"I… I have questions for you," I said. "And, you know, you are my grandmother."

She snorted, and I got the distinct impression she felt our familial relationship wasn't enough to seek her out. "I'm a busy woman. Make it quick."

"Why did you erase our memories?"

"Side effect of a barrier spell. I wanted to make sure you three forgot where our compound was in case you were tortured into revealing it."

I shivered. "Gavon wouldn't torture me."

"Gavon isn't the one who worries me. There's been a lot of activity from the tear," she said simply. "People coming and going."

"P-people?" I said. "Not person?"

"Your father, of course, continues to traverse back and forth. His apprentice as well. And also that…other man."

I licked my lips nervously. "Cyrus?"

"Whatever his name is. He's been holding meetings all over the place, so my sources are telling me. Trying to rouse the rabble."

"And you aren't…doing anything to stop it?" I said, aghast and concerned all at once.

"Of course I am. Our barriers are secure. There's no one getting into my compound and as soon as this conversation is over, I will strengthen them again."

"That's not doing anything," I replied with a frown. "That's covering your own ass and leaving the rest of us to fend for ourselves. What kind of meeting are they having? What's he trying to accomplish?"

"I'm sure nothing good. But thanks to the Danvers Accord, there's little he can accomplish with magicals here. The pact ensures their magic remains dulled."

"So you aren't doing a thing, then?" I shook my head. "So glad you're on my side."

"I'm on the Carrigan Clan's side, and I've made sure that none of my people are involved in that mess. They have been expressly forbidden to speak with that man, or any of his underlings."

"He has *underlings, too?*" This all sounded bad, although I wasn't sure what to do with this information. I couldn't go to Gavon, but at the same time, I didn't want to confront Cyrus by myself. And I sure as hell didn't trust James with this information.

"You're a Warrior, aren't you?" she said, and a foreign presence poked at my magic. "You've been training, I see."

"With myself," I added with a scowl. If Gram still thought I was a ticking time bomb, just a push away from joining the Dark Side, I probably shouldn't tell her that I'd become sparring partners with the enemy. "Any chance you could lift the embargo on us? We're not going to bring the plague."

"And what would you do if I did?" she drawled. "You've already surpassed most of the magicals in the Guild, save myself and a few others."

"Yeah, that's the thing. I haven't. There are giant, gaping holes in my magical tutelage."

"You have a sister who could instruct you on such things."

I resisted the urge to roll my eyes. Nothing had changed, it seemed. "Marie is missing."

"Have you checked with your father?"

I swallowed my initial response. "I'm sure she's not with him."

"Are you? How can you be sure?"

"Because I found a spell that tells me so," I said, forcing myself to keep calm. The more I spoke with Gram, the more I remembered our last blow-up encounter. "But maybe if you could help me—"

"I won't be able to help."

That earned a frown from me. "Can't or won't?"

"Both," Gram said, and had the grace to look a little sorry for it. "You three are no longer in my clan, and therefore, I have no control over you. Beyond that, Marie seems to have cast some powerful spells to hide herself, more than the usual amount."

"She…she has?" Where would she have learned to use spells like that?

"Your father, however, has the ability to locate her by virtue of his parentage. I suggest you start there—"

"No, wait!" I said, nearly spilling my coffee as I reached over the table to stop her from leaving. She lifted a brow. "I mean… Maybe you could just lend me some books, or maybe I could have an afternoon to pick your brain on some things—"

"My dear, as powerful as you are, the less you know about magic, the safer we all are."

I let go of her, stunned. "Are you kidding me?"

"No. Your mother would've taken the Clanmaster role after me. She was powerful enough. And with your fathers undiluted bloodline, your magic is greater than some of my best clansmen." As she spoke, her gaze betrayed no emotion. "Frankly, I would've been satisfied to have never told you about magic at all. You're a danger to us all, if only because you can't be stopped."

"I can be," I said, defiantly. "Gavon's apprentice and I are evenly matched. You'd better be glad I'm on your side."

"You were children then," she said. "I'm sure that boy is far stronger than you now."

Wanna bet? I didn't voice that thought. "Gram, I need help.

If Cyrus is planning something, if he's gathering magicals on this side—we have to *do* something." Helplessness finally seeped into my voice. "I have no idea what I'm doing."

"Your sister will turn up when she's run out of money or handsome men to give it to her," Gram said, brushing the front of her jacket as if removing my presence from it. "In the meantime, get out of my town."

"It's not your town," I snarled. "It's a free—"

But I couldn't even finish that thought. Before I knew it, I was being magically transported out of the coffee shop, landing on my rear on the outskirts of the town.

And, horrifically, the memories of the conversation floated away like clouds on the breeze until I couldn't remember why I'd come to Salem in the first place.

Fourteen

Before we'd eaten all the turkey leftovers, Nicole had turned on the holiday spirit. I awoke the day after Thanksgiving to a house covered in red and green, and a fake tree that Nicole was adorning while singing Christmas carols. At first, I thought it was just Nicole being her overly cheery self, but then I began to sense an ulterior motive.

"Isn't it so nice that we're together during the holidays?" Nicole said. "Imagine people who don't live with their families. How hard it must be to have to celebrate Christmas alone?"

I decided not to remind Nicole that both Marie and I could be home in the blink of an eye, should we choose to be.

Her holiday merrymaking (and guilt-tripping) was getting on my nerves, so I decided to head to New Orleans to find some new books to read. Even in late fall, the city was sticky, hot, and uncomfortable. But the tourists were few and far between, and I had a little bounce in my step when I saw the same cute guy at the counter.

He glanced up at the open door, and I could've sworn his eyes lit up. "Haven't seen you around here lately."

I gulped and my cheeks grew warm. He remembered me? "I…uh…I've been busy at school."

"Yeah? You go to Loyola?"

I had to laugh at that. "No, I'm in high school."

"Really?" He eyed me. "You sure? You look twenty."

My face grew even hotter; I was sure I looked like a tomato. "No, I'm seventeen."

"No way." His smile sent my pulse into overdrive, and I knew if I didn't get away, I'd probably do something stupid—like blurt out that I was a magical teenager or that I thought his eyes were pretty. Instead, I awkwardly laughed as I inched closer to the back staircase and then made some flimsy excuse as I darted up.

Once I was out of view, I replayed the conversation in my head and regretted even engaging Cute Bookshop Guy at all. Still, he'd thought I was in college. Maybe when I went to Georgetown, I'd emerge from my awkward cocoon into a beautiful, socially confident butterfly.

Grinning to myself, I reached the top of the stairs and breathed in the scent of old books. Closing my eyes, I released magic into the room, searching for something with even the smallest hint of magic.

Instead, it ran into something green and powerful.

"James?"

"What are you doing?" He stood in the center of the room, his head tilted to the left. Although his amused smile told me he'd been watching me for some time.

Oh crap, had he seen my awkward flirting?

"I'm looking for magical books," I snapped, annoyed that I'd embarrassed myself not only in front of Cute Bookstore Guy, but also James. Although I couldn't have cared less about what James thought.

"Why don't you try summoning?" he asked, barely containing his laughter.

My already flustered face grew even more hot. Summoning. Of course that would've been easier than what I'd been doing, which didn't really have a name.

"I don't know why you always do the hardest things first," he said, stuffing his hands in his pockets.

"What are you doing here?" I grumbled, not wanting to summon a book in front of him.

"I'm bored."

"Don't you have a girlfriend?" I asked.

"Callista and I are..." He squinted as he trailed off. "She's complicated. Too complicated for me. I think it's over."

"Uh-huh. And how does this affect me?"

"Because although I'm here, I don't have magic," James said with a devilish grin. "And you do, so..."

I didn't like where this was going. "So what?"

"So let's *go* somewhere! Let's do something fun!"

"We are somewhere," I said, although New Orleans wasn't the kind of city I'd want to spend the day in. "And I'm going home."

"C'mon, Lexie, don't be like that. It's not like you have anywhere else to be."

That was kind of true. I'd planned to spend most of the day

avoiding Nicole's guilt-trip, and now that I wasn't so interested in this bookstore anymore, my options were fairly limited.

James wiggled his eyebrows, and the last brick in my wall of resistance came down.

"Fine. Let's go walk around."

"I read a book about New Orleans once," James said as we walked down Royal Street. The sun was setting, casting an orange glow over the streets. "A lot of magicals immigrated here from French Canada."

"That explains the magical bookstore," I said, pausing to watch a horse-drawn carriage roll by with tourists.

James snorted and peered into a shop. "This voodoo stuff... Magic or not?"

I shrugged and let my gaze wander to a cheap Chinese-made skull decoration. "To be honest, I have no idea. There are giant holes in my magical understanding. I feel like I'm walking around blind most of the time."

"No kidding. I can't believe how little you know."

I stopped and crossed my arms over my chest. "If you're going to be an asshole, I'm going home."

"No, I mean...it's weird to me how you can be such a strong sparrer and yet don't know things like summoning," James said.

I frowned. "I know how to summon—"

"I mean, you do, but it's like...you don't instinctively know to use magic." He put down the candle. "But when we spar, it's like you've been using it your whole life."

I picked up a photo frame and chewed my lip. "That's because...well... It's because my mother used my magic when she was pregnant with me. I think."

James turned to look at me, confused. "What?"

"That's the only thing I can think of," I said, very interested in the details on the frame. "Because I remember the night she died, and I wasn't born yet."

James stared at the wall, his face twisted in thought for so long that I thought he might turn and call me insane, but then he nodded. "I guess it's because she didn't have a specialty. Gavon said that the magicals here were a lot less powerful than the ones in New Salem."

"If I knew any magicals, I'd agree with you," I said quietly.

If James had a question about my comment, he didn't voice it, because he was already out the door and headed into the store across the street.

"I think all these shops have the same stuff," he said, picking up another skull candle almost identical to the one across the street. "Don't think this is magical."

I half-smiled; I could've told him that.

"What about that grandmother of yours?" James asked.

"Who?" Why hadn't I ever heard anything about my mother's mother?

"Your Gram. Leader of Clan Carrigan. The… Oh…" He nodded in understanding. "Wow, that's…rough."

"What are you talking about?"

"Do you remember the end of our match? Do you remember how it ended?"

"Yes, you were about to kill me when…" I stretched my memory. "Something…happened? Somebody stopped it. That's so weird. Why don't I remember who it was?"

"Your grandmother. And I'm guessing when she put that powerful barrier spell around her compound, she also tossed in a memory charm." James shook his head. "You should be able to break it though."

"How?"

"Try."

I concentrated, mentally reaching for the wisps of memory that danced away from me. Last weekend, I had been in Salem, perhaps that was when... I tasted pumpkin spice on my tongue, I heard an argument...

Gram.

"*Crap*," I wheezed, grabbing the nearest shelf. "What the hell was that?"

"You broke her charm," James said with an impressed nod.

"Not all of it," I said, shaking my foggy head. "Just enough to know I went to go talk to her about something. Whatever it was, she obviously didn't want to help." There was something else I was forgetting, something she'd said that had made me nervous.

"Why did you go see her in the first place?" James scoffed. "She kicked you out of her clan."

"Yeah but..." I stopped trying to grasp the memories. "You're right, I'm completely idiotic when it comes to whatever Gavon *didn't* teach me—which is a lot. Nicole's useless, Marie's gone, Gavon's gone, and all I wanted was someone to help me."

James rubbed the back of his neck. "Gavon's not gone."

"Haven't seen him." Again, something at the back of my mind tickled in recognition, but I couldn't quite place my finger on it.

"Yeah, but…you know those magical books you've been 'finding' all over the place?"

I stopped in my tracks. "You've got to be kidding me."

"Nope, they're all his," James said.

I glared at the floor. "Why?"

"Probably because he thought you needed some help."

"You know what would be helpful? If he came here and had a conversation with me," I snapped. "I can't believe he thought it was easier to hide books in some library than to just come *talk* to me."

"Look, I have no idea how Gavon's mind works, and he raised me," James said. "But if he's giving you these books, it's because he thought it was the right thing to do."

"Well, that explains why all the books came from before the Separation." Why hadn't that tipped me off? I shook my head. "I can't believe I didn't realize it sooner. I'm such a moron."

"Don't be too hard on yourself. You are a pretty pathetic magical in basic spellcasting."

"Thanks," I said, dripping sarcasm as James grinned at me. I yanked my necklace out from beneath my shirt and glared at it. "Does this spell even work?"

"You know it does." He cleared his throat. "I, James Riley, think Lexie is a really fun person to spend the day with."

The gem warmed, and I glared at him, although it wasn't as hot as usual. "Asshole. I can only imagine that he wanted me to find the truth-telling charm so we could have a conversation."

"I'm sure."

I stewed in my anger for a moment, still unable to believe I'd missed all the signs. Every book had been *exactly* what I'd been looking for. He'd probably charmed the store. I wonder if Cute Bookshop Guy knew.

"What's the big deal? So Gavon's been giving you his library. Who cares?"

I glared at him. "Well, in the first place, books only do so much. And in the second place…I don't know." Some of my anger deflated. "I guess I was hoping I'd find some hint of the magical world today. Do we still have councils? Are there other clans than Carrigan? Right now, I'd even take a book on the subject."

"Well, why don't we go find one?" James said with a mischievous look. "You've got magic, I've got time to kill. Let's find you a magical book."

I wasn't sure how to respond to that. "I mean…I've been trying—"

"No, you haven't. You've been fumbling around in the darkness like a child." He grinned, even as he insulted me. "It's quite simple. Use your magic to summon exactly what you're looking for."

"Like it's that eas—" I started, but stopped when James quirked a brow. "Fine. I'm sure it's that easy."

"Try it for yourself. Just use your magic to find the thing you want."

I stopped on the sidewalk and closed my eyes, more out of spite and wanting to prove James wrong than because I wanted to. I concentrated on a book from after the Separation. Almost instantly, I felt the tug toward something to the north. But I couldn't wrap my magic around it, couldn't pull it to me like I'd done so many times before. It was like yanking a rope tied to an anvil.

I furrowed my brow. "I can't."

"Yes, you can, just concentrate—"

I opened both eyes. "No, I mean, I found something, but I can't…bring it or whatever. It's stuck."

James' eyes lit up. "Then you found more than just a book. There's only one reason a summon won't work—an anti-summon spell. Which means we'll have to go there ourselves to get it."

"Hang on," I said with a nervous laugh. "If there's an anti-summon spell on it, it's obviously somebody's property. We can't just take it—"

"Who said anything about taking?" James said, standing. "I just want to see where it is."

I narrowed my eyes, sensing something was wrong. "Why?"

He let out a loud sigh. "Be*cause* you're not the only one who wants to know what happened in the centuries since New Salem was created. So far, all I've seen of this world is the nonmagical parts. I'd like to see the magical parts, too."

Something about this felt dangerous and stupid, but also kind of exciting. It was the first hint of something that wasn't Clan Carrigan or New Salem, and I was curious, too. And as much as I hated to admit it, having James around—who might not have had magic at the moment, but knew more about it than I did—was convenient.

Case in point. "How do we get there?"

He laid his hand on my arm. "Have you ever transported

someone else before?"

I shook my head.

"If you leave half my body behind, I will haunt you forever," he said with a warning glare. But patiently, he explained the steps. First, I sought his body out with my magic, and for the first time, I realized the green aura around him was contained, unlike mine, which seemed to move and throb with every thought. Then I searched for the source of the book, or close to it, and pinpointed the location.

"Ready?" he asked, nerves evident in his voice.

"Ready," I whispered, and, with a prayer, I transported the both of us. I landed wrong and toppled over a pair of stones. Beside me, James yelped in pain.

"Great job, Lexie. Next time, look before you land."

"Don't be shitty. It's my first time," I snapped, wringing out my hands. "And something stopped me from getting into the building."

James sat up and craned his neck to a spot behind me. I followed his gaze, and my breath caught. Even though it was dark, I could tell it was a formidable building with tall spires and thick stone. It didn't look like it belonged in the US, either—almost like an old Irish castle.

"Wow," I breathed. "What is this?"

"I have no idea," James said, walking up to it. "But there's a lot of magic in here."

"It doesn't look like someone's house," I said cautiously. "It looks like—"

"The Boston Magical Library," James said with a grin. He pointed to a spot on the outside of the building. "Says so right there. Looks like you hit the jackpot."

The building was dilapidated, covered in overgrown weeds and vines. Upon closer inspection, even the iron on the windows looked old and rusted.

"Iron," James said, tapping the bars. "That's why you couldn't summon. Simple, effective anti-magic."

"What does that mean?"

He grinned. "Means I doubt anyone is home. Let's see if we can't get in."

"I'm not so sure about this…" I said, eyeing the iron locks on the windows. "I mean, what if we get caught?"

"By who? The nonmagicals? I doubt they can even see this thing. Probably a lot of Look-away charms on it." James procured a vial from his back pocket. He poured the liquid onto the lock, and it fizzled as it melted away.

"So you carry around iron-dissolving potions just because?" I said with pursed lips.

"Basic defensive precaution," James said, pulling the lock off the door. "You never know when someone will put you in a jail cell."

"James, I really don't think this is a good idea."

"C'mon, Lexie. Live a little. Who knows? There might be books in here. I know how much you love those. Maybe you can take a few new ones home that didn't come from Gavon."

I pursed my lips, still sore about Gavon and his book scavenger hunt.

James wrestled open the door and walked inside. "Cast a light in here, will you?"

I created a ball of magic, illuminating the large space with a bright lavender hue. Once beautiful tile lay dirt-covered and faded beneath my feet. Gold-leaf arches drooped overhead with cobweb-covered chandeliers. But the shelves were empty. This place had long since been abandoned.

"This must've been something at some point," James said, his voice echoing off the high ceilings. "I wonder what happened to all the books?"

"Me too." I ran my hands along the empty shelves, grimacing when they came back dirty. "It kind of fits, you know? It seems like the entire world has moved on from magic. I bet there hasn't been a magical book written since before the Separation."

"Oh, don't be glum," James said. "I'm sure there's something around here. Why don't you try summoning a book?"

"I tried that—"

"Not in here, you haven't. The iron on the windows was preventing you from removing the object. But now that you're here, you should be able to summon one from inside the building."

I let my magic wander away from me in search of the original book that had alerted me to the presence here. I saw a box, straw stuffing, and then before I could blink, the book was in my hands.

I gasped and grinned. "I got one!"

"Hey!" James said, walking over. "See? Summoning is a lot easier than hunting around in the dark. What's it about?"

"*Magic and the Steam Power*," I said, reading the cover. When I opened the book to the first, page, I grinned. "This was written in 1845. This is perfect! This is—"

"Stop where you are!"

Fifteen

The voice was unfamiliar, but full of authority. James and I glanced at each other, his face a mask of surprise. Then, slowly, we searched for the source.

A police officer, Boston's finest by my guess, walked into the room with a gun in his hand. I swallowed nervously and dropped the book.

"Officer, we—"

Something tightened around my hands, and then around my feet, knocking me back to the floor. I gasped and called out, but something *magical* muffled my words. I twisted onto my side, searching for James, but found him in about the same position.

The officer approached us and put away his gun. He picked up the book and to my complete surprise, it disappeared from his hand. "Now, I don't know what you kids thought you were doing here, but this is private property."

I opened my mouth to word-vomit apologies and beg forgiveness, but thanks to the spell on my mouth—

The spell on my mouth.

This policeman was *magical.*

"C'mon, I'm taking you two down to the station." He knelt in front of me. "Are you going to walk, or am I going to have to carry you?"

Station. *Station.* I opened my mouth to speak but no words came out. He waved his hand in front of my mouth, and the binding released. "What do you mean *station?*"

He quirked a brow. "You're trespassing."

Suddenly all curiosity about this magical man went out the window, replaced by pure, uncut *panic.* I was being arrested.

Arrested.

As in, handcuffs, jail cell, police car, *arrested.*

Words spilled from my mouth almost faster than I could speak. "I wasn't trespassing. Trespassing is illegal and I swear I don't do anything illegal. I promise, I don't—" My words ended abruptly as he replaced the binding spell on my mouth. Tears gathered in my eyes as I watched all my college dreams go up in smoke. I was being arrested for trespassing. I doubted Georgetown would look past that.

This might top the list of dumb decisions I'd made in my life.

"Are you going to walk?" the officer asked again.

I nodded vigorously, hoping good behavior would lessen the severity of my punishment.

"What about you, son?" he said to James. Based on the officer's response, James wasn't the least bit concerned. The tightness around my legs released, and I scrambled to my feet, keeping my head down and sniffing back tears. Out of the corner of my eye, I saw James leisurely get to his feet, neither looking chastised nor smug about the whole situation. If anything, he looked bored.

"Let's go, you two."

I followed with my head down, my heart sinking to my stomach as I saw the police car parked outside. How stupid could we have been? Of course this was private property. I should've known better than to trust James. Hot tears dripped down my face, and I sniffled silently as the officer held the door open. He wore a stern expression, but there was a hint of kindness in it as he helped me sit in the backseat.

As the car lurched forward, my sniffling turned to silent sobs. I was grateful for the binding on my voice, because I was fairly sure I would've been making a scene without it.

James nudged me and offered a confused expression. I glared at him and faced stonily ahead.

When we arrived at the police station, fear settled in my bones. Would I be locked in a cell? Would I be sent to juvenile detention? Was there a magical jail? Did I need to get bailed out? Could I call Nicole? How would she even get here? How would she *pay* for this? Yet another horrible screw up by one Alexis Carrigan. Now I'd be stuck in that apartment forever.

I refused to look up, hoping if I kept my eyes on the back of the officer's shoes, I could disappear completely. It wasn't until he stopped abruptly that I realized I was facing a jail cell.

My sobbing renewed.

"Get in," he said, holding open the door. "And this is iron, so don't even think about trying anything funny. You got any more of that iron-dissolving potion, son?"

To my left, James shook his head, although the officer checked his pockets regardless. Then he left us standing in the empty cell, and released the bindings on our hands and mouth.

The sobs that had been silently shaking my body broke through my mouth, and I wailed loudly.

"Oh, calm down," James said, plopping down on the metal bench. "It's just trespassing. It's not that big a deal."

I screwed up my face and wished I could blast him all the way back to New Salem. "*Don't talk to me.*"

James sighed and leaned against the wall. "Hopefully this won't…" His eyes flew open. "Shit."

Before I could ask him what was wrong, I heard voices approaching. One was the officer who'd arrested us and the other was…

"…sure she isn't blonde?"

"She's about seventeen, had a boy with her around the same age."

Gavon walked around the corner with the officer, looking for all the world like a very confused upper-middle-class father who'd just gotten a strange phone call. His gaze landed on me then James, and something akin to annoyance and disappointment settled on his face.

Turning to the policeman, Gavon offered his hand. "I appreciate the call, and your leniency. I promise it won't happen again."

The officer half-smiled in my direction. "See that it doesn't." He unlocked the cell door and left it open. "This is a warning, ladies and gentlemen. Stay out of places you don't belong."

I couldn't help the sigh of relief that reverberated through me, but I knew the worst was yet to come. The officer glanced at Gavon and muttered something about kids before leaving the three of us alone in the cell block. I wasn't sure if any of the other rooms were occupied, but somehow, I wished they weren't. I didn't want an audience for this.

I snuck a look at Gavon then averted my eyes. He wore a look of consideration, as if he were running through a litany of responses and trying to come up with the best one. By the tightness around his mouth, he was on the verge of an epic diatribe.

He cleared his throat after a moment. "Anyone care to explain how the two of you ended up in an abandoned library?"

I found the hem of my pants incredibly interesting, but James shifted next to me.

"It was an accident," he said.

"Trespassing is rarely an accident, that's why it's trespassing," Gavon said, sounding sharper than I'd ever heard him before. Even when I'd drunk a shoddy potion, he'd been more worried than angry. I chanced another peek at him—he was radiating fury. But not at me, at James.

"So this is my fault?" James said with a careless drawl. Perhaps he was more used to Gavon's anger than I was, because he seemed incredibly unconcerned about the furious magical standing in front of him.

I braced myself for an argument between them, but Gavon said, "I want you to go home and wait for me there. I will deal with you later."

"Whatever," James said, giving him one final rebellious look before walking out of the jail cell. He crossed his arms over his chest and glared at Gavon. "I need my magic back to—" He disappeared in a puff of purple smoke before he finished his sentence.

Gavon stared at the space James had vacated and clicked his tongue. Then he closed his eyes, inhaled deeply, and turned to me.

Despite myself, I gulped.

"Are you okay?" he asked softly.

"O-okay?" I squeaked, realizing that I wasn't going to get the brunt of his anger. In fact, based on the concern now replacing the fury in his eyes, I was pretty sure he would whip me up a calming draught if I asked for it.

"I'm fine," I muttered, returning my attention to my jeans.

"Alexis…" He sighed and entered the cell, taking the spot next to me. "I wanted *you* to be a better influence on *him*. Not the other way around. I don't know how he convinced you to trespass, but…"

How had James convinced me so easily? *Oh, that's right.* I'd been angry because I'd found out Gavon had been slipping me books instead of coming to talk to me. I supposed a girl had to get arrested in order to get a conversation with the man. Funnily enough, now that I had him in front of me, I suddenly wasn't all that interested in what he had to say.

"So do you want your books back or what?" I said, hot anger churning in the pit of my stomach. "Or are you content to make me stumble upon them like a moron."

He considered his response. "I thought it best to do it that way."

"You thought it best?" I actually laughed, although there was no humor in it. "Did you also think it best to let me worry for months on end that a deranged psychopath was going to come back and murder my whole family when, surprise! You'd already resolved that little problem a damn *week* after and didn't think to tell me about it?"

His eyes hardened. "You had the barrier spells. There was no need to worry—"

"How the hell was I supposed to know they were going to work?" I said, my voice rising an octave. "Gavon, I had *nobody*. Gram excommunicated us, Nicole doesn't want to admit she *has* magic anymore—"

"You have Marie."

"No, I don't," I said with a shake of my head. "She's *gone*, Gavon. She ran away, and we haven't heard from her in almost two years. The only thing I know is that she's safe, and that's thanks to some bullshit spell I hope is telling me the right thing and her damned read receipts."

Gavon's mouth fell open. "Marie's not with you?"

"Some father you are." I snorted with a heavy roll of my eyes. "Guess you just show up when it's convenient—"

"This is hardly what I would call a convenient occasion," Gavon said evenly. "You were arrested, in case you forgot. And it's a good thing you got off with a warning. Do you even know what this would do to your chances at Georgetown?"

I couldn't believe my ears—not only was he lecturing me, but he had the audacity to care about my college admissions? As if he were somehow interested in my hopes and dreams.

"Oh, fuck off—"

"*Excuse me?*" Gavon said, his voice rising. "I am your father, and you *will* not speak to me—"

I laughed, incredulous. "Father? You really want to pull that? I didn't even know who you were until I was fifteen! And then you disappeared again! For another two years!"

"Alexis—"

"My name is *Lexie!*"

"Your mother named you Alexis, and that is what I will call you."

I swallowed, tears brimming in my eyes. "How can you even talk to me about her? You let her *die*."

He recoiled as if I'd slapped him, but I couldn't stop the words spilling out of my mouth.

"Do you know what it was like having to relive the day my mother was killed? I remember *everything*. I have a great magical memory that starts and ends with *my mother* waiting for you while she's fighting off Cyrus. Do you know how scared she was? Do you know how she kept waiting for you? And she *died*."

"Enough," he said, his voice rough.

"No—"

He took my shoulders firmly. "*Enough*, Alexis. I understand you hate me. And you have every right to—"

"Damned straight I do."

"But that doesn't mean you should ruin your future by making stupid decisions. And this was, by all accounts, a very stupid decision."

I wanted to blast him away, to scream and rage until I had no energy left and, at the same time, I wanted to burst into tears and ask him why he was acting like he cared when he didn't. My conflicting emotions boiled inside me, threatening to explode into hysterics or magic, and it was all I could do just to stand there silently.

"Go home and stay there for the rest of the weekend. You and James are restricted from sparring until you can both demonstrate a bit more restraint."

I glared at him, wishing I had the focus to argue with him. My walls were wearing thin, and if I didn't leave the jail cell soon, I wasn't sure what I'd do. So I pushed myself to stand and marched out of the cell, not even bothering to give him a final look before transporting myself home and dissolving into tears.

The next morning, still bleary-eyed from crying myself to sleep, I braced for the worst. I was fairly sure that Nicole was aware of what I'd done, and if getting a lecture from Gavon wasn't enough, now I had to face Nicole.

But not just about trespassing. I would have to come clean about everything—Gavon returning, James, sparring. Hunting down magical books behind her back. Practicing magic every chance I could get. More lies, more secrets. More of the same bullshit behavior that had gotten me in trouble before. I would tell her that I thought it was for her own good, but I doubted that would get me very far with her.

I had two options: Hide in my room for the rest of my life or face the music. Sadly, putting things off would just make them worse, so I readied myself for the hurricane waiting for me in the kitchen.

"Morning!" Nicole said brightly. "You got in late last night."

"Uh…" I glanced around, confused. "Yes?"

"Out with friends?"

"S...something like that," I stammered, taking a seat at the counter. "So...um..."

Nicole went to the toaster and added a few pieces of bread. "What's up?"

It was then that I realized Nicole *didn't* know that I'd been arrested in Boston the night before. Gavon hadn't told her, and thanks to him, she hadn't received a phone call either.

I didn't forgive him, but damn. He'd done me a real solid.

"I hate to ask you this," she said with a small frown. "But would you mind taking me to work tonight? My car is still making noise, and I'm a little afraid to drive it. Next place we move needs to have a bus or something."

Nicole wanting to use magic? That was odd. "Why don't you take it back to the shop?"

"Because I think the guy is ripping me off," she said, taking the seat across from me. "Last time I was there, he spent more time flirting with me than fixing the car."

I brightened. "There's a *guy* flirting with you? Nicole!"

"I'd be more interested if he could fix my car right," she muttered. "Six hundred dollars I'm up to. That's...well, that's a lot of money that I don't have a whole lot of right now."

I felt like such an ass, but I said, "Do you want me to give you some? I mean, I don't pay rent or anything—"

"No way," Nicole said firmly. "It's fine. I'll take an extra shift."

The stone at my neck burned—Nicole was lying through her teeth—but what really grabbed my attention was it hadn't even warmed during my conversation with Gavon.

Sixteen

After being arrested in Boston and seeing Gavon again, returning to school seemed completely silly. But I was looking forward to the distraction. I hadn't been able to erase the memory of what I'd said to Gavon—or what he'd said back.

"Your mother named you Alexis, and that is what I will call you."

He'd said it so easily, like a real father would. Wasn't that what sitcom fathers said? "Go ask your mother." And honoring my mother by calling me the name *she'd* given me…I supposed that meant he hadn't named me after his mother.

"How can you even talk to me about her? You let her die."

I might never forget the look on his face. There was shock there—pure, unadulterated shock and pain. My own words echoed in my head, reminding me that although I'd finally gotten to tell the man off after two years, I didn't actually feel any better about it.

In fact, I felt *guilty*. There was this horrible, overbearing need to apologize to Gavon for speaking my mind and saying what needed to be said. And he'd done more than enough to deserve what I'd dished out. But the small voice in my head—the one that still wanted to be important to him—wailed with remorse.

James had been absent for the first two class periods, but I saw him at his locker at the third. Even from a distance, I could see anger radiating off him as he yanked his books out of his bag and thrust them into the locker. I debated turning and running in the other direction, but he caught my gaze and softened just enough to invite me over.

"So, I'll have you know that I'm without magic for a *month*," James said, closing his locker.

"A *month*?" The longest I'd ever been grounded was two weeks by Jeanie and I'd thought I was going to lose my mind. "That's pretty severe, don't you think?"

James snorted. "He's trying to send a message. Remind me that I'm not supposed to be getting his *precious daughter* in trouble."

"Father? You really want to pull that? I didn't even know who you were until I was fifteen!"

I winced at the memory. "That, or maybe his precious daughter pissed him off."

"What'd you say?"

I sighed loudly and glanced at the ceiling in shame. "That he doesn't have the right to call himself my father. Couple other choice phrases like that."

James stopped, staring at me for a moment before slowly nodding. "Yeah, that might do it."

He came up beside me and we walked in silence for a

moment while I continued to self-flagellate for what I'd said and then self-flagellate for self-flagellating.

"So…you aren't on good terms, then?" James asked, almost hesitantly.

"What makes you think we were?" I gaped. "Have you *not* been paying attention?"

"I mean, I know the thing with your aunt but…you really… you hate him?"

Again, guilt pressed on my shoulders, and I shrugged it off. "My feelings for him are complicated. But it's…I mean, it's his fault they're complicated. He shows up in my life, doesn't tell me he's my father then ruins everything and disappears until… well, until the day you showed up."

This all looked to be news to James. "Huh."

"You really had no idea?" I said.

"He's always leaving to come over to this side, has been for months now. I guess I figured he was coming here…"

"Nope," I said, before glaring at the floor. That familiar tickling in the back of my mind reemerged, as if I were trying to remember a word I'd forgotten. I shook my head to try to clear the uncomfortable feeling. "And apparently, he had no idea my sister was gone either. So who knows what he's up to?"

James was silent, his brow furrowed in concentration and curiosity. When he finally started walking again, he wore a smug smile.

"What?" I asked.

"Just, I guess I always thought you and he were…" His smirk grew into a genuine smile. "I think we're going to be good friends."

"Just as long as you don't get me arrested again."

"Hey, you asked me to help you find magicals and books, and I delivered, didn't I?"

At that, I had to laugh. "Fair enough, I guess."

December arrived with cool nights and pleasant days. Since James was still grounded, we couldn't spar, so I didn't see much of him outside of school. But I noticed a marked difference with him. He actually spoke to me at school, asked me to be his lab partner once in physics, and seemed to enjoy conversations with me when he wasn't with his girl-of-the-week. He and Callista had broken up over Thanksgiving, and he made no secret of his hunt for his next conquest.

His latest fling was with Gee, the drop-dead gorgeous editor of the yearbook, who straight-up asked me if there was anything going on between James and me.

"Nope, just unwilling friends," I said with an amused laugh.

I considered, perhaps, having "the talk" with James and making sure he was using protection. But that just conjured up images of Gavon having the same talk with him, and I pushed that out of my head.

The best thing about December was it meant the end of my second-to-last semester of high school. My grades came in perfectly, as predicted, and I maintained my position at the top of the class. Unless I did a total nosedive in the second half of the year, I'd graduate valedictorian.

The winter break started and I found myself rather...bored. James obviously wasn't around (still grounded) and my tutoring had ended for the semester. I spent a few days in the apartment, but all the downtime drove me batty. The spell books couldn't keep my interest, as they just reminded me that Gavon had tricked me into taking them. I even attempted a sparring session with myself, but it just didn't have the same impact as sparring with James.

To stay busy, I signed up for extra hours at the kennel and actually did the work, versus letting my magic do it for me. It made for sweaty hours, but I left every day feeling accomplished, and that counted for something.

The day before New Year's, I was wiping down the cat cages when I heard an annoyed sound behind me.

"Ugh," James made a face, "it smells like dog in here."

"Yeah, that's because it's a kennel," I said, but I couldn't help the smile on my face. "Did you get released?"

"Probation. No magic, and I have to be back in exactly three hours. Plenty of time to get into some trouble."

I glared at him.

"Okay, no trouble. Because if I'm a good boy today, Gavon will let me attend a New Year's Eve party tomorrow. Gee might give me another chance."

"You broke up?" I wasn't necessarily surprised about that, more that they'd lasted this long.

He shrugged. "I mean, the texts she sent weren't good. Mostly because I didn't get them until ten minutes ago."

That answered my question about cell reception in New Salem. "You should've told Gavon. I know he wouldn't stand in the way of true love."

James' dry look made me laugh.

"I try not to converse with him about that if I can help it,"

James said. "But how about it? If I go with you, at least if Gavon comes looking for me, he'll know you're keeping an eye on me."

I played with the mop handle. "Would he come looking for you?"

"Doubtful. I haven't seen much of him. I think he'd just prefer not to get another call from the police. Which I *promise* won't happen this time." He wiggled his eyebrows, his boyish charm drawing an unwilling smile onto my face. "C'mon…"

I gripped the mop and frowned. "I really need to get the volunteer hours…"

"Use your magic," James said with a grin. "It's not as if you're not doing the work. The place will get clean. Just quicker."

"The point is I need the hours."

"For what? You already sent in your college applications. Why do you need to keep working here?"

I chewed my lip, surprised he'd remembered something like that. "Yeah, but…"

"Yeah, but what? You've done what you can. Now it's time to have fun."

I looked around the kennel. James was right. I'd logged over two hundred hours this year alone, and I'd already submitted all my applications. And to be honest, I was volunteering because it got me out of the house and away from Nicole, who'd continued her insufferable campaign to make the holidays cheerful.

I sighed. "Fine. Let's go."

True to his word, James picked one of the most mundane

places possible—Starbucks. We found a table in the back of the shop, and he took a few minutes inhaling and savoring his coffee.

"There's nothing like this over there," he said, gently sipping his americano. "Nothing. Just disgusting brown liquid they substitute for tea."

I sipped my sugary peppermint mocha thoughtfully. "So what was it like…growing up there?"

"Terrible. Next question."

I put down my coffee. "Sorry I asked."

He actually looked a bit repentant. "Sorry, I just… I forgot what it's like. It's been horrendous back there. Boring as *hell*."

"What's there to do? Sparring matches?" I asked.

"No, those are rare. Gavon wouldn't allow an audience when he and I trained, and I was very rarely allowed to spar with Cyrus. Our introduction matches were the highlight of the decade." He shook his head. "Mostly they spend their days toiling dirt and trying to make food from whatever they can grow in the harsh conditions. Bunch of animals."

They'd looked poor and uneducated when I was there, but still human. "That's not fair, James. They can't help what kind of magic they were born with."

"It's not just their magic, it's…" He shook his head. "The Council does a good job of keeping them uneducated. Most of them think the world ends at the town limits. None of them know about, well…all this. If they knew, they might do something drastic, like revolt. Even though Gavon dotes on them. The Council thinks he's an idiot, but I think it's smart."

"Who…are the Council, exactly?" I asked, playing with the

rim of my coffee. "What's their purpose?"

"Supposedly, it's made up of the most powerful Warriors in New Salem," James said with a smirk. "But since the only Warriors around are me, Gavon, and Cyrus, we've had to add some Charmers and Enchanters to the mix."

A horrible, curious thought entered my brain. "Gavon's not your father, right? And neither is Cyrus…I hope…"

James looked at me, surprised. "What gave you that idea?"

"I mean I…" My face warmed. "Just checking."

"No, they're not," he said with a laugh. "But even Cyrus would've been a vast improvement over my actual parents. They're both worthless."

I chewed my lip, toying with the white lid on my coffee. "Was James Riley your ancestor?"

"My father claims he's directly descended from Riley, but so do half the residents there. He's nothing but an enchanter, so there's a good possibility he's lying or misinformed." James heaved a breath. "But on the other hand, there haven't been a whole lot of Warriors, so who knows?"

There was no mistaking the contempt in his voice. "Do you talk to him often?"

"Never, if I can help it. Both he and my mother were quick to hand me over to Gavon once I was off the teet."

I gasped, covering my mouth. "He took you from your parents so young?"

"He didn't take me. They practically tossed me at him," James said with a sardonic laugh. "In New Salem, Warriors are highly coveted, especially as there haven't been a lot of them born in the past hundred years. So when one comes along, they're snatched up pretty quickly by the surviving Warriors and trained. And the parents get a large sum of money every month. They've been living easy ever since."

"But it can't be all bad over there," I said. "Don't you have friends?"

He snorted. "We're about as close as my friends over here. Over there, everything's about magic. It's hard to find common ground when you're better than everyone else at everything."

He looked completely serious, and I barked a laugh. "I don't know, maybe you should try treating people like humans instead of magic?"

"Do you really want to talk friend-making? You live here and you don't have any."

"I have *friends*," I said. "My sister is my friend."

"Mm. Yeah. That doesn't count."

I grit my teeth and decided to change the subject. "What's Cyrus been up to?"

"Odd change of subject. You'd rather talk about Cyrus than your lack of friends?"

I shrugged and took a sip. "Why not? We're talking about uncomfortable things. Why not check in on the madman who ruined my life?"

"Well, we don't chat often. Gavon's forbade me from seeking him out. And he's been absent over the past few months."

"That doesn't…worry you?"

"Why should it?" he asked. "I'm not the one he wants dead."

I leveled an icy glare at him, which he laughed at.

"What are you so worried about? He can't touch you. And if

he ever *did* figure a way to do it, you'd kick his ass."

"Oh right…"

"I'm serious," James said, leaning back. "We're about the same level, and I'm amazing."

I rolled my eyes. "Humble, too."

"I know you think I'm lying, but I'm being serious. Even if Cyrus were more powerful than you, he's still got a good thirty years on you. Magic can help slow the aging process, but not by that much. Besides, you really do kick ass."

I smiled, oddly charmed by the compliment. "You think?"

"I think you're a force to be reckoned with, absolutely. One of the most powerful magicals I've ever seen." My suspicions rose as he reached across the table to take my hand. "And so smart, so brilliant—"

"Out with it. What do you want?"

"Would you take me to Gee's party tomorrow night?"

I parsed his words for a moment, because he couldn't mean what I thought he meant…until I realized he didn't. "Oh. You mean you need me to bring you to the party because you don't have magic."

"And Gee won't tell me where it is either. I think she's trying to play power with me."

"Power play," I corrected. "Or, and this is just a stab in the dark, perhaps she's decided you aren't worth her time because you ignored her for two weeks."

"But it wasn't my fault!" he said quickly. "That's why I need you to take me there so I can talk to her in person. Please?" He squeezed my hands. "It's not like you have any other plans tomorrow night."

"I'll have you know I was planning on watching Netflix and going to sleep at ten."

"*Lexie*," he whined. "I need your help. And you need to get out and spend time with real people. It'll be good for you."

"Look," I said, taking my hands out of his. "I'm not... Parties aren't really my scene. The last one I went to was a complete disaster."

"That's because you left after fifteen minutes. I can't believe I have to explain this, but in order to make friends, you have to actually *talk* to people."

"I have…friends," I said lamely. "Besides, what do you care?"

"Seeing you alone all the time is depressing."

"Go to hell."

"How about this: you're obviously unhappy, and that makes me, as your friend, unhappy. So let's both go to the party and have some fun?"

He was back to his charming smile, and it was hard to say no to it. I tried a diversion tactic. "Didn't you say there would be something in it for me?"

"Yes, isn't that obvious? You get to attend a party. See? Win-win." I rolled my eyes, but he took my hands again. "Stop fighting it, and come with me."

I couldn't resist any more. "*Fine*. But if it's lame, I'm going home and you're on your own."

Seventeen

For the second time in three months, I found myself digging through my closet, searching for something to wear to an actual party. This time, I was slightly more excited. At the very least, I would have James to hang out with. Our conversation had warmed me to him a little, if only because it might've been the first honest one we'd ever had.

"Oh…" Nicole appeared in my doorway, a bottle of cheap champagne in her hands and her excited smile turning into a frown. "I didn't know you had plans…"

"Yeah," I said, standing and feeling a little guilty. "Last minute invite."

"Well…well, good." Her fake smile was back, but I saw right through it. "Have fun. Is it a date or…?"

"Absolutely not," I said with a laugh. "One of my friends needs…me to play wingman. I guess."

"Really? Who's your friend? Have I met her before?"

Yeah. "No. Just someone I go to school with. We're in a lot of the same classes. He's—"

"Oh, *he* is it?"

"Calm down," I said with my hands in the air. "This is the guy I was telling you about a few months ago."

"The one who burned you in the past?" She frowned. "I thought you weren't going to work with him or whatever?"

"He made a compelling case," I said. "And at the end of the day, it's better if we work together than apart. Turns out, once you get past his ego, bluster, and womanizing ways—"

"I thought you said he was gay?"

Damn Nicole and her good memory. "Turns out, he's bi…I guess." I needed to end this conversation before I slipped up again. "Anyway, he's really not a bad person. I mean, he's still a pain in the ass, but it's actually kind of fun to put him in his place."

"Uh-oh, Lexie, sounds like you're developing a crush on him," Nicole said with a wink. "Just be careful. Even if you think he's changed, people rarely do. I don't want to see you get hurt."

I smiled. "I won't, trust me. I'm keeping my distance. It's more fun to see him get destroyed by the girls in my class." I chuckled. "I have to say, I really like watching them dump him. Sweet justice."

"Have fun." She kissed me on the forehead. "Please stay until midnight, at least."

"I will." I frowned. "Are you going to be all right by yourself?"

"Sure. May not be sober when you get back, but I'll be fine."

She left me to my devices and I finished checking my

makeup in the mirror. I wasn't the kind of girl who spent hours contouring and defining, but I figured for a special occasion, I could add a little extra. Once I was happy with my appearance, I transported myself to the beach and waited for James to arrive.

He showed in a puff of black smoke not five minutes later, dusting the remnants of his transport potion off his shirt and coughing into the darkness.

"You've got to teach me how to do that," I said, walking over to him.

"You're better off driving. This is no way to travel." He coughed again and shook his head as black soot fell from his dark locks. "I'm counting down until I get my magic back. One week, five days left."

I smiled, recalling my own brief grounding. "Hopefully you can forget about it tonight."

"I don't know," he said, his face lit by his phone's backlight. "Gee hasn't responded to any of my texts."

"I doubt she will. She doesn't seem like the kind of girl who'd accept an apology over the phone."

James slid the phone into his jeans and took my arm. "Good thing I've got you, then."

"Yeah, yeah."

Gee lived in one of the nicer subdivisions in the city, so it was easy to locate a dark spot to appear in. James even commented on my improving abilities to transport others, before he ditched me and nearly ran into the house. I followed slower, knowing that us arriving together would kill his chances of getting back together with Gee. To be honest, I wanted them back together. He seemed a lot less willful in her presence.

The house was already full of people, most of whom I didn't know. I found out from some overheard conversations on my way to the kitchen that Gee's older brother was visiting from Florida State, and had invited his friends to stay for the weekend. They were supposedly chaperoning, but from the looks of them, they were more drunk than the high schoolers.

I found a few of Gee's friends in the kitchen, and they waved me over, offering me a super-sugary alcoholic drink.

"So, I hear James is trying to get back together with Gee," Tamara said with a shake of her head. "Doesn't he know to leave well enough alone?"

"No," I said with a snort. The bubbles in the drink tickled my nose and the sugar sat unhappily in my stomach. I'd probably only have one.

"Look at them out there," said Emily, peering over the countertop curiously. "Gee does *not* look happy he showed up. How did he even know where she lived?"

I tried not to look too guilty. "He's resourceful. And determined."

"So what is the deal with you two?" asked the other Emily. "Are you friends, are you—"

"Friends, believe me. I'm not touching that. Ever." I shivered. "He's not the kind of person one should date."

"Yeah, I hear Callista was heartbroken. He apparently wouldn't ever take her out except on Friday nights and wouldn't introduce her to his parents."

I imagined what it would be like for Gavon to meet Callista and had to laugh, which I covered up with a cough. "Sorry, went down the wrong pipe."

"Oh, she's coming in," Tamara said. "She looks pissed."

The three girls went to do their best friend duty, and Gee tossed one very evil look in my direction, which I responded with an "I'm-sorry" expression. But I could hear the sound of her stomps all the way up to her bedroom.

"Well, that went well," James said, walking up to me. "Guess I'm back on sale."

"Back on the market," I replied. "Honestly, how am I the only one who gets to hear you make mistakes like that?"

"Because you're the only one I'm comfortable making mistakes around," James said, grabbing my drink from me and downing it with admirable gumption. "Ugh, this is gross." He drank more.

"So what happened?"

"I tried to tell her I'd been grounded, and didn't have my phone until the other day. She then tells me I was supposed to come over on Christmas and meet her family. Is that a thing?"

"I'll explain later," I said with an amused smile. "Then what happened?"

"I said she was the first person I'd texted and when she didn't respond, I came to you—"

"*James*!" I cried, throwing my hands in the air. "Leave me out of it!"

"Why?"

"You *can't* be that stupid."

"I'm not, but I don't see why anyone would think there's something between us. I mean…look at you and look at me."

"Yes, one of us is a well-adjusted valedictorian, and the other is a selfish asshole."

James glowered. "That's not fair."

"Neither is the insinuation that I'm somehow less attractive than you are. Or less datable."

"I didn't mean you weren't cute. But you're my friend. We spar and we talk magic. And, oh by the way, your father is my master."

A fact I let myself forget most days. "Yeah, that would be kind of weird."

"We're close because we're both magical. That's all. But there's not really an easy way to explain that to Gee without her thinking I'm hiding something."

"James…you *are* hiding something."

We stared at each other for a moment before bursting into laughter. I wasn't even sure why it was so funny, but after spending so much time living half-truths and sneaking around, it was nice to admit it out loud. Especially with someone in the exact same boat.

Friends. James had said we were friends. And for the first time, I realized that I did consider him my friend. Sure, he was self-absorbed, but he'd also made a compelling case for me to go out and socialize. In his own warped little mind, I supposed he thought he was doing me a favor.

"What's that on the TV?" he asked, nodding toward it.

"New Year's Eve celebration in New York," I said. "Thousands of people watch a giant glass ball drop. Everyone celebrates at midnight."

"Looks like fun. We should go."

"What? Right now?"

"Yeah," James said with a devilish grin. "This party is boring anyway."

"Right now."

"*Yes.*"

"I can't find a spot," I said, standing in the dark outside of Gee's house. "The whole place is crowded. There isn't an empty place anywhere in the city."

"So...let's just appear," James replied. "Nobody will notice."

"Isn't that..." I bit my lip. I'd never consciously attempted magic in front of non-magicals, but I'd always lived in fear of some unknown consequence. "I mean, there's a law against it. A magical one."

"One that, I would suppose, doesn't apply to you," James said. "Considering none of the others do."

He had a point. After the Separation, the remaining magicals created an agreement to prevent the same thing from happening again. That meant no magic until fifteen and no specialties, among other things. But since my father's ancestors had been stuck in New Salem, I was exempt from the pact. Another pesky loophole.

"Look," James said, adjusting his grip on my arm, "why don't you try again? Maybe find somewhere dark and crowded, that way no one will notice us showing up."

"I looked—"

"Try. Again." His smile was encouraging, as if he was sure I could do this and I was just doubting myself. "And stop controlling your magic so hard. You look like you're taking a—"

"All right, that's enough," I snapped, glaring at him. Closing my eyes, I released my magic again, concentrating—

He brushed the center of my forehead with his fingers, relaxing the concentrated tension he found. "Relax. Magic isn't this difficult."

"Easy for you to say," I grumbled, but his gentle touch had worked. Free of the control and with a simple request, my magic darted through the city, landing on an empty broom closet in a building right in Times Square. "I found one!"

"See? And you doubted your—"

I didn't want to lose the place, so I transported the two of us before he could finish. The air sucked out of my chest as he crashed into me, our bodies filling the tiny space. I heard something crash behind him as we both got our bearings.

His breath tickled my cheek as he coughed. "Well...this is awkward."

I glanced down; my legs straddled his, and his thigh was pressed very firmly against the more sensitive parts of my body. Uncomfortable, new feelings rose in my stomach. "I think we should get out of here."

"Waiting on you, magical."

"Oh, right." Using magic, I unlocked the door from the inside, and we spilled out onto the tile floor. I nursed my bruised elbows and hands, but James just lay on the floor, laughing.

"This is already much more fun than that party. Why don't we do this more often?" he asked, turning to look at me.

At first, I thought he meant the intimate moment in the closet, which increased the new squirming in my stomach. Then I realized he was speaking more generally.

"Because, apparently, you hated me," I said after a while.

"Oh right," he said. "Because I thought you and Gavon were conspiring to make my life miserable."

"You know," I said, propping myself up on my elbows. "In order to conspire, people actually have to communicate."

"Enough of that. I don't want to think about him," James said, popping deftly to his feet. He grabbed my hand and pulled me up too, so fast I got dizzy, so he placed both hands on my shoulders. "We have a city to explore."

The crowd was audible from the seventh floor (where I'd transported us), and even louder when the elevator doors opened. The lobby was empty, but just beyond the glass double doors, people were crammed in tight on the street outside. I wasn't even in the crowd, and already claustrophobia welled in my chest.

"C'mon," James said, grabbing my hand and pulling me toward it. I magically unlocked the glass doors (then locked them again; no need to get a poor security guard in trouble), and we entered the fray. Crowded didn't even begin to describe it. This was *insanity*. Lights and flashes blinked down at me from everywhere, and the din of the crowd was so loud it made my ears ring. My only tether to sanity was the pressure of James' palm in mine, and the tug of forward motion as we walked through the crowd. I was over it in seconds, but he seemed drunk on the activity of it all.

"You're sure you don't want to go back to the party?" I yelled over the din.

"No way," he called, glancing over his shoulder. "You don't think this is fun?"

I offered a half-smile, and he tugged at my hand.

"C'mon! Live a little. You have all this power to go anywhere you choose and you choose to stay home."

"I like being home!"

"You aren't living. This is living!"

He stopped short, and I ran into him. Again, I found myself in close quarters with him, pressed against his back as he held tight to my hand. But his attention had gone upward, to the moving signs and tall buildings. He turned to me with a wide-eyed innocence I'd never seen before. Gone was the cocky and brazen boy who swaggered around my school as if he owned it. James was gawking at New York City as if it were the most fascinating thing he'd ever seen.

He finally noticed my closeness and took a step away. "What?"

"You're…actually excited about something," I said over the loud chatter around us. "It's weird."

"I get excited about lots of things. But I can't very well act like everything in school is brand new to me, can I? Might invite some questions."

"Yeah, one of these days, you're going to have to tell me how you managed to fool my school into thinking you're a normal kid from the twenty-first century."

He grinned. "Later. After you tell me what *that* thing is!" He pointed to one of the large movie screens on the building, counting down the minutes until midnight. "And that! What is that over there? And—"

"One thing at a time," I said with a laugh. I drew his attention to the main event, pointing over his head. "See? That's the ball that drops at midnight."

"And why is that important?"

"I...have no idea," I said with a frown. "Just tradition, I guess. New Year's means everything starts over. People like that."

"I like that, too." His attention was still on the ball, as if willing it to move sooner. It might be a good thing he was without magic. "This year is going to be weird."

"Tell me about it," I replied with a sigh. "Graduation, going to college. Moving out."

"Getting inducted into the Guild."

I looked at him sharply, but he hadn't moved. "You're getting inducted?"

"On my eighteenth birthday in March." He finally wrenched his attention away, and for a split second, I saw uncharacteristic uncertainty. But it was quickly replaced by his usual carefree smile. "But let's—"

A loud cheer rose from the crowd, and we turned to the main billboard. There was one minute left until midnight.

"Now what?" James called to me.

"Now we count down to midnight," I called back.

"Oh. What happens then?"

What did happen then? People usually cheered, toasted... and kissed.

Oh crap, this was going to be awkward.

"Ten! Nine!"

James joined in the chanting and I did too, half-heartedly, dreading the impending moment and wishing I could transport myself out of there.

"Six! Five!"

James turned to me, a curious look on his face, so I wiped the worry from mine. This year was going to be better. I'd be getting into Georgetown. I'd be graduating high school. My new life was going to begin.

Yeah, things were going to be great. Just after this awkward moment passed.

"Three! Two! One!"

The world exploded in cheers and confetti, and next to us, couples moved together in celebratory kisses. Before I could even question it, James grabbed my face between his hands and planted his lips on mine.

My first kiss was over before it began, and it was all I could do to stare wordlessly at James. He turned away as if nothing interesting had just occurred and wrapped my hand in his, tugging me forward to do another lap around the crowd.

But even as I dumbly followed, I pressed a finger to my lips, wondering if it had been my imagination, or if a bit of magic had passed between us.

Eighteen

By the time I woke up on New Year's Day, I'd all but forgotten the kiss. And by forgotten, I meant tried my damnedest not to overthink what it meant or how it had felt. It had been spur of the moment. A friend kiss. A peer-pressure induced meeting-of-the-mouths. There hadn't even been any tongue and it had lasted about two seconds.

So why couldn't I stop thinking about it?

This was *James*, apprentice to Gavon. Future leader of the Death Eaters. I couldn't come up with a better example of "Bad Boy." Not to mention he was arrogant, selfish, and the worst kind of womanizer. The polar opposite of anything I should've even considered being attracted to.

Yet, he was incredibly charming when he wanted to be. He was also handsome, although his personality overshadowed that most of the time. Something drew me toward his arrogance, too, especially because I knew I was his equal and could put him back in his place. There was something so delicious about watching him stew in defeat when I bested him—verbally and magically.

But did that mean I was developing a crush on him? And how could one develop a crush on someone who was so obviously a terrible choice? It was almost like I had no control over my own decision-making. Like seeing disaster ahead and not being able to find the brakes.

That son of a bitch must've put a potion on me. Or a charm. Or something. Because I was *not* this stupid. Maybe he'd coated his lips, and I was simply feeling the aftereffects. But after searching my potion book, I discovered that most potions that affected the brain weren't permanent. They only lasted a day, maybe two if the dose was made strong enough.

Which meant that after three days of fighting a goofy, lovesick smile when I thought of James, I determined that he hadn't potioned me, and I was simply being an idiot.

"You're distracted today," Nicole said one morning over breakfast.

My kingdom for a sister I could be honest with. "Yeah. Just getting excited about the year, I guess. Nervous."

"Nothing has to change, you know," she said. "I mean, it's okay to stay here and go to school—"

"It's not okay," I said, complete with the familiar surge of annoyance that came with the idea of staying where I was.

She pursed her lips, clearly wanting to say more. Instead she said, "I think I'm going to take my car in again."

"R-really?" I blinked. "That's what? Three times in three months?"

"It's still making noises and..." She chewed on her lip.

"Demand that the mechanic do something about it," I replied. "You shouldn't be paying him if he's not doing his job."

"I think it's just an old car."

"Nicole," I said with a frown. "Don't let him push you around."

"He's not pushing me around," she said hotly. "I'm going to demand that he fix the car and not charge me this time."

"Absolutely."

"Just…I'll go in later," she said, wilting into her coffee.

"I could go threaten to blow him up," I said after a few minutes of silence.

"Don't you *dare*."

When the first day of my final semester in high school arrived, I awoke with a pit of dread in my stomach. Not because I was nervous about school, but it had been over a week since I'd seen James, and I was still thinking about him with infuriating frequency. I'd have to face him eventually, but if I limited our exposure as much as possible, perhaps I could build up an immunity to him.

I waited until the last minute to transport to the bathroom and squeaked into my desk during the morning announcements. I kept my head down, but I felt his gaze on me as I settled in across the room. The heat was palpable, or perhaps it was just my embarrassment, and it took all my willpower not to look up. Finally, out of the corner of my eye, I saw him turn back to the front.

My gaze landed on his neck, and I wondered what it would be like to kiss it—

I blinked, blushing for even thinking that way. I suddenly felt exposed, as if everyone in the room had just heard what I'd thought. Turning my attention, I tried my very best to focus on the teacher, and not on the way James' arms so slightly moved as he scribbled down notes.

Those arms, connected to those hands, which had taken me and kissed me so—

Stop it, Lexie.

In the first place, no matter how friendly we'd gotten, he was still in line to be the next Guildmaster, with all the repercussions thereof.

In the second place, I saw him share a glance with Mary Catherine, a tall, skinny girl who I thought was a dancer. Our kiss had obviously changed nothing for him and he was on the prowl for his next girl. As class wrapped up, he turned to her, smiling in that way that said he was very interested, and said, "What's happening?"

As I packed my books up, I told myself it was a good thing, because if he was distracted with someone else, he wouldn't be able to flirt with me and make me daydream about him. And then perhaps I could return to seeing him as just a friend, and not someone I wanted to push up against the wall and make out with.

"Are you mad at me?"

I jumped nearly out of my skin, as James had appeared in front of me as if by magic.

"You've been avoiding me all day," he said with a frown. "Did I do something wrong?"

I yelped then busied myself with my locker. "I mean, no. I'm not. Just trying to get back into school."

If he found my bashful behavior strange, he was clearly upset over other things. "I'm so glad to be back. Gavon's been relentless lately. My induction match is three months away."

"You mentioned that," I said, cautiously.

"Final test before I'm officially admitted into the Guild." He chewed his lip and glanced down at me. "You aren't going to get mad at me if I talk about this, are you?"

"Me?" I squeaked. "Why would I get mad?"

"I just… I know how you get when I talk about Gavon, and I don't want to upset you."

Words left me in favor of shock, and I stared at him for a long time before I noticed he'd started walking away. I jogged after him, still unable to shake the strange feeling in my chest.

"Look, we're friends. And friends talk to each other about stuff that's bothering them. You've heard me talk about my issues. So…yeah. Fire away."

"I've been allowed to spar with you once a week again, because Gavon has taken an interest in my training. Tuesdays with him, Fridays with you. And when I'm not doing homework, I have to study magical theories and potions." He rolled his eyes. "Wouldn't surprise me if he popped an exam on me either."

"Why the worry?" I asked as we walked to our next class. "Has Cyrus done anything…?"

James heaved a sigh and I feared the worst. "He asked me over for tea the other day. He hasn't done that in several months, not since I started attending school."

"I thought you were forbidden to go over there?"

"I'm forbidden, but if Cyrus asks Gavon, Gavon has to let me go. Guild rules and all that. Anyway, Cyrus asked if I would consider taking over the Guildmastership."

"But, I mean…you will one day… Oh." I licked my lips. "You mean…"

"Yes. Kill Gavon and take over now."

I swallowed. The last words I'd spoken to Gavon had been in anger, and if that was the last thing I *ever* said to him…I shuddered. Even now, I still felt guilty about it, even though I knew I'd been mostly in the right.

"Which means either he thinks he can sway me to whatever plan he's got, or he thinks *he* can challenge me in a duel and finish me off." James chuckled. "In both cases, he'll find himself sorely mistaken."

I actually sighed in relief. "Thank God."

"Which part?"

"The part where you aren't killing Gavon."

He stopped in the middle of the hall. "Do you really think I could do something like that?"

"Well…"

He stopped and took my arm. "Do you not understand me? Cyrus wants me to kill a man in cold blood. Despite my issues with Gavon, he's still the only father I've ever known. And you really think I'd be able to take his life simply so I can ascend to my rightful position twenty years sooner?"

I didn't know what to say to that, except to ask, "You were ready to kill me."

"I was a child then. I didn't understand…" James released my arm. "Gavon… He took me to a sick house. Our poor excuse for a hospital. Without potion-makers, sick villagers die slow, painful deaths. Gavon told me if I was so eager to take innocent life, there was a house full of them, each ready for it, unlike you."

I shivered as James released a shaky breath. "Did you do it?"

"I couldn't," he said, staring at the floor in shame. "Just like I can't take Gavon's life. Warriors aren't supposed to be killers. We're defenders."

"Cyrus did it so easily," I replied, tightening my hold around my books. "My mother, my aunt. My *grandmother*—"

"Cyrus is insane," James said, though he nudged me gently with his elbow. "I'm not him. I'm not going to take lives simply because I can."

I heard Gavon in his words, and had to smile. James may have hated him, but it was clear he'd learned a lot.

James shook himself, and the haunted look fell from his eyes. "Besides that, I don't want to be Guildmaster yet. I'll be eighteen and this world requires a lot more exploring." He grinned at me but I didn't reciprocate.

"What are you going to do when you become Guildmaster?" I asked. "Eventually."

"Take over the world."

I stopped short and gaped at him, fear spreading like wildfire until I saw the turn of his mouth.

"You're too easy," he said with a laugh. "Probably the same thing Gavon's done. Keep the idiots happy and the powerful ones in the dark. They may think the New Salem Guild could come back with a roaring vengeance, but it's clear there's more of you than us. They'd have us back inside the tear in a heartbeat. Surprised they haven't come and cleaned us out already."

"I guess that makes sense."

"You don't have anything to fear from me, Lexie. Besides, the nonmagicals get by pretty well without magic." He pulled his phone out of his front pocket. "This thing is pretty cool."

"Yeah, I guess it is," I said with a smile.

"Honestly, thinking I could kill Gavon. You probably still think I'm evil, don't you?" James asked with a sad shake of his head.

I shrugged, noncommittal. "Maybe not evil anymore. A dick, sure."

"You wound me."

"You've got a potion for that, I hear," I shot back then stopped myself. I was flirting. With *James*. What the hell was wrong with me? A little kiss, and I'd all but lost my mind.

"So what happens after you're inducted?" I asked, after we settled into our seats. "Assuming you don't take over for Gavon."

"Then I am a fully-fledged member of the Guild. Get a vote on Guild matters and everything."

"Like what?"

"Oh you know, what to call the semi-monthly meeting of the Charmers." James sniffed. "And how much wine we will conjure for the annual celebration." He grinned at me. "You know, evil stuff."

I laughed, although his smile made me blush.

"So, are we on for Friday night?"

"Friday?" I gulped. Had I missed him asking me out? Was he

asking me out? What was going on?

"Sparring? I mean, unless you're still mad at me." He winked. "You know, for being evil and whatnot."

"S-sparring. Sure." I nodded, already dreading my idiotic reaction to it. "Friday it is."

But James had already forgotten about me, glancing over my shoulder to make eyes with Mary Catherine.

Nineteen

James moved from flirting to dating in the span of two days, which suited me just fine. This was not a crush I wanted to nurture and grow, and the more he showcased his disgusting behavior, the quicker it would disappear. However, the looming issue of our Friday sparring sessions weighed on the back of my mind.

It had never occurred to me that he and I were alone together for long periods of time, usually ending up winded, sweaty, and exhausted. But now it was all I thought about, and my brain ran wild with images of what else we could do to end up winded, sweaty, and exhausted.

And the flirting—goodness, we flirted. Or it felt like flirting. The back and forth, the need to one-up him. Before our kiss, it was strictly two Warriors using every strategy in the book to confuse and distract their opponent. Now? I was fairly sure my own distraction levels were going to be at an all-time high without his help.

Skipping wasn't really an option either, so Friday evening, I arrived at the beach early to have a few minutes to myself. I watched the waves lap against the shore and reminded myself of all the reasons James was a horrible person—not the least of which had to do with his New Salem connections.

He was selfish and had an ego the size of the moon.

He went through girls like tissue paper.

He didn't do anything unless it benefitted himself first.

There was nothing cute about his attitude or his pride.

"Oh, you're here."

But damn, there was something really cute about his face— and the way he smiled at me from across the beach. The breeze tousled his hair, as did the lingering magic that had brought him to me. He stuffed his hands in his pockets as he walked closer, and I swore my pulse would never return to a normal rate.

Focus, Lexie!

"Shall we?" I asked, standing and brushing the sand off.

"Yeah, but let's not overdo it. I've got a date with MC."

Despite my best efforts, my smile faltered. "Of course. I've got a date too. With Netflix."

"You do know you don't have to be so pathetic, right?"

"Shut up and let's spar," I snapped.

I'd hoped that focusing on my volleys, dodging, and return fires would distract me from him, but it was like every sense I had was heightened—and attuned to him. His particular scent filled my mind when he attacked at close-range. His smile when he landed a good blow sent butterflies into my stomach even as pain tore through me. His magic felt rough and familiar against mine as they collided with one another, and his body mesmerized me as he moved fluidly across the beach.

Meanwhile, he was kicking my ass. Literally.

"*Ow!*" I cried as a light spell zapped me in the rear.

"You're rusty," he said with a devilish grin. "One month off, and you're losing it?"

"I'll show you rusty," I muttered, but he was right. I had lost it. I couldn't get my brain to focus on the problem at hand, as it was too busy doing backflips because James was sparring with me, talking to me, close to me, looking at me.

"Gah!" I cried, transporting out of the way of his magic. I was barely getting any volleys in myself, too busy overthinking about him.

"Stop for a second," James called, holding up his hands.

He appeared in front of me and put his hands on my shoulders, sending chills down my spine and my already elevated pulse into overdrive.

"What. Is. With. You?"

"I…" Words failed me, as the warmth of his fingers seeped through my shirt. The sane half of me was failing to contain the smitten half, and if the latter won, I knew I'd do something stupid. Like kiss him again.

"I'm fine," I breathed. "Let's go."

I concentrated on the consequences of failing to keep my urges in check, and my magic responded in kind. The more focused I was, the easier it became to stay that way, until there was nothing but the need to win this match.

"That's more like it!" James called from the sand dune I'd thrown him into.

"*That's more like it!*"

I paused, a flash of an unfamiliar memory crawling past my brain almost like déjà vu. A man lay sprawled in a sand dune, his laughter filling my ears with joy and my heart with warmth.

Almost too late, I came back to myself, just in time to duck out of the way of a bright green burst of magic.

"Are you sleeping over there?" James taunted. "C'mon, Lexie, I want a challenge!"

"I want a challenge. You're being too easy on me."

"Pardon me for wearing kid gloves with my pregnant wife."

"Lexie?"

The man before me changed. He was familiar to me, and yet something was different. He was younger, happier. His eyes sparkled with amusement and something else. The magic in his hand was purple, as was mine. The feeling of Warrior magic invading my own had been as strange as the healing and potion-making before it. But every day, the magic grew stronger, and the nightly matches with my husband grew more intense. And I savored every moment of them.

His gaze softened slightly. "Mora, please don't overdo it."

"I'm not overdoing it," I insisted. "I'm in complete control."

"I have a potion ready if you need it."

"Did you make it, or did Nicole?" A foul taste in my mouth recalled the first healing potion my daughter had made me. Just four years old, she'd been so proud of what she'd accomplished, although the results left much to be desired. Gavon said the more she practiced, the better she'd be at it, although I worried about what her life would be like without magic. Still, it warmed my heart to see her father so invested in her. I'd taken great joy in watching my mother get proven wrong again and again.

"Are we going to spar or are we going to chat? I'm here for a

fight, McKinnon."

The challenge reawakened in his eyes, and he licked his lips, sending warmth right down to my core. "As you wish, my love."

"Lexie. *Lexie!*"

I was back in my own mind, staring at the stars. A rush of pain burst through me, and I groaned as I clutched the ache in my chest. But it wasn't completely magically-induced, either. This was longing, loss, and the unmistakable need to vomit and cry at the same time.

"What the hell happened?" James asked, hovering over me. "You froze, and I couldn't… Are you hurt?"

I couldn't even find the words to explain it. It had been a magical memory, that much was clear. But unlike the one that had haunted me for weeks after Jeanie died, this was more… warm and fuzzy. I was left with mixed emotions of joy and disgust—especially as I parsed out the voices.

"You look like you're gonna be sick."

"I might be," I muttered, allowing him to pull me to sit up.

"Should I get Gavon—"

"*No!*" I screamed, grabbing his shirt. "Not Gavon. Never Gavon."

Not when I'd heard him *flirting* with my mother. They were sparring, trading banter. Flirting. I felt such…such…*love* for him. My mother had been absolutely crazy about Gavon, and based on the undercurrent of her thoughts, sparring was some kind of…(gag) *foreplay.*

"I really hurt you, didn't I?" James sounded concerned, but I couldn't bring myself to wipe the horrified look off my face. He handed me a vial he'd summoned, but I didn't take it.

"No, I'm fine," I said slowly.

"You don't look fine. You completely froze then got the shit kicked out of you. What *happened?*"

How was I to explain to James what I'd just seen? I didn't want to explain it, I just wanted to forget it. But to placate him, I sucked in a breath and closed my eyes, whispering, "I…had another magical memory."

"Of Cyrus?"

I snorted. "I wish. No, this one was…of Gavon and…my mother. They were…" I gagged. "Flirting."

James quirked a brow. "Flirting?"

"Flirting. And then some." I rubbed my face in a vain attempt to remove the lingering feelings from the back of my mind. As if I wasn't already confused enough about Gavon, I didn't need to add my mother's attraction to him to the pile.

James did not sound like he pitied me at all. "You completely lost it because you had a magical memory of your parents flirting?"

"Yeah, I did," I snapped. "I don't know if you've ever had someone else's memories in your head before, but it's not fun. Especially because you get left with whatever feelings they had at the time. This? What I'm feeling right now? This is *disgusting*. I don't want to know how I was made."

"If she was using your magic, that means you were already… *made*," he replied with a snicker.

I cried out in anguish and buried my face in my hands. "Stop it. Seriously. Never again. I don't want to think about it."

James laughed and plopped down beside me, pressing the vial into my hands. I knew if I didn't take it, I'd regret it, so I popped the cork and downed it. It did a lot to ease the bruising, but not the horror.

"Do you get these kind of magical memories often?" he asked.

"N-no. Last one I ever had was when I was fighting Cyrus. I get dreams sometimes though." I looked down at the empty vial, horror turning to sadness. My mother had been so happy with Gavon that I'd forgotten how the story ended. It was no wonder she kept looking for him the day she'd died. She'd thought he'd loved her.

"Wonder why you thought of that particular memory?" James asked, popping my thought bubble.

Heat flooded my face. I'd probably had that memory because I was nursing some strange attraction to James, and sparring had increased it.

Oh God, was I just like my mother?

Did I get off on that kind of thing?

Ew.

Suddenly, James seemed a lot less adorable to me now. Perhaps it was my brain reminding me that if I sparred while twitterpated, I'd have another magical memory of my parents getting frisky. And also that my mother had fallen for a man from New Salem and ended up dead.

That threw cold water on me rather quickly.

"So do you think this will be a regular occurrence?" James asked.

"God, I hope not," I replied with a frown. "Sorry. I'll get myself together by next week."

"It's just as well. I have to get ready for my date," he said.

"What are you supposed to talk about with a dancer?"

I shrugged. "What did you talk about with the other girls?"

"I just let them talk and acted interested," he replied. "There's not really much I can say to them about myself without lying."

"So why are you dating them?" I asked, genuinely curious. "If you can't have an honest relationship with them, what's the point?"

He quirked a brow. "You really have to ask that?"

"So it's just about sex, then?" I said with a nod, grateful for this reminder of his true nature. Unlike Gavon, James had been nothing but honest about how much of an asshole he was. "Then why are you asking me what to talk to her about?"

He shrugged and said, "See you around," before disappearing in a cloud of green smoke.

"Are you okay?" Nicole watched me over the top of her coffee mug.

"Yeah," I said without looking at her.

I was the farthest thing from okay in reality, but yet again, I couldn't talk to Nicole about it. I'd left the sparring beach feeling like I had a handle on all my magical memories, but the dream I'd had the night before painted a very different story. More sparring, more flirting. More…ugh.

The worst part was I'd woken up with the smallest desire to hear their voices again. I had never been able to stomach the sound of my mother's dying pleas, but this memory, while disgusting, was intriguing. My mother had always been this intangible thing that was often talked about, but never seen.

I knew from the first magical memory that she had been an expert magical, but it became clear to me how I became such a quick learner at sparring. My magic already had the benefit of Gavon's tutelage before I'd been born.

It wasn't hard to see why my mom had fallen for him. He was a handsome guy, and there was something humble and genuine about the way he carried himself. At least, it felt that way to me. And if my magical memories were real, he'd acted like he cared for Mom. But was that just because she was pregnant with his future Guildmaster or because he actually did?

The questions had bothered me so much that it had prompted me to leave my bedroom and have breakfast with Nicole. She'd been surprised to see me—as I'd been all but avoiding her for the past week—but eventually we'd descended into silence as I tried to figure out how to broach the subject.

"Hey, can I talk to you about something?" I said, although I was already sure I knew how this conversation would end. "It's about…Mom."

Nicole glanced up from her phone. "Yeah?"

"And…Gavon."

Her gaze darted back down to her phone. "No, Lexie. I don't want to talk about it."

"Nicole, come on. I don't have anyone else to talk about them with. Gram's excommunicated us and—"

"What do you mean excommunicated?" Nicole replied. "And who is Gram?"

Crap. I'd forgotten about that. "Look, I think, as a seventeen-year-old girl, I have a right to know about my parents. Even if you don't like one of them—"

"Hate."

"Fine, hate. But maybe, just this once, you could…I don't know, suck it up and tell me how it was."

Nicole's brows rose and her mouth fell open. "Suck it up?"

"Bad choice of words," I said quickly. "But I mean—"

"Why do you want to know anything about what life was like? It was a *lie*. It was all one big ploy to make a Guildmaster. And as soon as he got what he wanted—"

"But he didn't," I said. "I grew up here."

"That's because…because…" Nicole's eyes searched the room, and I knew she was butting up against the charm Gram had placed on her. I half-wanted her to beat it, just to spite Gram and show her we were more powerful. "It doesn't matter. Gavon is a horrible person, and the less you know about him, the happier you'll be."

"But was Mom happy with him?" I asked, realizing I'd better ask what I wanted to before the situation devolved any further. "I mean, she loved him, right?"

Nicole was silent for a long time, chewing on the inside of her cheek in thought. "Mom was crazy about him. And to be honest, so was I. He was the best dad…he'd always make time for me. He taught me how to make potions. He told me that potion-makers could do anything a regular magic user could. And he just…he acted like he loved Mom."

And you, too, I wanted to add, but I thought that might make things worse. It was clear why this conversation brought Nicole so much pain, but I just needed to know the truth once and then I'd never bring it up again.

"But you know what? None of that matters because he's

never done a damned thing to help us since."

"He's the one who told Gram about the loophole," I offered mildly.

"Who is this Gram you keep talking about?" Nicole asked. "Look, I don't like talking about this stuff. It reminds me how thoroughly he played all of us, and just reopens a lot of hurt that I've done a good job healing."

"Yeah right," I muttered, but unfortunately, it was too loud.

"Don't take that tone with me," Nicole said.

I almost dared her to try to ground me, but I stopped myself. "I'm sorry. It was wrong of me to bring it up and to be disrespectful. I won't ask again."

"That's right, you won't." Nicole seemed pleased that she'd placated me.

But I was just relieved I'd never have to experience an awkward moment where Nicole tried to ground me—because I wasn't sure that she could.

Twenty

"Lexie!"

The memory of my parents cleared too late, and the force of his magic hit me hard.

"Another one?" James said with a frown. "This is becoming a problem."

I stared at the stars above my head, unwilling to look at James in the eye to tell him the truth. Two weeks and four sparring sessions later, I wanted to hear the voices. I needed to understand, to search my memories of Gavon's face for any sign that he'd been lying about the way he felt. On some level, I thought maybe if Gavon was capable of loving my mother—really loving her—then…

"Hello? Are you in there still?" James waved his hands in front of my face. "You realize my induction is soon. This half-assed training isn't helping me."

Of course I knew that. It was all he'd talked about, becoming almost an obsession over making himself perfect. If I hadn't been so caught up in my own memories, I would've been more enamored with how adorable insecurity was on him. Thank goodness for small miracles.

"I don't understand why you're so worried," I said, brushing the sand off my pants as I stood slowly. "You said Cyrus doesn't want to fight you."

"That's what he said, but who knows if he means it? That would be typical Cyrus. Let me think I'm fighting Gavon until the last minute." He frowned and ran a nervous hand through his hair. "It's just strange. He hasn't spoken to me once since our tea."

"Is that…odd?"

"Cyrus has always been rather obsessed with me," James said. "He had to be careful around Gavon, but he'd always find his way to a conversation. But now, it's almost like he wants nothing to do with me."

"That's a good thing, right?" I only wished I could say the same.

"If he's not interested in me, what else might be holding his attention?" James asked with a quirked brow.

Knowing Cyrus, that was actually a good question. My pulse began to flutter with nerves and the reminder that there was something about him I'd forgotten. "Have you told Gavon about it?"

"I did, but Gavon doesn't really listen to me anymore," he replied. "More interested in his own projects, I think."

"What kind of projects?"

"Who knows? Gavon isn't concerned about him, in any case."

But Gavon had shown a surprising lack of urgency for Cyrus-related things. "I don't like it. If Cyrus is up to something, we need to figure out what it is."

James chuckled. "That's a change. I thought you were terrified of him?"

His observation struck a chord in my brain. It had been a while since I'd had a Cyrus-related panic attack, or dreamed about him coming to hurt my sisters. Perhaps in sparring with James, I'd become a lot more confident in my abilities to keep my sisters safe.

"I mean, he's still dangerous. He's a cold-blooded killer. I'd rather be prepared than sit around and wait for him to strike."

"Do you think he'd go after your family again? It's been over two years. If he was going to make a move against you, he would have by now."

"Doesn't mean he won't ever. Maybe he's just biding his time."

"Maybe you're paranoid."

I glowered at James, and he laughed again.

"Look, I know Cyrus and he's an opportunist. He's not going to do anything unless he's sure he can get away with it. And the only way he'll get you in the dueling ring is if you agree to be inducted into the Guild."

"And *that's* never gonna happen."

"Exactly. So why are you worried?"

"Because…I don't know." I sighed. "Because even though I could probably take Cyrus, my sisters are defenseless. And it would be really easy to get me to do anything if they were in danger."

"The pact protects them, too."

"I guess...I don't know. I haven't seen Marie in months. What if she's been in Cyrus' basement all this time?"

"Well, I can assure you she's not down *there*," James said.

"How do you know? All she does is send back read receipts and never answers my texts and..."

"Didn't you say you had a health spell on her?"

I nodded. "But what if it's wrong? What if she's been hurt or dead all this time and—"

"Why is your first instinct to doubt your own magic?" James asked.

"Because I have no way of knowing if what I'm doing is right." I sighed. "James, I'm a girl who thrives on empirical evidence. If I can see and replicate the results, I'll believe it. And sure, this spell has shown me the same thing. But I haven't seen Marie in years, and—"

He closed his hand over mine again. "Sometimes, Lexie, you have to just believe in your own magic."

"How?"

"I think you are a terrible magical."

I opened my mouth to ask why he'd say something so mean, but the stone at my neck grew warm. I began blushing from embarrassment, and also from the feel of his hand covering mine.

"If you don't trust anyone else, you have to learn to trust yourself. Otherwise, what's the point?"

James was right, I didn't trust myself. Not since I'd been completely wrong about Gavon. I'd not been concerned about him, not when he'd shown up on Magic's Eve, not when I found out we were both Warriors. Not even when I'd woken up in New Salem. And even with Nicole and Jeanie telling me how bad he was, I still couldn't shake the underlying feeling that he wasn't. There were too many inconsistencies in his behavior, too many times the ulterior motives they said he had didn't make sense. While I was angry at him for abandoning me, I didn't believe he would ever physically hurt me.

And despite all his flaws, James no longer concerned me either, which terrified me. I refused to make the same mistake twice, and yet there I was. Trusting and spending time with a magical from New Salem.

Perhaps even growing attached to said magical.

"Fine, whatever. But I tried the locator spell you gave me and it didn't work."

He winced and looked away. "Yeah, I knew it wouldn't."

I stared at him. "Excuse me?"

"The spell I gave you was intended to be used by a charmer, maybe an enchanter. Your magic is too blunt." Before I could snap an insult back, he clarified, "I mean, your Warrior magic. Charms and those kinds of things require precision. Warriors don't have precision. Or at least, not without a lot of concentration and skill." My breath caught as he leaned over, but he simply hooked a finger on the chain around my neck. "You nearly destroyed this thing when you charmed it, remember?"

I swiped the chain away. "But that's because I'm untrained."

"No, it's because you're a Warrior," he said.

I nodded, my words stuck in my throat until he released my necklace. "So what should I do about Marie?"

"We could try a different locator spell, but I doubt we'd be successful. I think there might be a potion that would work better. I'll see if I can locate it in Gavon's library."

"Why are you so interested in finding her?" I asked. It did strike me as odd that he would go through all this trouble.

His gaze captured mine. "Because you are."

My mouth went bone dry and I knew my shock was written all over my face. But while I had extensive experience in sparring with James, this new, thoughtful person was unfamiliar territory. And based on the amused turn of his mouth, he was enjoying catching me off guard.

"Well, that's just…" I began once I figured out how to move my mouth.

"And maybe, if you talk with your sister, she can help you figure out why you keep having these magical memories so we can get back to business."

There it was. Arrogant James I could deal with. "I'll look in my books as well. Maybe I missed something when I searched them before."

"Let's do this on Friday. After all, if you aren't going to get your head out of your ass and spar, what good are you?"

In response, I flung an attack spell at him.

I looked and looked but couldn't find anything useful to locate Marie. Not that it surprised me. It was the first thing I checked for in every new book. But James had assured me he'd found the right potion and that I would see my sister again on Friday. And the look he'd given me had sent warmth right into the pit of my stomach.

The more of himself he showed me, the less sure I was I had him pegged. I could think of a thousand reasons why he'd want to find Marie, from the selfish (he wanted her to heal him after sparring) to the evil (he wanted to hurt her), but none of them felt true. What had seemed real was when he looked me in the eyes and told me that he was interested in finding her because I was.

Friday came too soon, and before I knew it, I was peering into a cauldron with James, torn between optimism that this potion would work and fear that it would.

I did like watching James brew potions. His eyes darkened in concentration, barely noticing my presence as he measured out herbs and liquids like a professional. A few times, I thought to ask him what he was mixing, but I didn't want to disturb him.

"There," he said, a little breathlessly. The concoction was a pale yellow, almost like melted butter, but smelled of the daisies and sunflowers he'd added. "I was a little worried I'd added too much goldenrod."

"You? Worried?" I snorted.

"Yeah, potions are damned difficult," he replied. "I can pour it out if you're going to be rude."

"No, no," I said, with my hands in the air. "It's just…you're good at everything. I'm surprised to hear you admit otherwise."

"I am not good at everything, and I never said I was." James plopped down on the table and flipped pages in the book.

"Well, you're better than me. Some days I feel like I know my magic, and others it's like I'm discovering new things every day."

James actually smiled. "I think it comes more from practice.

To be honest, I actually tried to use that same locator spell on you once before. I found out the hard way it didn't work that well."

I flushed. "When?"

"The first time I found you in New Orleans. I spent three hours wandering around the city. But when I saw that bookstore, I was pretty sure you'd be in there. You're a creature of habit."

"I am *not*."

"You were usually in one of four places: your apartment, school, the kennel, though thankfully you've decided to end that relentless torture, or the library. Weekends if you aren't in one of those places, you're at that old bookstore in New Orleans or," he smiled, "with me."

I didn't share his smile. "It's creepy you know me so well."

"Lexie, *anyone* who spent more than one week with you would know your patterns. It's only thanks to me that you've actually had any fun this year."

I frowned, but had nothing to say in response because another idea popped into my head. "So is that how Gavon knew where we were when we'd been arrested? He used a locator spell on me?"

"No, in that case, he was probably alerted by the officer through your magic. Because he's your father, there's an inherent connection people can tap into, especially as you're still young." He didn't look up as he talked, and I got the distinct impression that James wasn't pleased I was bringing up the arrest thing.

"So he could find Marie if he wanted to?" I asked quietly.

"Do you want to ask him?" James asked. "Or would you rather summon me a lock of your sister's hair so we can complete the potion?"

I didn't want to see Gavon, so I summoned her hairbrush. After all this time, I was nervous about the idea of talking with my sister. Would she even want to speak to me? Would it be another fight that would irreparably damage our relationship?

"I'll take that." James plucked the brush out of my hands and pulled out a single strand of hair, dropping it into the potion. I held my breath as the concoction bubbled and gurgled. Smoke rose from the sides, but instead of dissipating into the air around us, it gathered and formed a sphere.

"Is it supposed to do that?" I asked him, and he nodded.

"It will show us exactly where she is," James said, not taking his eyes away from the smoke. "Kind of like Google Maps. I just learned about that recently. But all you have to do is look into the sphere and use your magic to locate her. Focus on her, and let your magic and the potion do the rest."

I took his hand suddenly. "James, what if she doesn't want to see me?"

"She will." He squeezed my hand. "You have to trust yourself, otherwise the potion won't work."

I closed my eyes and forced away all of my nervous thoughts, centering on my sister. The potion tugged at my magic, inviting it closer, as it melded together inside the cauldron.

A flash of something crossed by my mind's eye, and I scrambled to hold onto it. "I see something!"

"What is it?"

"I… Lights…a lot of lights. Activity. It's blurry but…" A

familiar sign rose in the distance, as cars drove down a central street. It was hot, too, even in the middle of winter. A desert. "She's in Las Vegas."

"Let the potion pinpoint her."

"How?"

A warm hand covered mine. "Just let your magic do the work."

At his instruction, I released my subconscious control, and it was like putting on a pair of glasses. In front of me was the city of Las Vegas, with all the glittering lights and activity even as the sun was setting in the distance. I was momentarily distracted by the glitz, before a tug on my hand reminded me of my purpose. If my magic had gone to this spot (I guessed it was there in some disembodied form), then Marie had to be close.

I felt, rather than saw her first. The tug of familiar magic, the yin to my yang. My sister's magic was so close I could taste it. The doors of a fine apartment building opened, and she walked out. Her face was a mask of confusion until she looked right at me.

And she smiled.

"Well? Don't just dawdle there like an idiot," she said. "Come on."

I opened my eyes and gasped. "I found her. James, I found her."

"Go get her!" he said, releasing my hand. "I'll clean up here."

"James, I..." There were a thousand things I wanted to tell him in that moment, but all I could come up with was, "You're an asshole for not helping me with this sooner."

Then I transported away.

Twenty-One

I appeared in the street where my magic had led me, and almost immediately, Marie's magic surrounded me and transported both of us. I landed with unsteady feet on a white plush carpet and a swankily-decorated apartment.

"For crying out loud, don't you know you aren't supposed to transport yourself into the middle of the street?" came the reply from my totally alive, totally not-being-tortured older sister.

Tears gathered in my eyes as I drank in the sight of her. She was skinner than I remembered, a bit more mature and weathered, but still retaining that callous haughtiness. Although she'd been sarcastic, her smile betrayed her true feelings.

I crossed the room in three steps and collapsed into her arms. She embraced me tightly and I cried into her shoulder.

"You've been practicing," Marie said, pressing her cheek to my forehead. "That's some powerful magic you've got there."

"Where have you been?" I asked. "Why haven't you come home?"

"Here and there. Settled on Vegas a few weeks ago." The stone at my neck warmed, but I wasn't surprised. Marie had always dealt in half-truths, so I wasn't surprised she was keeping stuff from me now. I also didn't care.

"This is a nice place," I said. "Do you still have the convertible?"

She chuckled. "Oh yeah. I take it for long desert rides every so often."

Before magic, Marie's car had been a mystery to me. Namely, how she could afford it—or why Jeanie had seen fit to buy it for her. But I'd found out later that she'd fixed it up with magic. I could only assume the apartment was procured the same way. After all, there was no way she could've afforded this on her own, and I doubted anyone would find her *that* enthralling to pay for it.

The view itself had to be worth a million dollars. I went to the window and pressed my fingers against the glass. Her apartment was at least twenty stories up, and the entire strip folded out in a sparkling, beautiful oasis.

"You're gonna get slobber marks all over my window," she said, coming to stand beside me.

"Sorry. Pictures don't do it justice." Even though I stepped back, I kept my attention on the outside. After a few moments, I noticed her staring at me. "What?"

"I can't believe how old you are," she said with a frown. "It's like you suddenly got hot when I was away."

Classic Marie. "Thanks."

"I don't mean that as an insult. It's like…you were a kid and now you're not." She handed me a glass of brown liquid that smelled foul. "Please tell me this isn't your first drink."

"No," I said, taking a hesitant sip. It tasted like motor oil. "But I don't like this."

She waved her hand, and the glass grew in size and the liquid changed color. "You'll be a whiskey girl eventually."

"Doubtful." I sipped the concoction and found it much sweeter and palatable than before. But even after one sip, my brain hummed and I decided against drinking any more. "So…"

"So."

We stood in silence for a moment. Then I erupted.

"Gavon's apprentice enrolled in my high school, and we've been sparring for a few months and I think I might have a crush on him and now I'm having magical memories of when Gavon and Mom used to spar, and I'm wondering if Gavon really loved her or if it was a ruse."

I watched Marie's reflection in the mirror. Her face had gone slack as she processed what I'd just told her. She chuckled and took a long sip of her drink. "And I take it Nicole doesn't know any of this."

"It's not that I *want* to lie to her—"

"It's that she's too wrapped up in her own shit to see outside the bubble," Marie finished for me. "You can't even make a G sound without her having a coronary."

I smiled. "It's really nice to talk to someone who understands."

"So you've been going to school with Gavon's apprentice and now you have a crush on him." She closed her eyes. "I can't picture him."

"He's cute. Really cute. Really obnoxiously, stupidly cute.

And funny, but kind of an asshole. But kind when he wants to be."

"Uh-huh. And how did we get here from you waking up in the middle of the night with nightmares about Cyrus?"

My face warmed. "A long, arduous tale."

"I have all the time in the world."

So I told her everything, from how James had shown up on the first day of school, to our pact, to when Gavon had bailed us out of jail (she found that highly entertaining) to the impromptu kiss and my strange magical memories of our parents.

"You remember him, don't you?" I asked. "Is that why you've always been so pro-Gavon?"

"I don't remember a lot, obviously," Marie said. "But you know, when you're a healer, you sort of...know things about people. Like I always knew that Jeanie resented us a little and it made me resent her."

"I don't blame her," I replied. "She was really young, and there wasn't anyone else to take us."

"Dad could've taken us," Marie replied. She took a long drink then sighed. "I thought, anyway."

I stared at her. I'd never heard Gavon referred to as anything other than his name.

"He made it pretty clear to me taking us wasn't an option for several reasons. I didn't really understand a few years ago when I went to his place and argued with him about it."

"I'm sorry, you did *what*?"

She laughed, and played with her straw. "After Nicole and I had that last big fight, I crossed the tear and found him. He was so pissed..." She chuckled again. "And then we got into it.

Really bad. So I disappeared for a few years." Her eyes grew a little sad. "I kind of kept waiting for him to show up, but he never did. Until one day, out of the blue, there he was. We had a good talk about a lot of things, including the reasons Jeanie had to be the one to take us, and I forgave him."

"I wish I could forgive that easily," I said.

"Like I said, it's weird when you're a healer. You sort of have this overbearing knowledge of people's intentions. And I know that his are genuine."

"Did he tell you about the edict?" I asked.

She nodded. "Pretty genius, if you ask me. They can't screw with us, and, in case you got any wild hairs, we can't screw with them. Dad said it was his finest bit of political manipulation to get it approved."

There it was again. "Why do you call him that?"

"Because he's Dad. He's been Dad since I was a little girl, and I don't plan on changing that any time soon. Used to drive Jeanie *crazy* when I said it."

I frowned. "Marie… Jeanie's gone."

"I know," she replied softly. "I just…it makes it a little easier if I pretend like she's still around, you know?" Marie shook her head. "I do miss her."

"Me too." I went back to my glass, which was mostly liquid now. "I wish I could talk to someone about what life was like back then. I get some idea from these magical memories, but it's all what Mom felt. How do I know how much of that was real on his part?"

"I don't know, you tell me." Marie's eyes danced, as if she knew something I didn't. Or something I was unwilling to accept.

"If I knew, I wouldn't be asking you," I said, a little hotly.

"Does this have anything to do with that apprentice you're crushing on?"

I blew air out between my lips. "Yes. Part of it. I don't know. It's still weird that I like him, because I know I shouldn't. I mean, he tried to kill me. But he apologized—poorly, I might add—and he's been…well, somehow he's become my friend. And ever since we kissed, it's like I can't even think straight."

Marie nodded thoughtfully. "Any change on his part?"

"No. Yes? Maybe." I wished I was a little more together in my memories of him. "He found out Gavon and I aren't on speaking terms and that was a big deal for him. He's the one who helped me figure out how to find you." *Because you are.* I shivered at the memory.

"If he didn't want to kiss you, he wouldn't have kissed you. And I'd say helping you find your sister is a pretty big green flag that you're more than a friend."

"But he's so selfish," I said. "And rude, and—"

"Selfish people don't do nice things for other people," Marie said, looking at her glass. "At least, not unless there's something in it for them."

Sure, he'd said he wanted us to have a conversation because I was dealing with the magical memories, but was that the truth?

Because you are.

"Despite his flaws, I feel like he's the first person who's ever really understood me." I chewed my lip. "Well, not the first."

"You're lucky. I'm the only healer I know of."

I took a step back. It had never occurred to me that Marie

would feel the same pressing loneliness I did.

"But I doubt it's just about that," Marie said, lifting her fingers off the glass. "It sounds like you and he have more to talk about than just flinging spells at each other."

I nodded. "It started out with just that. But I guess we're on the same wavelength. We think the same things, we have the same sense of humor. Being with him brings out this competitive urge that drives me to be better, to be stronger. I don't—"

"You're in love with him," Marie said simply, and my heart skipped a beat. "It happens."

"I shouldn't be. He's… I mean, I couldn't make a *worse* decision, Marie." My breath hitched. "I mean, Mom—"

"Lexie, a word of advice," Marie interrupted. "Your apprentice is not Gavon, and you are not Mom. Don't let the fear of what happened to them prevent you from experiencing something beautiful. Especially if you've got such a deep connection."

I sighed, the discussion prompting a deeper look at my own feelings. "It's not just about Gavon. I mean, that's part of it. But I think the biggest fear I have is…what if he doesn't feel the same? It could completely ruin our friendship."

"That's a risk we take with honesty. You have to ask yourself: is it worth it not to say anything? Sure, he might not feel the same, and you'll be humiliated." I frowned, but she smiled. "But he also could be in love with you, too. And neither of you would ever know if one of you didn't take a chance."

I tapped my fingers to the glass, drawing outlines of the lights below. Marie's words settled uncomfortably in my mind, perhaps because I knew how true they were. There really was nothing keeping me from taking the next step except fear of rejection.

"Look, don't just plant a kiss on him the first chance you get," Marie said after my uncomfortable silence. "Take small steps. Hold his hand. Kiss his cheek. If he freaks out, you'll know. If he lets you, there's your answer."

"Wow," I said, stepping back. "That…actually makes a lot of sense."

"You sound surprised," Marie said with a daring raise of her brow.

"More like…happy to see you." I tore my gaze away from the reflections to look at her again. "I really missed you."

Her magic surrounded me and pushed me closer to her, and she wrapped an arm around me once I was within reach. "I missed you too, loser."

I spent most of the weekend in Las Vegas with Marie. We window shopped and ate good food, and she introduced me to three different kinds of wine. But beyond that, it was a relief that our relationship could be repaired. Whatever grudge she'd held against me had faded, and it was nice to actually have a conversation with my sister without feeling like we were on the brink of war.

But the war, I felt, would be right there when I got home. I'd texted Nicole that first night to let her know where I was, and the terse reply was telling.

K

Marie wouldn't enlighten me on what exactly their fight was

about, only that it had been long and a lot of hurt had been caused on both sides. I asked her if she'd ever consider making amends with Nicole, but she was noncommittal.

Sunday evening, I transported myself back to my room and braced myself for the fallout. I put a bright smile on my face and cracked open the door, listening for the sounds of my sister. The TV was on in the living room, so I threw my shoulders back and walked out of my room.

"Hey," Nicole said, without looking up. As expected, she did not look pleased. But now that half my family was at least talking to *me*, I wanted to try to mend fences.

"Hey…so… Marie—"

"I don't want to talk to her or about her."

I recoiled as if she'd slapped me. "I mean, she's our sister—"

"Yes, and I love her, but that doesn't mean I have to like her."

"Okay, but not even to—"

"This isn't up for debate, Alexis. I don't want to talk about her, and if you have a problem with it, you can just move in with her."

I swallowed, the acid in her voice bringing me to tears. "Nicole, I didn't mean to…"

"No, you never mean to, but you do anyway." She pushed herself off the couch and stormed into her room, slamming the door behind her.

Twenty-Two

Nicole apologized the next morning for her outburst, but it wasn't one I would soon forget. Although Marie and I were now texting regularly, I didn't mention it to Nicole, and I didn't mention Nicole to Marie. I felt like the strangest middleman alive.

More pressing was having to go to school and face James in the wake of this new…something. I obviously couldn't avoid him forever, especially as he all but cornered me in front of my locker.

"Well?" he asked.

"Well?"

"I can only assume things went well with your sister."

I nodded. "Yeah…"

"So why aren't you happy?"

Closing my locker, I chewed on the side of my lip. "Mending fences with one broke them with another."

"Ah. Nicole, right? The potion-maker."

"Yeah." I squinted at him. "When did you get so interested in my sisters?"

"I've always known about them," he replied pointedly. "Just…making conversation. Sorry if I offended you with caring about your life."

"You didn't, I just…" Damn, but he was confusing me. I needed to change the subject—fast. "Did you spend the weekend sparring?"

"And then some." He cocked his head to the side, stretching out his muscles. "I'm still sore. I can't figure out who's more worried about it—me or Gavon."

"You? Why are you worried about it? You'll spar with Gavon, and that's that."

"I'm not worried about the match, I'm worried about what happens after it." He stared at an unseeing point in front of him. "Gavon reminded me last night that I'll be a fully independent member of the Guild. He won't be able to restrict my magic or order me around as his apprentice, though he'll still retain some control as Guildmaster." He finally lifted his gaze to me. "And in that capacity, he might restrict me from coming back here."

"Oh."

James might never come back? I wasn't sure what surprised me more: that I was upset about it, or that he was.

"Why would he do that? You're supposed to be learning, right?"

"Sometimes I think it was just a way to keep me out of trouble until the induction match. I feel like he no longer wants anything to do with me, so if I was over here, he wouldn't have to waste his time."

"What makes you say that?

"He's always criticizing me," James said. "I mean, you saw how he treats me. Everything is always my fault. I'm never good enough for him. Even when I do the right thing, there's always room for improvement."

I chewed my lip, unsure what to say. So I decided to go with humor. "And here I thought you were learning all the secrets of this world to take over."

His far-off look disappeared and he cracked a grin. "And what, pray tell, shall I do with my knowledge of social media and how to take an advanced placement test? Because, I assure you, that's *all* I've picked up in my year over here."

"That's not…entirely true," I said. "You also know the particulars of football."

He laughed, and I was glad to see some of the tension leaving his face. "I just don't see how it's in the Guild's best interest to keep me enrolled in high school. And Gavon is pretty particular about who he lets over here. He doesn't want to bring the wrath of the Carrigan Clan down on us needlessly. And seeing as Gavon doesn't quite believe I'm a good influence on you—or so he says…"

"It's been weeks since we got in trouble," I said with a huff. "He let us spar again. Besides that, I don't think Gavon would stop you from finishing the year. He values knowledge over strength, after all."

He glanced at me. "You think?"

"Yeah," I said firmly. Then, nervously, I asked, "You still aren't going to…challenge him for the Guildmaster, right?"

James snorted. "No. I'm not ready for that yet."

"Good," I said with a relieved sigh. "I'm actually starting to like you. I'd hate to have a reason to loathe you again."

He flashed me his charming smile again and my face turned into a tomato. "I'll try my best to stay on your good side."

James' induction match would be on his eighteenth birthday, the fourth of March, and while that was his main preoccupation, mine was checking the mailbox every day for my admissions decision. Both of us were nervous balls of anxiety, although we did our best not to show it.

At school, James spent more time talking with the friends he'd made, a little less time studying, although most of the teachers were well aware of the senioritis permeating the entire class. After school, we'd stopped by my house to check the mail, and when I hadn't received my letter, we'd go to the sparring beach. Most of the time, we read or did homework. Sometimes, we'd spar a little, or James would help me practice charms. I still didn't get them, but it made me feel better when he wasn't much better at it than I was.

My favorite afternoons, we'd just sit quietly and watch the sun set, content to be with each other in silence.

I began to wonder what life would be like with James *not* in it. He'd gone from my arch nemesis to the closest thing I could call a best friend in a matter of months. Sure, I had Marie back, but it wasn't the same. James *got* me, the same way Gavon had. And knowing I was facing the loss of such a friend hit me hard.

Especially because I hadn't moved forward on my feelings for him. Whenever I got the urge to take his hand or say something, I chickened out. By James' birthday—the last day I might ever see him—I was still waffling as to whether I should say something to him.

That day, he showed up at school with a grim expression, and I could only offer a sympathetic smile. He made no mention of the day to any of his school friends, and when I wished him a happy birthday, he just nodded.

After school, we met by my locker and said nothing to each other while our classmates gathered their things and left. Some of them stopped to talk to us, asking if someone had died, to which I just shook my head.

When the halls were empty, James finally spoke. "Let's go see if you've gotten your acceptance letter yet."

"Really?" I shook my head. "I mean, it's not—"

He grabbed my hand. "Don't say that. I have five hours to kill. Might as well."

He didn't let go of my hand all the way to our secret transport spot behind the band room, nor did he let it go when we crossed the parking lot of my apartment building. But when I crossed through the barrier, he finally had to let go.

There was no mail waiting for me, and when I returned with the news, James actually looked dejected. "I wanted to see your face when you got in."

"I don't know—"

"You'll get in."

We stood on opposite sides of the barrier, and I took in just how far we'd come. This protection wasn't even necessary anymore—it hadn't been for months—but seeing James on the other side of it was jarring. He was about to become a fully-fledged member of the Guild that had tried to enslave the nonmagicals. He was on his way to becoming the next Guildmaster. There were no guarantees that he wasn't another Cyrus.

Except I knew him. I'd spent nearly every day with him, had countless conversations. I'd begun to see glimpses of the real James, the one who cracked under the pressure of being the future leader of his guild, the one who relished in the glow of popularity, but was still lonely from all the lying. And this person—who'd stuck by my side over the past few weeks, who cared about my sisters and my college applications, was the one I'd stupidly fallen for.

"Will you come sit with me?" James asked, not meeting my gaze. "At the tear? Until it's time?"

I reached through the barrier and took his hand. "Sure."

Unsurprisingly, it was still cold in March in Massachusetts, but I cast a warming charm on my shirt and settled in next to James. The tear was as violent as ever, but the old fear of the man who lay on the other side of it was tempered. I'd overcome that particular fear, thanks to James.

He wore a pensive look, the lines tense around his mouth as his gaze swept from the tear to the darkening beach. The dull, gray waves proved a better scene than the pristine green waters of the gulf, punctuated by a crackle or hiss from the writhing magical tear in front of us.

"I think I'm going to miss this," he said, breaking an almost twenty-minute silence.

"What?"

"The sun setting. I'd never seen it before until I came here.

It's really beautiful."

Breathing shallowly, I reached over and took his hand. "You're going to be able to come back."

He glanced at our joined hands and smiled. "It's that, and it's also…I just keep imagining that Cyrus will come up with some backwards plan to force me to fight Gavon," he said, chewing the nail on his other hand. "That's what he does, you know? He finds your weakness, exploits it, and then makes you do his bidding. And—"

I gently reached up to pull his hand down. "He can't make you do anything you don't want to. You can choose not to challenge Gavon after the induction. And he, and the rest of the Guild, will have to accept your decision. What are they gonna do? There aren't any other Warriors to take your place." I swallowed. "Right?"

"Not that I'm aware of," James said. "But—"

"Stop worrying," I said with a shrug. "That's my job."

"Your paranoia has rubbed off on me."

We descended into silence again, and as the seconds ticked by and he didn't drop my hand, my pulse sped up. Was he holding on because because he needed comfort or because he wanted comfort from me specifically?

These thoughts were idiotic, especially in light of what James was worried about.

"I'm gonna miss you," he said quietly.

"Stop it." I rolled my eyes to keep the shock off my face. "It's not like the tear's gonna close for—"

He yanked our clasped hands and suddenly I was in his arms. I froze, because if I moved, I might wake up. James rested his cheek on my forehead and released a loud breath.

"I'm taking it as a good sign that you haven't blown me into the water."

I chuckled and relaxed just a little. "I might, still."

"You won't."

I lifted my head to look at him. "You know me so well?"

He didn't respond, but his eyes danced as they looked into mine. I waited for the nervous voice, the one that would tell me this was a terrible idea and I should back away while I still had the chance. But even it was silent in the face of James' sincere eyes and the sound of the tear crackling before us.

"Lexie, I…"

"What's the big deal?" I whispered, but only because I had no air. "You kissed me in New York, remember?"

"Oh yeah."

His lips brushed mine. Unlike in New York, which had been shocking and over quickly, this kiss lingered. I savored the experience, from the way his lips felt against mine, to the way his scent filled my brain, to the way my magic moved against his. And it was unique—our own special connection. I relaxed into his arms, and my magic moved against his, earning me a breathy chuckle.

"I've never made out with another Warrior before," he said against my lips. "What are you doing?"

"I have no idea."

He recaptured my lips, and this time, his tongue slid between my lips. I was sure I was doing it all wrong, but he didn't seem to care. His magic pushed against mine, and mine pushed back, until not-uncomfortable feelings started stirring in my stomach.

I broke the kiss first, these new feelings taking me down a path I wasn't sure I wanted to go yet. I licked my lips and regretted it, as they tasted like him still.

"I'm glad I got to do that before…"

I finally looked at him. His lips were red, as were his cheeks, but there was a bittersweet look about him.

"You're gonna be allowed back," I replied with just a hint of exasperation.

"But just in case I'm not…I'm glad." His eyes pierced mine as he spoke, his voice rough and full of emotion. "I, James Riley, request induction into the New Salem Warrior's Guild."

Just like that, he released me and stood, facing the tear. He didn't look back as he walked through it, leaving me with the ghost of his lips on mine.

James didn't show up at school the next day, sending my already frayed nerves into overdrive. I'd spent most of the night dreaming about all the horrible things that could've gone wrong (as well as spending more than a little time thinking about all the new feelings he'd stirred up). So as first period turned to second and he didn't show, then lunch and he didn't show, and then the day was over and he'd missed the entire day…

There was probably a logical explanation for it, but the anxious voice in my mind had taken all his fears and wound them up into a knot of panic in my stomach. I fidgeted and chewed my thumb. I barely paid attention in class. I even half-considered going to the tear and finding him myself, before the rational half of my brain reminded me what a stupid idea that was.

By the end of the day, I was exhausted from worrying and on the verge of tears. I wanted a nap, I wanted to—

I stopped, dropping my backpack. James sat under the oak tree in front of my house, napping in the early afternoon shade. As I approached, he cracked open an eye then let out a large yawn.

"Took you long enough," he said, checking the time on his phone. "You're late."

"Didn't realize we had an appointment," I replied, unable to keep the smile off my face. "So…?"

"I'm in the Guild," he said, pushing himself to stand slowly. "And Gavon says he wants me to continue learning over here." He shrugged. "Who am I to argue with my Guildmaster?"

I laughed, both in happiness that I'd have James for a few more months and that he'd resisted the urge to claim the title from Gavon. But I didn't run to him like I wanted to. Marie's voice sang in the back of my mind, egging me on to kiss him, but I remained where I was. I wasn't completely sure where we stood on that.

"I'm glad you're back. Things have been boring without you."

"Yeah. And you know, Gavon even mentioned he might want me to attend college." His happy smile turned into a smirk as he drew closer. "Tells me he can magically enroll me in a certain school—"

I shot him an icy glare. "Don't you dare."

"What, you don't want me to show you up in every class at Georgetown?"

"Like you could handle Georgetown. Please."

Despite my smile, I was panicking. Not because James was back or going to cheat his way into Georgetown. But because if Gavon allowed him to be in my life permanently…

"So…about what happened before I left…" he said, as if reading my mind. "I'm sorry if—"

"No, no…I understand." I chewed my lip, desperate to get off this conversation before my heart broke any more.

"I hope I didn't freak you out."

"N-No way…"

"So you wanna do it again?"

Something loud cracked in my mind, and I lost the ability to speak. Finally, I forced out, "You mean, like…as friends?"

His face flushed. "No, as…not friends?"

"O…oh."

"It's okay if you don't want to, but…"

"N-no!" *What is happening?* "I mean, I just…I don't…"

"You're inexperienced, I know."

My awkwardness evaporated and I glared at him. "You ass."

Instead of responding, he transported himself right in front of me. Before I could yell at him for using magic without checking, he took my cheeks in his hands and kissed me.

Full-lipped, open-mouthed, hands-on-face kissed me. Shock froze me at first, but it melted away. Somewhere between his tongue and his magic and his hands, I accepted this strange new reality. It was obvious how James convinced so many girls to date him (*Gah, don't think about that right now*), he was an expert kisser. Whereas I was—

"You kiss like you wield magic," he said with a shake of his head. "You think too much."

"Thanks for the—"

He kissed me again, this time soft, sweet, quick. "I've got to get back home."

"Do you?"

"You aren't gonna let me through that barrier, are you?"

My eyes grew wide and I used magic to smack him in the shoulder. "Pig."

He chuckled, but then sobered a little. "Look, let's just…not think too hard about this right now. I like what's happening." He turned his head in confusion. "Do you?"

Knowing I was going to sound like an idiot, I replied, "I guess I'm still a little confused what's happening."

"I like you."

"Oh."

"It's okay, I know you like me, too," he replied, with a self-satisfied smirk.

"And how do you know that?" I asked, still scrambling to find my footing in this conversation.

"I can read you like a book. See you at school tomorrow." He bent his head once more to kiss me before disappearing in a puff of green smoke, leaving me standing beneath the oak tree confused, exhilarated, and a little bit excited.

Twenty-Three

I awoke the next morning, plagued by questions about how James might act or what he meant by "I like you" or if I'd just imagined the whole thing. But when I met James by my locker, he erased all of my questions with a simple kiss.

"So, I didn't get a chance to tell you about my match the other day," he said, turning to his locker to switch out his books.

I was still stunned by the impromptu kiss, so I let him describe in vivid detail every moment of his match. And as he went on and on, I was fairly sure embellishing the number of times he got the better of Gavon (and leaving out a few instances of the opposite), I supposed that's how it would be. Our regular joking with the added bonus of making out every so often.

Of course, there was one big question that had to be asked.

"So…you aren't going to tell Gavon, right?"

"Are you kidding me?" James snorted. "The only way this works is if I forget you're in any way related to him."

Ugh, why do I like him again? I pursed my lips. "The only

241

way it works for me is if I forget you belong to an evil gang."

Something like admiration crossed his face, and my pulse skipped a beat. "Anyway, he's not the one I'm really worried about. Cyrus didn't look too happy when I declined his request to challenge Gavon."

I closed my locker. "Let him come."

"Seriously?"

"Yeah, you said I could kick his ass, right?"

"I mean, sure, but you shouldn't go looking for a fight. He'd still do some serious damage. And, of course, there's that pact. You can't go causing trouble, either."

"I know, I know."

"What's all this newfound confidence from?" he asked. "I thought Cyrus made you piss your pants."

"Crude," I said. But it was true. Over the past few weeks, I'd began feeling more in control over my life. Marie was speaking with me again, Nicole and I were on rocky, but decent terms. James and I were…well, the kiss had said a lot. And magically, I'd finally gained a baseline understanding that I'd been missing.

"I guess spending time with me rubbed off on you," he said.

"Everything isn't always about you," I replied, elbowing him. So he kissed me.

I still wasn't used to that.

Nor was I used to the death glare I received from Callista, who muttered something about me being a liar.

During first period, I let my mind wander back to James, and this time, I didn't fight it. So this was what it was like to be on the other side of things. To be the girl that James doted on.

But there would be more than just hand-holding and stolen

kisses. I was most looking forward to our next bout in the sparring ring, and what that might result in.

Slow down, Lexie, you've barely started dating the guy.

Besides not wanting to rush with someone so unpredictable, there was the other, larger problem. Despite what I'd said about Cyrus, I was a little worried about what he might do if he found out James and I had moved beyond friends.

James, on the other hand, seemed confident enough that neither Gavon nor Cyrus made a habit of spending a lot of time spying on us, because he kissed me three times before lunch.

Then again, he might've just been drunk on newfound freedom. Occasionally, I spotted him using magic while taking notes, and when I admonished him about it at the end of the day, he just threw an arm around me and pointed to the glazed looks of our classmates who were just trying to get through the last few weeks of high school.

"They aren't even on this planet," he said. "Speaking of… you and I are due for another adventure."

"Oh, are we?"

"I promise I won't get you arrested this time," he said with that dazzling smile of his.

"So Gavon has no control over you anymore?" I asked while pondering what kind of adventures we could get into. A moonlight stroll in Paris came to mind. "That's it, huh?"

"That's it. It's in case I decided I wanted to overthrow him. It would be hard for me to beat him if he could ground me."

"True…" I chewed my lip. "But then why does Gavon have control over me? I'm not in the Clan or a Guild."

"Parents always retain some control, especially if they're

powerful like Gavon is. That's why it's always been tradition for Warriors to go with a different master. That way, once the apprenticeship ends, so does the control."

"Hm." I wasn't sure I liked that. "So are you still living at his mansion or what?"

"At the moment, yes," he said. "It won't surprise you that there aren't a lot of available properties in New Salem. Gavon could evict a lesser magical, but he won't do that."

"He could evict Cyrus," I suggested. "I'd bring the papers for him.

"Look at you," James said. "All confident. I like it."

I flushed at his compliment. I supposed that wouldn't change overnight. "So do you think you'll just live with Gavon for a while?"

"That sounds awful," he said with a blanch. "Besides, if I'm going to college with you…"

"Don't say that," I snapped. "I worked really hard to get into Georgetown, and that you could just *magic* your way into it—"

"Lexie," he said, stopping me. "I'm just kidding."

"Still though," I said, furrowing my brow. "I don't know what I'll do if I don't get in."

"You will," he said with almost infuriating certainty. His faith did nothing to dissolve the worry in the pit of my stomach. "C'mon, let's go to your place and check."

I nodded, grabbing my backpack and following him to a secluded spot behind the gym where we transported to another secluded spot near my apartment complex.

"You could, you know, let me inside the barrier," James said as we crossed the parking lot.

"I could," I said, without elaborating.

"You still don't trust me, do you? After all we've been through together."

"I..." I trusted him a lot, actually. I'd even stopped wearing my charmed stone after he'd helped me find Marie. But the barrier felt like the last defense, the one thing that reminded me of who he was and why I'd been hesitant to trust him at first. If I allowed him into my house, that meant I no longer held the small nugget of fear about him. And I wasn't sure I was there yet.

Instead of answering him, I scurried into the building, making a beeline for the mailboxes. I opened the small door and my heart skipped a beat.

There was a large white envelope in there.

I swallowed and pulled it out, feeling faint at the Georgetown logo emblazoned on the top. I absentmindedly stuck the rest of the mail back in the box and stumbled back out to where James was waiting for me.

"What's wrong with you?" James asked.

"It's my college admissions decision," I said quietly.

"Oh, did you get in?"

"I don't know yet." I looked down at the potentially life-changing envelope in my hand. "Maybe?"

"You should open it."

All of my doubts came roaring back. Had I completed my application correctly? Were there typos? Had I not volunteered enough, had I—

James ripped the envelope out of my hand and before I could stop him, tore it open and began reading. The smile on his face told me everything I needed to know.

"*No way!*" I screamed, backing up three steps.

"You got in," he said, handing me the paper. All I got to was "Congratulations" and I nearly lost it. I buried my head in my hands, laughing and crying, and feeling like I could fly to the moon and back. I'd done it. I'd gotten into Georgetown.

"Did you really think you wouldn't?" James asked, but he looked genuinely happy for me, and my heart melted a little.

"I had my doubts, yeah," I said, reading over the paper again. "I can't believe this. I'm going to Georgetown."

And that was when I saw the second page, and my heart stopped. "Oh…yeah. That."

"What?"

I showed him the amount of the first deposit to retain my place in the graduating class.

"Ouch," James said, horrified. "That's… Why do you want to go there if it's that much money?"

"Pride," I said, unashamed and undeterred. "That's all right. I'll…figure something out. Loans and scholarships. There has to be information about scholarships in here."

But there wasn't—not even an insert about how to apply for them.

"That's…odd."

"Hey, don't let it bother you," James said, throwing an arm around my shoulder. "If worse comes to worse, you can always —"

"Not asking him."

"Fine, but he's an option."

"This makes *no* sense," I said. "Why wouldn't they put

financial aid information in the packet?"

"Well…why don't you go ask them? I said I wanted to go on another adventure."

I chewed my lip. "Right now?"

"Yeah. Better to know than to worry, right?" James held out his hand. "Let's go."

The summer before, I'd gone to the university to take a tour and solidify my decision to apply there. Now, as then, I was entranced by the tall spires, the architecture, the beautiful campus—the bustling city, the shops and markets in the city outside the university. Everything about this neighborhood was alive and different from anything I'd known in Florida. This was the place for me, where I would truly find myself.

And as the reality of my financial situation sank in, I could feel my well-laid plans slipping away.

James was equally entranced, although he was less impressed by the university itself ("It looks like a prison"). He took in the sights and sounds as readily as I did. If, by some miracle, I resolved this little financial issue, and he magically enrolled himself into the school, I decided it wouldn't be the worst thing in the world. After all, I could see myself traveling around the city, hand-in-hand with him…

I stopped myself before I got too far ahead. Before I could get to happily ever after, I needed to pay for it.

We found the admissions office after asking several people for directions, and I signed in to meet with an advisor. The office was stale and uninviting and it renewed the nervousness in the pit of my stomach. The sheer mountain of money I had to come up with was staggering, even for one semester. I had money in the bank, but it was a fraction of what Georgetown would cost.

More concerning was the lack of scholarship information in the letter itself. I was, by all accounts, a needy student. My guardian made absolutely nothing, we lived in a tiny apartment. I was exactly the kind of student that aid was meant for.

So why hadn't any been in there?

"Stop worrying," James repeated again and again. But it was easy for him to say. He didn't have his entire future riding on the line. But when I began chewing my thumb, he reached over and took it from my mouth, much the same as I had before his induction match.

Damn, but we were really similar.

"Alexis Carrigan?" A tall, willowy woman with dark skin appeared in the hallway.

I popped up so fast I almost got dizzy. "Right here."

She waved me over, and I followed her into her office, leaving James behind to read through some old magazines about the school. I sat down in the chair across from her, fidgeting as I replayed every grade, every note on my application. There had to be a misunderstanding. There was no way they *wouldn't* give me aid.

I exhaled and forced my worries down to a dull roar.

"Well, we're excited to have you this year as a Hoya," the admissions officer said, folding her hands over her desk. "What can we do for you?"

"I just got my acceptance letter and I noticed it didn't have any financial aid offers," I replied. "Just wondering why that was."

"Oh, well, let's take a look." She entered my information into the computer and we exchanged polite small talk on where I was from and why I chose Georgetown.

"You're from Florida?" she asked, pausing.

"Uh. Yeah. Was visiting on a school trip.

She squinted at her computer and shook her head. "Well, it looks like we've declined to offer you any aid."

My chest seized. "W-what? Why not?"

"Says your guardian doesn't meet the minimum requirements for need-based scholarships."

I laughed, nervously. "That's…impossible. My sister works at a pharmacy."

"It says here she makes in excess of a hundred thousand a year."

"That has to be a mistake," I said, swallowing hard. "I mean, there's no way that…"

Something thudded in the back of my mind and I saw Marie's extravagant apartment. I saw the way my stone lit up when Nicole talked about taking extra shifts at the pharmacy. A conversation with Gavon two years ago about how he'd been left a sizable fortune and was meeting with an investment banker to manage it.

"I can resubmit your application and see if we can find something somewhere," she said with a frown. "But—"

"No need," I squeaked out, caught between pure fury and wanting to bawl my eyes out. "Thank you."

I stormed out of the admissions office, and felt James take his place beside me. "What's the deal?"

Balling my fists, I seethed. "I think my sister has been getting money from Gavon and not telling me about it."

I sat at the dining room table, my phone in front of me with a group text to my sisters asking them to meet me at home. I'd been so angry I couldn't even speak to James, and he'd simply cautioned me to take a deep breath and calm down before I threw him a death glare so cold he actually shivered. I was grateful he couldn't follow me into the apartment, because I needed to have private words with my sisters, and I didn't want him here with his logic and reason about why I shouldn't scream at them.

Marie arrived first, helping herself to some food in the fridge while I stewed at the kitchen table. She was smart enough not to speak to me once she saw my face, and made herself scarce while we waited for Nicole to arrive home.

When she finally did, she glanced at me and Marie nervously. "Lexie, what's going on? Marie, what are you—"

"Have a seat," I said quietly.

Nicole sat and shared a glance at Marie, who shrugged as she joined her. Neither said a word as I gathered my thoughts.

"So as you know," I started evenly, "I applied to Georgetown University."

"You've only mentioned it fifteen thousand times," Marie said with a smirk.

I glared at her and she shrank back in her seat. "I received my admissions decision today," I said, summoning the paper and sliding it toward them.

"Oh my God, you got in," Nicole said with a gasp. "Lexie, that's...that's incredible! Congratulations!"

"Why don't you look happy?" Marie said, eyeing me.

"I'm not happy," I said, staring at the table and willing myself not to set it on fire. "Although I got accepted, *paying* for it is an entirely different story."

Nicole's smile faded. "Lexie, we talked about this. You knew how much money it would be. This can't be a surprise to you."

I snorted. "No, the surprise wasn't the cost. The surprise was what I found out when I went to the financial aid office to ask why they hadn't given me any assistance. Turns out, my guardian doesn't meet the minimum requirement for need-based financial aid. Turns out, she's been getting a lot of money every month."

The faded smile on Nicole's face disappeared entirely. "Lexie, I can explain."

"Oh? Please *enlighten* me." I summoned the other paper I'd rustled up—Nicole's tax return. At the time, I hadn't questioned why she had been so evasive about letting me see it. Now it was clear. "Enlighten me how eight thousand dollars just *appears* in your account every month?"

Nicole swallowed. "I didn't ask for it. He just put it there. I haven't touched it."

"Bullshit," Marie said with a snort.

"Don't *you* start with your fancy apartment in Las Vegas," I snarled at her. "You didn't tell me either—"

"Why do you think she kicked me out?" Marie said with a death glare to Nicole. "Dad gave me money, too. Only I'm not too proud to use it."

I couldn't believe what I was hearing. "So all this time, all the conversations about how I needed to work through college and save my money and…and you could've just paid for it?"

"Do you really want Gavon's money paying for your education?" Nicole said. "There's no telling what he'll ask for in return."

"Oh yeah? What did you get in exchange for this money?"

"A promise that he would leave us alone."

Twenty-Four

Silence echoed in the room, and I honestly thought I'd had a stroke. "I'm sorry. What?"

Nicole continued, but it was less sure than before. "I told him I would take this money if he left us the *hell* alone. And he has, so as far as I'm concerned—"

"But you lied to me," I said. "You told me Gavon didn't want anything to do with us."

"It was for your own good—"

"*How?*"

"Because the sooner you got it through your head that he's a bad person, the better."

"You maybe could've *asked* me about it first," I said. "After all, he's my—"

"Don't you *dare* call him your father," Nicole snarled, rising to her feet. "He hasn't been a father to any of us. He's done nothing but ruin lives and make things worse for us. Everything was fine until he came back, and then Jeanie ended up dead."

"He didn't kill Jeanie, Cyrus did," I said. "And it's thanks to some bullshit political beef."

Nicole's face grew pale. "How…how do you know that?"

"Because guess who's been at school with me all year," I said, too angry to even care about the consequences. "James, Gavon's apprentice. He's the one who's enlightened me about all the stuff you two decided to keep from me."

Nicole gasped, covering her mouth, and Marie shook her head.

"Did you know that Gavon passed an edict so no one would come after us?" I said. "One week after Jeanie died. But nobody thought to tell me that, so I spent a year studying every book I could find and erecting at least twenty barrier spells around you and this house to keep us safe. And now I find out you're taking money from him and forcing him to stay out of my life?"

The whole thing became riotously hilarious to me. All this time, I'd assumed Gavon had kept his distance because he didn't want me in his life. His actions had left me confused and angry, too—especially when he acted like he really cared what happened to me. Now, to find out that he did care, but Nicole had been the one…

"I can't believe you didn't tell me," I said with a shake of my head.

"And I can't believe you didn't tell me his apprentice was skulking around your high school," Nicole said. "Lexie, he could've hurt you—"

"We're evenly matched," I replied hotly.

"Lexie," Marie spoke up for the first time, "look, I didn't agree with what Nicole did either, but—"

"And then you ran away for two years. Like you get a say in this conversation, Marie."

"Wow, fine," she said, holding up her hands. "You're on your own."

"Yeah, I am on my own," I said, standing up. "Because, apparently, my sisters think that I'm still the same kid they can keep secrets from. Well, you know what? I'm seventeen, and I'm one of the most powerful magicals in a generation. I come from not only a Clanmaster, but two Guildmasters. I'm not helpless, and I'm not an idiot, and I'm *definitely* not a child."

Nicole jumped to her feet. "You're seventeen, and until I say otherwise, *you're grounded.*"

I waited for my magic to peter out, to disappear as it had with Jeanie. But it remained as powerful as ever under my skin. So I'd been right all along—Nicole didn't have the power to ground me.

"You can't ground me," I said with a scoff. "You're nothing but a useless potion-maker."

As soon as the words were out of my mouth, I regretted them. I might as well have slapped her.

"What the fuck, Lexie?" Marie cried. "*Uncalled* for."

"I think it's time for you to leave," Nicole said, eyeing me coldly.

"You know what? Fine. Here." I waved my hands, recalling all the barriers around the apartment. "See what happens when you don't have my magic keeping out all the bad guys."

And with that, I transported myself to the sparring beach and burst into tears.

"Went that well, huh?"

I lifted my head, knowing I was already red, puffy, and ugly, but only caring that James was there for me. I stumbled forward, sniffing and hiccupping as I sobbed, and fell into his arms. To his credit, he didn't pull away, but held me close to him while I got tears, snot, and who-knew-what-else onto his shirt.

"T-t-t-they've been l-l-l—" I started, but I couldn't get the words out.

"Deep breath," James said, wiping the tears from my face. "Can't have you passing out."

I sniffed, gulping down as much air as I could. "Nicole's been lying to me…"

"Yeah, and?"

My gaze shot to him. "You knew?"

"No, I didn't know, but this is the kind of stuff your family's always done," he said. "They lied to you about Gavon, they lied to you about this. What's new?"

He had a point there. I laid my head back on his chest, listening to his heartbeat and grateful for his presence. "I guess I thought…I don't know. I thought they'd changed. I thought after everything that happened, everything I've done…they'd…" I shook my head. "And *Gavon*. He never told me either."

"What are you babbling about?"

"Gavon gave my sister money, and she told him to leave us alone," I said, looking up at him. "All this time, I thought he didn't want me. But now…now… Now I don't know what to think." I sucked in a breath. "I took down the barriers around my house."

"Why?"

"Because I was mad. I should go home and put them back

up. Apologize to my sisters. Fix this—"

"No. You want them to know how much you've done for them? Let them think they're in danger." He squeezed my hand. "Besides that, there's the edict, remember? Cyrus can't hurt them."

I frowned. "Yeah, but—"

He cocked his head to the side, brow furrowed, as if considering what to say. "You know what I think? I think you should forget them."

"W-what?"

"Forget them. You got into your top school. If being in high school this year has taught me anything, it's that that sort of thing is important. And you'll figure out the money." He gently brushed away the tears still falling down my face. "No more of this. You're a Warrior, damn it. We don't cry."

"Yes, we do."

"Look at me," he tilted my chin upward, "you are a strong, powerful magical. You could take on the entire New Salem Guild if you wanted to, and they know it. Your own Gram is terrified of you. And you're upset because some people lied to you?"

"But—"

"But what?"

"But it hurts," I whispered.

He pressed his lips against my forehead and my knees almost buckled at the gentleness of it. "Then let's do something to help you forget what they've done. We should celebrate."

"I don't know if I have the focus to transport right now." Or the energy. But I had nowhere else to go. Nicole had kicked me out. Something ached in my chest. Perhaps my heart was breaking

James tightened his hold around me, crushing me to his body. "Lucky for the both of us, I have plenty of focus to go around."

Cold air hit me first, freezing both my lungs and my tearstained cheeks. The rest of me was still surrounded by James' warm embrace. I didn't know if he was being kind because I was a mess or because he wanted to be; either way, I probably would've done anything he asked.

"Are you going to look or are you going to stare at my chest all night?"

I lifted my head and sucked in a breath. We were in a city—New York, by the skyline—on a rooftop overlooking what appeared to be the Brooklyn Bridge. But what had taken my breath was the table and chairs, the dinner, the candles—the wine.

"What…is this?" I said.

"I saw it in a movie once. Right? Girls like this sort of thing, don't they?" He released me to walk over to his setup, and held out the chair. "I'm supposed to do this."

"Did Gavon throw some rom-coms into your education?"

"I had to watch a few with…with the others," he said, and I was glad he didn't mention their names. Because this was looking an awful lot like a date.

"Did you really put all this together for me?" I asked, crossing the roof and sitting down.

"Yeah, I said we'd celebrate, didn't I? Although I wasn't

expecting you to be hysterical when you returned from talking with your sisters."

"Sorry to disappoint."

He flashed a grin across the table as he magically uncorked the wine. "You never disappoint."

Okay, now I was sure this was a date and I was also sure my heart was about to explode from pumping so fast. I took the glass of wine from James and sipped it, trying not to look disgusted by the sour taste.

"Yeah," he said with a similar reaction. "I wasn't sure which one to buy."

"Buy? You mean you didn't…"

"Somebody told me that you can't just use magic to get what you want all the time."

"*Is this a date?*" I blurted, my loudness falling over the edge of the rooftop.

James chuckled as he took my hand, and kissed my knuckles. "Do you want it to be?"

I ripped my hand out of his and stood quickly, backing up a few steps. "James, I don't know what this is, and you're freaking me out."

"Ah shit," he said, throwing down his napkin. Suddenly, the charming James was gone and he was back to normal. "I was trying to do something nice for you. I'm sorry if I… But I thought that you…"

"I don't know what I think," I said, turning away from him and leaning over the roof. He came up beside me and we watched a ship putter along the river. "But this is…yeah, this is freaky."

"So is how I feel about you." He sighed deeply. "Lexie, I think I'm in love with you."

My eyes widened, and I became very interested in the ship. There was no way I'd just heard what I thought I'd heard.

Sure, I'd been crushing on James for a while. But that was firmly in the boyfriend-and-girlfriend, let's-hold-hands-and-go-to-the-movies kind of crush category. With one phrase, James had just leapfrogged over that into a much more serious and terrifying world. A world where I let him past the barrier into my apartment, where I trusted him not only with my life, but with the lives of my family.

"Lexie."

I shook my head, gaze still rooted on the ship and hoping it wouldn't burst into flames, because I was fairly sure I wasn't in control of my magic.

"Damn it, you're making me feel like an idiot here."

Finally, I glared at him. "You can't spring that kind of thing on me without warning."

"I already told you I liked you!"

"Like isn't love, James," I said. "You said you loved me. That's…"

"I know exactly what it means." He swallowed. "You haven't blasted me off the rooftop, so that's a good sign."

"I don't understand. You…we're just…we're friends?"

"My best friend," he said. "And somehow along the way, I fell in love with you. As much as I tried not to."

I snorted. "Thanks."

"You know what I mean. You realize this isn't…I mean, this isn't the most ideal situation." He closed his eyes. "Disaster waiting to happen."

"Then why did you tell me at all?" I said, folding my arms over my chest.

"Because I couldn't not tell you. Not the way you look right now. Not after seeing you so upset." He unfolded my arms and pulled me closer to him. "I'm going to kiss you again."

"Why are you asking all of a sudden?"

"Because you don't like it when I surprise you tonight."

He didn't wait for my response, pressing his lips to mine. Over the past few days, I'd become used to the soft pecks and brief flashes of something more passionate. Tonight, he was testing the waters, moving slow and deliberately to see if I'd object.

And although I didn't object, I also didn't know how to reciprocate.

He released me. "I'm sorry. I shouldn't have said anything."

"It's not that. It's just…" I whispered, staring at the skin on his cheeks instead of his eyes. "I really thought you just thought of me like all the other girls you've dated."

He chuckled, and the vibration tickled my stomach. "I haven't dated anyone but you in weeks."

I glanced up at him, realizing he was right. The last girl he'd dated was Mary Catherine in January, and that had been a one-week thing. I'd thought he'd just been too preoccupied with his induction match but…

"Halfway through that date with MC, I realized I wanted to be with you instead. I don't want to be with someone I can't be honest with or someone I can't be myself around. I can be myself around you." He brushed a hair behind my ear. "And you don't give me an inch."

"I don't, do I?" My heart pounded in my chest. He was so close, and I was about to fall off the edge. Would it be so bad if I did? "What makes you think you're in love with me?"

"That's easy," he said, slipping his hand down to rest against my neck. "I love watching your mind work. The way you carefully consider every move before you make it. It's what makes you such a terrible sparrer." His eyes glittered. "And such a horrible person to fall in love with."

"Oh?" I said weakly. "Why's that?"

"Because I told you I loved you five minutes ago, and you haven't responded," he whispered with a feather light kiss on my lips. "But you know what I love most about you?"

I swallowed, my tongue stuck to the roof of my mouth.

"That your emotions are always written on your face."

His kiss was not innocent this time. Instinct took over and I leaned into him, sliding my hands around his waist. He pulled me against him, and I melted into this new feeling and trying to scare away the questions and fears—because I knew I felt the same. I had fought it tooth and nail but he was right. There was no hiding how I felt.

I took his shirt and pulled him back to me, granting him permission to take things a little further. His fingertips brushed my back as they slipped under my shirt, and I pressed myself even closer. There was something stirring, something he'd awakened back at New Year's, something that I was both ready and not ready for.

"We shouldn't... This is already so complicated," he whispered against my cheek. "I should go—"

"I don't really want to be alone tonight." The words came out before I could stop them.

"Lexie, I don't know if we should—"

"I mean, I don't know if that means I want to..." I swallowed. "But I don't want to stop. Not yet." Because we stopped, I might've wised up and realized this was going to be an epic mistake.

But I didn't care. I was in love with James Riley.

Smarter instincts be damned.

"Would you come back to my apartment with me?"

Twenty-Five

I cracked open an eye, but the absence of warmth next to me told me I was alone. And for that, I was kind of grateful.

There was a lot to process in the early morning light.

I'd had no intention of sleeping with James. None. Even in the throes of passion, with his lips drawing forth new and exciting feelings, I'd remained sane and promised myself that I wouldn't take things too far.

But it kind of…happened.

We'd lain in bed, cuddling and talking. Then cuddling had turned to kissing. Kissing turned into his hand up my shirt. Once my shirt was off, so was his. Then the rest of the clothes, and so on, and so forth.

I'd never really had any great opinions about virginity, and I didn't feel any different about not being one anymore. Especially since the actual act had been, well…not as romantic as advertised, or at least, not as nice as the snuggling before and after. If I hadn't seen James' philandering on display over the past six months, I might've guessed he was as clueless as I was.

I traced the outline of what I presumed was James in my pillow. He was in love with me, and he had been for some time. We'd laid bare our emotions, our fears of what this new complication to our already weird relationship would bring. And as we'd drifted off to sleep in each other's arms, we'd agreed to take it one day at a time, even though we'd already taken a huge step forward physically.

All I knew was I wanted to make out with him more. The sex part could use some improvement.

A giggle erupted from my chest, and it sounded strange in the silent room. Too silent, in fact. I usually heard Nicole walking around. But even after straining my ears, I heard nothing.

I supposed that was to be expected. She was probably pretty hurt and didn't want to talk. I reached for my phone on the bedside table and tapped out a message to Marie, *Can we talk*? Perhaps she could help me smooth things over, or at least help me come up with the right words to say to apologize.

I'd been wrong to say such hurtful things, but at the same time, I was hurt that they lied to me. That they still felt the need to protect me, when I was the one who'd been protecting them all along.

I wanted a rational, non-emotional conversation with Nicole about what Gavon had given to Nicole, why, and whether or not I could use those funds for school. But Marie was right; Nicole couldn't separate her own issues with Gavon. She was so convinced he was evil that she'd lied to make me believe it, too. I understood why, but I just needed her to think clearly for ten minutes while we figured all this out.

But first I needed to apologize.

I groaned and flipped onto my side. I'd apologize in a minute. Once I found my nerve.

I glanced at the text and furrowed my brow; it hadn't been read yet. Marie always checked her texts. And I hadn't gone overboard with her as much as with Nicole, so I doubted she'd be mad enough not to read them.

I sat up and summoned my shirt and pants from where they'd been thrown the night before. I wanted to talk to Marie about Nicole, but I also wanted to talk about James. I wasn't sure what happened next, but I was excited about all the possibilities.

I transported myself directly into her apartment. It was early in the morning, so I tiptoed over to Marie's bedroom, cracking open the door.

The bed was messy, but empty.

A sliver of fear trickled down the back of my neck, but I kept myself calm. She could've been out partying still, or perhaps she'd gone out and met a guy and was at his place. Or perhaps…

I released a shaky breath and leaned against the doorframe. Now was not the time to let those old fears take over. I'd made my peace with them. And there was an edict in place preventing anyone from harming me or my sisters.

But the barriers were down last night.

"That doesn't mean anything," I whispered to the empty air and the dragon-like voice in my mind. Before I lost my mind, I transported back home to Florida. I stood for a moment, breathing out the anxiety that was starting to churn like a hurricane in my stomach. I knew I just needed to put eyes on one sister, and it would all go away.

"Nicole?" I called, hearing the worry in my voice. I crossed the hall to her room and knocked, and when I didn't hear anything, opened the door.

Her room was empty.

Anxiety blossomed in my chest and I shook my head. There was an edict. There was no way Cyrus could get to my sisters. It had been over two years. Why would he choose to strike now?

The worry continued to bubble, especially when I saw Nicole's car in the driveway. That didn't mean anything; perhaps Marie took her to cool off. But would Nicole agree to a magical means of transportation, especially after what I said the night before?

Guilt joined worry in the pit of my stomach and I glanced at my phone, begging for it to light up with Marie's name and a text confirming that she was fine.

Then I shook my head, swallowed the panic. I had a solution for all of this—the health charm. The one I'd been using for months to make sure Marie was in good health. I could use it on both of them and know once and for all.

I retreated to my room and dug in my closet for Marie's hairbrush and the spell book that held the charm in it. I held both items in my hand and concentrated, as instructed, and I waited for the flash of white light.

Only this time, the light was yellow.

Not dead, but not safe.

I gasped and scooted away from them as if they were on fire. Spots danced in my vision as I envisioned the thousands of different ways they could be in trouble and I gasped for air. Fear and guilt took turns in my mind, knowing it was *my* fault, hating myself for being so trusting, for being too complacent. For letting James convince me they would be fine instead of returning to fix the barrier.

For James to—No. He had nothing to do with this. Of that, I was absolutely certain.

I had James on my side, maybe even Gavon. They could help me.

Or could they?

They were all in the same Guild as Cyrus, which meant they couldn't directly challenge him. And what would their Guild care if a potion-maker and a healer were in danger? To them, my sisters' lives were worth less than dirt.

I needed to think clearly about this, which was increasingly difficult the more my heart raced. Someone had taken my sisters, and the only logical explanation was Cyrus. But he hadn't killed them, which meant he was using them to get to me.

But even if I wanted to, I couldn't. Gavon's edict had also forbidden me from dueling with any of them.

Except if I requested an induction match.

Magic hummed in my veins at the idea, but I shut it down. To go to New Salem and request an induction match was absolute lunacy. No matter how strong I'd become in the past few months, I wasn't about to put myself in Cyrus' line of fire unless I absolutely had to. I'd go find James or Gavon, and we'd figure something out together.

Getting to my feet, I wiped away my tears and stared at myself in the mirror. I was a Warrior, damn it. And as James said, we didn't cry.

The tear crackled before me, drawing fear into my stomach for the first time in months. Perhaps it was because I would be crossing it by myself, and I fully appreciated the violent nature of it. If I hadn't gone through it already, I would've been doubtful there was any way to survive it. Knowing what lay on the other side of it, and what I was prepared to do, made it all the more terrifying.

Before I could move, a foot jutted out of the white ferocity. But I knew as soon as I saw it that it didn't belong to James or Gavon. I stepped back, watching the man who'd haunted my nightmares for months step out of the tear, brushing himself off before pausing. Slowly, his gaze drifted up to me, and a smile curled onto his face.

I swallowed my panic. "Where are they?"

"Shame you still haven't learned your manners," Cyrus said, intertwining his fingers in front of him. "It is customary for adversaries to exchange pleasantries."

In response, I shot an attack spell his way, and it bounced harmlessly off him. I'd known it would, but a girl could dream.

"Was that necessary?" Cyrus asked, with an infuriatingly unconcerned air. "You can't attack me and I can't attack you. So whatever issue you think you have—"

"You took my sisters," I snarled.

"Did I?" he asked with a chuckle. "Oh, how very interesting."

His amused smile sent the first shot of doubt down my spine. He could've been playing stupid, sure, but what if he wasn't? What if he hadn't been the one—

That's what he wants you to think.

"So here we are. You've got a grievance against me, and no recourse to take other than to waste your energy in useless offensive spells." He tapped his finger against his chin. "What shall we do?"

He was leading me to the obvious answer, the insane one that was my absolute last resort. If my anger got the better of me, I'd make a mistake. But his words had plucked something in my gut, and my Warrior magic was humming with the need to fight him for real. Especially as he looked older, less menacing than the last time I'd faced him. I was his equal—perhaps even his better. James had said as much, hadn't he?

Don't you dare, came the smarter half. *James never wanted you to get into a ring with him.*

"I could go to Gavon," I replied. "I could tell him what you've done."

"You could do that." He stepped out of the way. "Please, after you."

I took a step then stopped. Maybe that was what he wanted me to do.

"Well?" He waved his arm.

I hated him so very much in that moment. My gut was too jumbled from panic and nerves to tell me what I should do. Cyrus never had my best interests at heart, so if he wasn't trying to prevent me from doing something, that meant I shouldn't do it, right? I felt trapped between what I thought to be the truth and what I feared *could* be the truth.

"I wonder if your reticence is due to your lack of confidence in your assertions of my guilt," Cyrus said after a long moment. "Because if you were to go to Gavon, and he accused me when there was no proof, it might cast doubt on his position as Guildmaster. The rest of the Council might see fit to relieve him of his duties. Which would, in effect, put me in charge." He smiled. "And as much as I'd enjoy that, I doubt you'd feel the same."

I hadn't considered that scenario. Was Gavon's position really that precarious? Or was Cyrus lying to me again?

"Well, if you didn't take them, then who the hell did," I snapped, trying to buy myself some time.

"There are three possible scenarios. The first, as you've stated, is that I took them. Your father would have to prove such a thing in front of the Guild, and I'm afraid I've far surpassed him in covering my tracks." He smiled, and something tickled the back of my mind. "He has very little idea what I've been doing, I'm afraid. It would be easy for me to fool him and the idiots on the Council."

My memory pinged with something that I'd long forgotten, and I angrily brushed it aside.

"The second scenario, far less likely, is that your father took your sisters."

"He wouldn't."

"I said it was far less likely," Cyrus said with a glare. "And finally, the last option, which to my eyes seems the most likely since I am innocent, is that your new *friend* took them."

The way he said *friend* raised the hair on the back of my neck. Did he know about James and me? Was this some way to trap us both, to take advantage of our new relationship?

"And why would he do that?" I asked, even as the grain of doubt nestled in the back of my mind.

"Jealousy? Revenge? A spot of fun? After all, he's the only one with a pact to spar with you." Cyrus eyes glittered. "I could think of a few reasons he'd be envious of you. Not the least of which is your power, your intellect, and your relationship with your father."

I almost believed him. But I knew James. He might've been jealous of me at one point, but we were long past that. Now he loved me.

So he says…

Shut up, other me.

"Our pact stipulates that he can't induct me," I said, lifting my chin higher. "So what would he gain by kidnapping them?"

"Your pact says that *he* can't induct *you*. It says nothing about requesting an induction match." His eyes narrowed at my obvious surprise. "Did you think Gavon was the only one to review your little agreement?"

Something clicked in my brain, and everything fell into place. My original assumption had been right: Cyrus had taken my sisters to force me into an induction match so he could finally kill me.

But what he didn't know was I wasn't the same idiot he'd nearly killed. Or maybe he did know, and he didn't care. Either way, this entire song and dance was getting tiring. I was done with spending my life worrying about this lunatic.

"Fine," I snapped, praying that I wasn't making a mistake. "Induct me and let's get this over with."

"Ah, but we have to make it official, so your father won't be able to interfere." He glanced around as if expecting Gavon to appear out of nowhere. "We must make these things official, as it were. A declaration of your intent. Say I, Alexis Carrigan, request induction into the New Salem Warrior's Guild."

This was my last chance to back out. To go find Gavon and pray he'd have some magical solution to fix this.

Or, you could end this thing once and for all.

"I, Alexis Carrigan, request induction into the New Salem Warrior's Guild."

Magic sizzled in my veins as whatever old magic I'd just appealed to solidified my intent. There was no backing out now.

Cyrus' eyes glittered. "Well, who am I to argue?"

I was struck with the oddest sensation of déjà vu as I walked along a stony path, following Cyrus. He said nothing to me, although the catty smile on his face told me that either he'd been pleasantly surprised by my offer, or I was playing right into his hands.

"You look worried, my dear," Cyrus said, breaking our silence as we walked into the village. "Second thoughts about your intention statement?"

Like hell I'd let him know what I was thinking. "Not even one."

The sparring arena loomed in the distance, but Cyrus took another turn down a new road. This one was lined with houses much nicer than the rest of the village. There were fewer beggars on the street, although the stench remained. I absentmindedly wondered if Gavon had tried to implement plumbing, or if they'd even be receptive to the idea.

We drew closer to a large building, one more ornate than even the nicest on the block. The double doors opened, and Cyrus swept in, with me following slowly behind. His boots clacked on the old wooden floor, and as my eyes adjusted to the candlelight, I recognized the room as an old meeting space from history books.

That was when I heard a familiar voice.

"What is the meaning of this?" Gavon had risen to his feet, his face a rare mixture of shock and worry. There were others in the room I vaguely recognized as the Council.

"You tell me. She's your daughter," Cyrus said, as if he hadn't masterminded this whole thing. "She's come to claim her birthright as a member of our Guild."

"She can't, as long as she's in Clan Carrigan," Gavon said, almost too quickly. He shot a dark look at me.

"I've not been in the Clan for two years," I said clearly. "Ergo, there's nothing preventing me from joining your guild."

Gavon clenched his jaw. "We will have to confer—"

"*Actually*," Cyrus said, and my blood ran cold, "since she participated in an introduction match, there are no laws preventing her from requesting an induction match, assuming, of course, all previous hurdles to introduction are cleared." He glanced to me. "As it appears they are."

Gavon's red face had turned purple, and I distractedly wondered if that was where I'd gotten my coloring from. "I see."

"I think we should complete this match today. After all, the crowds have become thirsty for another match, since they were so deprived of a good one with our young master Riley." Cyrus glanced around before his gaze settled on Gavon. "And where is our newest member? I hope that his newfound freedom to explore the Old World hasn't interfered with your ability to control him. I'd hate for him to…go rogue."

Whatever conversation Gavon and Cyrus were having was lost on me, but it was clear they were speaking in a code they both understood.

"See to it this match occurs today, if that's what you desire," Gavon said with a glare to Cyrus. Then in a puff of smoke, he appeared next to me, grabbing me by the elbow. "While you're otherwise occupied, I'd like a word with my daughter."

And before Cyrus could respond, I was covered in purple smoke and transported out of the room.

Twenty-Six

"Are you *out of your Goddamned mind?*" he bellowed. "What could've possessed you to agree to such a thing?"

I wasn't fully transported into the room before Gavon started screaming at me, so I backed up and fell backward. Luckily, my butt sank into a chair instead of hitting the hard floor. I lifted my dizzy head and recognized his library before his purple face filled my vision again.

"Maybe because I woke up and my sisters were *gone*," I snapped back.

That got his attention. "What are you talking about?"

"He *took* Nicole and Marie," I said, helplessly. "They're in danger, or so says that stupid hairbrush charm."

"I..." Gavon's face melted into panic. "You're right. I can't find them either."

"See?"

"But then *why* not come to me first?" he said, his anger returning. "What possible reason could you have to want to endanger your life this way?"

"Cyrus met me at the tear," I said, wishing I had a stronger argument. "I couldn't just…"

"Just walk away and come to me?" Gavon finished with no shortage of fire in his voice. "Considering the edict prevented him from hurting you."

"But he could've—"

"Could've what? What possible outcome was so terrifying that you lost your *damned* mind and challenged the one person in the Guild who actually wants you dead?"

"Because I could defeat him," I replied, although my confidence was quickly slipping away.

"Oh? So you think you're ready to take someone else's life?" he asked, hotly. "Because that's the only way to truly defeat him."

I chewed my lip. "I mean…"

"And also if you don't kill him, he will most assuredly kill you. Was that part of your plan? Or did you just think you could announce your intention, knock him around, and walk away with both of you still alive? Because that's not what will happen. If you get into that match with him, someone will die. And it will probably be you."

Tears pricked at my eyes, but I didn't give him the satisfaction. "Thanks for the pep talk. Do you even know how powerful I am?"

He shook his head. "You've been spending too much time with James, it seems. You aren't powerful, Alexis. You're a kid. You're barely seventeen."

His words stripped away whatever false confidence I'd been

wearing, leaving me as nervous and unsure as the last time I'd been in New Salem. And without it, I was left with the real reason why I'd taken such a bold risk.

I stared at the floor and begged my lip not to tremble. "It was my fault. I took the barriers down last night after…after we'd had a big fight. And he… And I just didn't want anyone else to get hurt because I'd made another stupid…mistake. And I panicked."

His warm hands landed on my shoulders and I finally lifted my gaze to his. And I was grateful some of his anger had given way to determination.

"You aren't going to duel anyone today. Not if I can help it. It's a small village, so if they're here, it won't take long to find them. If I can prove it's happened under duress, the match will be null and void."

I actually sighed in relief. "So I don't have to fight him?"

"No," he said with an angry look at me, "you have to fight him. At least, you have to hold him off until I can find your sisters. But I won't be able to locate them before the match starts. If Cyrus took them, they're in his manor, presumably in his basement—"

"That's what I thought, too!" I said, then wilted at the glare he gave me.

"But I can't just walk into his manor. There are spells to undo, charms to break. And that's all presuming he's placed them there and not in some other iron-clad room."

I winced. "There are more of them?"

"Plenty more. We magicals like our prisons," Gavon said, releasing my shoulders. "I'm sending you back to Cyrus. Do not do or say anything that will inform him of our plans. It's best if you say nothing at all. He will try to goad you, to convince you that the truth is a lie and that lies are truth. You need to trust your own instincts more than what he says, no matter how much he tries to confuse you."

Again, I nodded.

"I'm very, *very* disappointed in you," he said before transporting me out of his library.

I landed in the same, small holding room near the sparring arena I'd been held in before my introduction match. Then, I'd been terrified that I was about to die. But now, staring out the small window, I mostly felt nerves, a little excitement, and the lingering disgust at myself.

I couldn't dwell on what I should or shouldn't have done. The only thing to do now was focus on the knowledge that I was here to put an end to Cyrus—at least until Gavon could clean up my mess.

Assuming he could before Cyrus made a mess out of me.

I paced the floor, scraping the bottom of my conscious for the confidence that Gavon had so effortlessly destroyed. I craned my neck to see the stands In the arena in front of me. James had said—

James. Where the hell was that kid?

"Don't focus on that," I whispered to myself, returning my train of thought to the audience gathering in the stone stands of the arena. I couldn't see much from this vantage point, but the roar was growing. Matches were the only bit of entertainment these people ever got.

The door swung open, but it wasn't Cyrus waiting for me, rather a young woman who would not look me in the eye.

"I'm here to get you, Mistress," she whispered.

I followed her out of the room, observing the woman with detached interest. Her clothes were nice but her frame was too slender. She'd gone hungry often, but she seemed well taken care of otherwise.

I couldn't help the burst of curiosity. "What do you think of G—the Guildmaster?"

Her eyes darted around before settling back on the floor. "Master Gavon is a kind man. He helped me find employment when no one would take me. My magic isn't…isn't very strong."

Despite my own nerves, I placed a hand on her shoulder. "Sounds like you've got plenty to me."

She squeaked, somewhat in fear, but a little in excitement, and scurried forward to hold the door open for me. The roar of the crowd echoed down the stone hallway, and I readied myself for the action.

My erratic brain reminded me how terrified I'd been to go to that party at Callista's. If only they could see me now.

The stands rose several tiers into the sky, but it was hard to see how many with the crowds already cramming into the arena. My gaze swept the arena until it landed on the Guildmaster's box. Gavon was nowhere to be seen, and neither was James. I hoped that was a good sign.

The crowd cheered loudly and I glanced to my left; Cyrus emerged from the other side with an air of smug calmness. Either he didn't know that I'd told Gavon about my sisters, or he didn't care. Perhaps all he wanted was to get into the ring with me. Perhaps he didn't know that Gavon could nullify the match.

Or perhaps he did, and there was some other plan afoot.

"As customary, we shake hands," he said, extending his.

I grasped it, infusing all my power into my grip, as he did the same. The dueling agreement solidified, and a large dome expanded from where our hands met. It was colored purple and dark gray, giving me just a hint of pride that this time, this duel, it was on me to sink or swim.

I retreated to my side, throwing back my shoulders and waiting. Cyrus glanced to the Guildmaster box and frowned; Gavon still hadn't arrived.

"I doubt he has the stomach to watch this," Cyrus called.

"I didn't think he cared for you that much."

Cyrus smiled. "I think, above all else, I shall miss that quick wit of yours, Alexis."

His confidence made me itch with the need to put him in his place. My own was pulsing and raging, fueled by my emotions, my protective instincts, and the knowledge that I wasn't just fighting for myself, but for my sisters.

I barely heard the "begin" before the dark gray power came for me. But I was ready, deflecting it with ease and wincing only when the loud boom of magic exploded against the protective dome.

"Little Alexis," Cyrus teased, walking closer. "You are quite powerful now, aren't you?"

Three more spells, three more deflections. This was proving almost too easy, and I knew he was testing me, feeling me out and waiting for me to show my weaknesses.

"You cannot win this fight by defense only," Cyrus said, circling me. "Perhaps you aren't angry enough. Shall I talk about your dear mother? That seemed to get you riled up before. Or perhaps we could discuss your late aunt?"

He will try to goad you, to convince you that the truth is a lie and that lies are truth. You need to trust your own instincts and keep strong to your convictions.

Gavon's words echoed in my mind, removing the anguish Cyrus' words had caused and replacing them with cool focus. This was nothing more than a sparring match, with my opponent mercilessly attacking me on all sides. Only instead of James, I was facing someone who didn't care if he bruised me.

But James had given me something to work with.

"We could talk about how you lost the Guildmastership to Gavon. How about that?" I called back, releasing my first offensive spell. To my surprise, it landed right where it was supposed to.

"Oh, so you've been informed of recent history, then?" The cool, calm, collected Cyrus was back, and I knew my hit had been a one-time deal. I wished James had shared more information with me, but I would have to rely on my own skills to defeat him.

Or—I glanced at the empty box—delay him as long as possible.

"I know you also killed my grandmother, your own master," I said, transporting out of the way of a fierce-looking gray ball of magic. "Did it bother you at all, or are you just so used to killing that it doesn't matter?"

There was another crack in his armor. Alexandra was a sore

point with him, it seemed, sorer than losing the Guildmastership.

"I would keep quiet on matters you know nothing about," Cyrus said through clenched teeth.

"I'm a teenager, we always talk about stuff we don't know," I parried, elation coursing through my body. I was actually winning, I was actually—

Something hard slammed into me, followed by the impact of my body against something even harder. When the magic dissipated, I fell forward onto my hands, coughing air back into my bruised lungs. *That* was probably what Gavon had been referring to with emotion and getting distracted.

"Oh, sweet child," Cyrus said, standing above me as I spat blood onto the rock. "As if someone like you could outsmart me. I've had years of working this antique system to learn how to get what I want from it."

"And yet here you are, second-in-command," I replied, rolling out of the way before another angry blast came my way. "By the way, I think I'm winning in the sarcasm department."

"Your mother had a mouth on her too," Cyrus said before his anger curled into amusement. "Turns out you two have more in common than I first thought."

I swallowed. So he knew about James. "And what of it?"

"Surprised he's not here. What oh what could be more important than watching his lover fight in an induction match?"

I tried to let the question roll off my back, but it stuck right in the forefront of my mind. I was sure he was…what? Helping Gavon? Yes. That was it. He was helping Gavon.

So why did my gut feel like it was on a ship in a storm?

Cyrus had lowered his attack spells, and when I sent two over, he easily deflected them. I was showing my hand, but it was hard to think straight with the question in my mind about James…and why he hadn't appeared since I'd arrived in New Salem?

"Nice try," I said with a smile. "But I know it was you—"

"How could I have possibly done so? There are some very powerful barrier spells around your home. Trust me," he smirked, "I've checked."

"I…" I swallowed my guilt in favor of the truth. "I took them down."

"Your healing sister put them back up," Cyrus said, placing his hands behind his back. I could've hit him with everything I had, but I lacked the mental focus. "The only way anyone could've gotten past them was if they were invited in by a member of your family."

"Marie doesn't know how to put up barriers," I said, although my conviction on that matter was a bit shaky.

"And you believe your father wouldn't have given her his knowledge on the subject?"

I shook my head. This had to be a trick, a way to get me completely unnerved so I would make a mistake. Or perhaps he just enjoyed watching me question every decision I'd made over the past six months.

"You're missing the bigger picture," I replied, as the crowd around us shouted for us to quit talking and start blowing each other up. "Why would James do something like that? What could he possibly gain?"

"You mean besides having one of his rivals dead in the ring?"

Cyrus offered.

"I'm not his rival. I never wanted anything to do with this stupid world."

"I am his rival for Guildmaster," Cyrus said with a shrug. "But you're his rival for the Guildmaster's affections."

His words landed a split second before the attack spell did, and I had no time to defend against either. As I flew backwards, the truth echoed in my ears as the ringing did seconds later when my head hit the hard rock. More spells came at me, and I could only muster enough focus to construct a barrier spell. I lay on my stomach, pouring all of my magic into the purple dome above my head and repeating to myself that Cyrus was a liar, and he wanted nothing more than to unnerve me so I wouldn't lose focus.

But damn, he was doing a good job of it.

Every questioning thought, every suspicion I'd ever had about James came back to the forefront of my mind. Both scenarios made sense: he'd either been completely honest with me this whole time, or he'd been playing me all along. He'd changed since his induction match, acting more interested, pushing the envelope with our pseudo-relationship. Sleeping with me…had it all been one elaborate hoax?

Get yourself together, Lexie.

I pushed myself to my hands and took a deep breath under the protection of my magic. Whether James was a lying bastard or my one true love, I would figure that out later. Right now, I was in a duel with a man who'd taken the lives of my mother, grandmother, and aunt, and if I didn't pull myself out of my funk, I'd be next.

I cast one glance at the box; still empty.

Come on, D…Gavon, don't let me down.

"Are you done hiding?" Cyrus called. "I would like this game to be over with."

I focused my energy on waiting for Gavon and the tug of the magical memory took me away. The smell of salt air filled my nose, the sound of the waves filled my ears. The competing feelings of knowing I was about to take my last breath and praying that it wouldn't happen. That he would come to save me before it was too late. I erased the hope I'd nurtured, knowing it was better to allow the memory to take me completely.

I opened my eyes, and I knew Cyrus could sense the familiarity in the way I gathered magic from every corner of my body. But to me, this was a new magical memory. It wasn't my mother's—it was mine. From the night Jeanie died.

I was filled with sadness, fear, hopelessness. Knowing that this was the end of my life. That my sisters would be safe, but I would not be. That my death would not be in vain, because I could destroy the person in front of me so he'd never bother them again. Back then, I'd been a child. Now, I was a Warrior.

I rose to my feet, nursing the sensation of calm. The memory no longer overtook my consciousness, but enhanced what I was seeing, how I was feeling. Perhaps I'd reached a new phase in my magical ability, finally able to utilize the breadth of magical training in battles like this.

"You look scared," I called over the crackling of my hands.

"I—"

"For once in your life, Cyrus, just shut up."

And I released the barrage. My magic seemed endless as it

pummeled and torpedoed him from all angles. I was moving faster than I'd ever thought possible, twisting and turning against his response spells and landing more of my own. I was moving forward and he was moving toward the edge of the ring.

When he fell to one knee, I had him.

I gathered magic from the top of my head to the tips of my fingers, down to the bottom of my feet. There was no need to conserve, no need to leave behind anything. I was going to end his…

Did I truly want to kill—

Do it, Lexie.

I took the last crumbs and opened my eyes, willing myself to look at the first life I'd ever take. Magic exploded from my body, rushing toward my opponent like a freight train, ready to do the thing I simultaneously wanted and didn't want to do.

And then…the ball of magic disappeared.

Exhaustion swept over me, and I collapsed to my knees, moaning and clutching my aching chest. Bleary-eyed, I looked up as two figures approached me, one blonde, one brunette. Healing magic swept through my body, and my vision cleared.

"M-Marie! Nicole!"

"We're here," Nicole said, wiping hair from my sweaty forehead. "You damned idiot. We're here. And we're fine."

I choked out a sob and fell forward, unsure which sister I landed on first. They held me tight as Marie finished her healing; just enough so I could stand, but not so much that I wouldn't be in pain. I could only suppose I deserved it.

"What happened?" I said.

"We…" Marie looked at Nicole. "One minute we were

sleeping on the couch, waiting for you to come home, the next thing we knew, we were in an iron cell."

I turned to Cyrus, who was leaning on a walking stick and looking beat up. I hoped nobody healed him for a long time. "Cyrus—"

"It wasn't...him," Marie said quietly.

Something thudded in the back of my mind and I didn't want to look. If I didn't look at who Gavon had bound and gagged in front of him, it wouldn't be real. If I didn't acknowledge what was happening, it wouldn't.

But my traitorous eyes turned that way anyway.

"I'm sorry, Lexie," Nicole said.

"There has to be an explanation for this," I said, pushing myself to stand even though every piece of me protested it. With the help of Marie and Nicole, I hobbled over to where Gavon was talking with the members of his council. He looked... devastated.

"...women have testified that James was the one who took them," he said. "There were traces of his magic on all the locks around Master Cyrus' house."

This couldn't be happening. My brain refused to believe this was happening. Cyrus had been lying about it; this was some elaborate ploy to nail both of us, or to...

My doubts died when I finally looked at James. There was no remorse on his face, only anger.

My knees buckled under me, and I was grateful for my sisters' arms.

"Guildmaster McKinnon," wheezed an old man with a long beard. "Let the boy speak on his behalf."

With a sigh, Gavon waved his hand and the gag around James' mouth disappeared. He straightened his shoulders and spoke clearly. "I am guilty of the charges against me."

The air left my lungs.

"I took the potion-maker and the healer so Carrigan would think that they had been taken by Master Cyrus." He spoke evenly, staring at Gavon without emotion. Just matter-of-fact. "After sparring with her for several months, I was sure she would be able to kill him."

"But why, James?" Gavon asked.

Gone was the boy I'd sparred with. Fallen in love with. All that remained was a cold shell. "Cyrus has a history of devious behavior that suits him instead of the Guild. I wanted him taken care of."

"And so you took it upon yourself to endanger our Guild by inviting the wrath of Clan Carrigan upon us?" Gavon displayed no affection in my direction, but for the first time, I noticed him holding back. Showing real emotion while saying something different. He really was a master of deception.

"She is out of the clan—"

"*She* is the Clan Carrigan I'm worried about," Gavon responded. "I don't have to remind you that Warriors are in short supply around here. By all accounts, she could kill half our village before any of us could stop her."

I would've argued with Gavon that that was impossible with my current injuries, but my brain was too focused on James. He had to be lying, right? This had to be some thinly veiled code I was missing, but unlike when Cyrus and Gavon had spoken before, Gavon seemed oblivious to whatever James was trying to tell him.

Other than the words coming out of his mouth.

"Guildmaster, might I remind you that the woman in question stands not ten feet from us?" wheezed the old man.

Gavon's attention turned to my sisters and me, and I could've sworn a sparkle appeared in his eye. "Unless you plan to launch an attack on us where we stand, please feel free to vacate our world."

"C'mon," Marie said, grabbing both Nicole and I and enveloping us in her white healing magic.

Twenty-Seven

I slumped onto the couch, feeling every bruise and ache as acutely as the pain in my heart. I'd thought I'd been idiotic before, but now…now I wanted to die.

How could I have been so stupid? How could sweet words and the promise of true love have taken me so far from my sanity? I was smarter than this. I was so much smarter than this.

"Lexie…" Marie started. "We're okay. He didn't hurt us."

He couldn't, not under the edict. I wasn't sure how he'd managed to get around that particular note, but perhaps if *he* wasn't out to harm *them*, he could've simply taken them. In the end, it didn't matter. He'd played me, and there was nobody to blame but myself.

"I knew you'd come for us," Nicole said. "Lexie, you were *incredible* out there. I've never seen you look so…so…"

"Fierce," Marie finished for her. "Girl, those sparring sessions have been paying off."

I closed my eyes, gently batting away the painful memories

that popped up. "Did you erect a new barrier around the apartment?"

"Yes, I did," Marie said quietly. "Dad said it was a good idea, even with the edict."

"But I'm sure he must've come into the house before she put it up," Nicole said.

All I could do was shake my head, resulting in a loud sigh from Marie.

"You slept with him, didn't you?"

Closing my eyes, I nodded. The twin groans were barely audible. I cracked open an eye to survey the damage. Marie was shaking her head, and Nicole's mouth was pressed into a firm line. Apparently, Marie had gotten her up to speed on my feelings for James.

"I'm sorry," I whispered, tears gathering in my eyes. "I should've known better. I did know better. But Gavon…and it didn't seem like…" I buried my head into my hands. I didn't really know what to say or even what to think. I was so embarrassed that I couldn't even look at my sisters.

The couch dipped beside me as an arm draped over my shoulders. "I think I've got it, Marie," Nicole said.

"You sure? I could talk about my dumbass decisions with men over the past few years."

"Then we'd be here for hours."

"Bitch," Marie said, but there was no fire in it. "Lexie, I'm here if you want to talk."

"Could you…stay?" I said, lifting my head. "I don't want Cyrus…"

"I doubt Cyrus is going to be moving any time soon," Marie

said. "You beat the shit out of him."

"But James—"

"Dad will take care of James," Marie said, and Nicole stiffened beside me. "Just like he came to get us. Besides, you aren't the only one who knows how to put together a barrier spell." She smiled at me. "Come visit this weekend, okay?"

I nodded and she was gone in a puff of white and I missed her instantly. Somehow, dismantling the web of lies was easier with her in the room.

"I'm sorry," I whispered to the silent room. "For everything. For what I said. For lying. For getting you…" I sniffed. "I'm just sorry."

"I'm sorry, too," Nicole replied, brushing the hair off my face. "I shouldn't have lied, and I shouldn't have…I shouldn't have acted like I didn't want you to go to Georgetown. I want you to go, Lexie."

"I won't go," I said, sniffing back my tears. "I don't deserve to, not after what I've done."

"You deserve to go precisely for what you've done. You've punished yourself for two years for Jeanie's death. It's enough."

I screwed up my face and released a sob. The long hours, the work, cleaning dog stalls and working with mean parents. I'd said it was for Georgetown, but it was really my punishment. I had been responsible for Jeanie's death, the same way I was responsible for letting another monster into my life. In some sick ironic twist, I'd been drawn to James because he was an escape from the self-punishment.

"Ssh," Nicole cooed as I laid my head in her lap. "You don't need to punish yourself anymore. Jeanie would want you to go to Georgetown. *I* want you to go. You have to live your life sometime, Lexie. You may be a Warrior, but you aren't the adult here. Not yet anyway."

"But I have to protect you guys—"

"No, you don't," Nicole said softly. "That's not your job."

"Then whose is it? Nicole, you couldn't *do* anything against Cyrus…no offense," I added quickly before she could overreact.

"Fine," she said with a resolute shake of her head. "But that doesn't mean whatever the problems are, we can't work them out together. You should've told me about James sooner." She closed her eyes as I winced. "That's the boy you've been telling me about. The one who burned you. The one who…" She sighed. "Crafty bitch."

"I thought if I told you, you'd just flip out, and you already had enough to worry about. Besides, I had a handle on him."

"So I hear," Nicole said with a smirk.

My face grew bright red, and I fought between embarrassment and despair. "Don't start."

"I will wait until you're recovered from your heartbreak to give you the proper amount of shit for your horrible romantic decision-making."

I wanted to smile, but the reminder of what James had done drew me lower. "I fought so hard not to like him. But he was really good at lying to me."

"Now do you see why I didn't want Gavon around?" Nicole said, taking my hand. "I didn't want to see you get hurt again."

"Gavon and James aren't the same person. Gavon genuinely cares about us—"

"Does he?"

"When I told him that Cyrus…James, I guess, had taken you, he sprang into action. He's been giving you money and honoring your wishes to stay out of my life, and…" Well, if we were being honest… "And also he bailed me out of jail a few months ago."

"I'm sorry, *what?*"

"James and I happened upon a magical library, but apparently, we were trespassing. Gavon got tipped off and got both of us out with a warning." I picked at my hands. "He was really…disappointed in me. Gave me a lecture about Georgetown and my future and…well…" A warning that James was not to be trusted. That he was a bad influence. If only I'd listened instead of falling deeper in love with him.

"Lexie, I swear…" Nicole mumbled into her hands. "You got really lucky."

"I know," I said. "Trust me, I refused any magical mischief after that. I mean…" I swallowed. "Besides the obvious lapse in judgement. But James… Nicole, I swear to you, it was like he really cared about me. He helped me find Marie…" I closed my eyes in a wince. "Yeah, brilliant job, Lexie. Led him right to her."

"And I'm sorry I made you feel like you had to use magic to find her," Nicole said. "I'm just…I'm sorry. Can we start over? Before you run off to college halfway across the country?"

I half-smiled. "I'm only a transport spell away."

Nicole shook her head. "It's not the same, Lexie. I've looked after you for seventeen years. What am I supposed to do now that you're gone?"

I stared at her like I was seeing her for the first time. I'd been too wrapped up in trying to get away from her that I'd never stopped long enough to wonder why Nicole was so clingy.

"I'm not gone yet," I said, softly.

"I just want things to go back to the way they used to be," Nicole said. "When you and I were on the same side. Ever since Jeanie died, you've been pulling away."

"You've been pulling away, too," I said with a frown. "I want to be honest, but I don't want you to overreact every time I mention Gavon. Or magic."

"I'll work on it, but it's going to take some time." Nicole sighed, then smiled. "How about this: First thing in the morning, you and I can go to this stupid bank Gavon's got and withdraw the money so you can pay for Georgetown."

I smiled. "Really?"

"How much do you need?"

"Twenty-five thousand."

Nicole exhaled loudly. "Per *year*?"

"Um…per semester?"

"*Good night*," Nicole wheezed. "Well, if it's what you want, I'll figure out a way to—"

Someone rapped on the door.

I froze and grabbed Nicole's arm. Cyrus wasn't known to knock, but I wasn't taking any chances. Not anymore. "Nicole, I'm going to send you to Marie's. I want you to find Gavon and bring him here as quickly as possible. I can hold him off for a bit —"

"Lexie, I don't—"

"Trust me," I said, steeling myself. "I can handle him."

I gathered magic in my hand and readied myself. Then,

inhaling, I swung open the door and fired.

"*Whoa!*"

The man standing at the door was definitely not Cyrus, and definitely not magical. The oil stains on his blue jumpsuit were clue enough, but the patch on his shirt told me he was a mechanic from the car shop Nicole had been fighting with. I lowered my hand and scanned his face—he was younger than I'd thought, though the wide-eyed terror made him look more innocent than he probably was.

"What…the hell…was that…?" he asked.

"Uh…firecracker?" I squeaked, quickly squashing the magic in my hand.

"Y-you!" Nicole appeared at my shoulder, although she looked much angrier than me or the mechanic. "You have a lot of nerve showing up here."

"I know, and I'm sorry," he stammered. "Look, I have a confession. I've been messing with your car."

Nicole took a step back and blinked. "You—"

"I thought you were really pretty, but I just never got the courage to say anything. So I drove your car back here to ask you if…well…to give you your money back."

He handed her an oil-stained check along with her keys, which Nicole took lightly. She stared at the check then the mechanic, and then back again. "Uh…if you drove my car here, how are you going to get back to your shop?"

"I…uh…" He scratched the back of his head. "I suppose I'll just walk."

"Nicole could drive you home," I offered, smiling as she gave me a frightened look. But I saw the surprise, and a bit of curiosity in her eyes, too. "Go on."

"But he…"

"I mean, it can't hurt to have a conversation with the guy," I said with a shrug. "I think I need to go for a walk anyway."

Nicole shook her head like she'd much rather I stayed, but I figured any guy who was willing to sabotage a car to be able to talk to my sister deserved some privacy.

I walked alone down the street, lost in my own thoughts. There were so many conflicting emotions. Relief that my sisters were safe, but morbid embarrassment that I'd been so completely blindsided. I'd been so careful, so sure of myself. I had overthought everything and still, I'd missed all the warning signs. It just made no sense to me, and yet again, I found myself questioning my own sanity. How could I have felt so strongly about something, only to have it blow up in my face again?

I glanced up at where my ambling had brought me and couldn't believe my eyes. I'd ended up in the park in my old neighborhood, the one where I'd first met Gavon. I hadn't been back here since before Jeanie had died, and seeing the old swing set brought forth a bittersweet nostalgia.

"Rough day?"

I pursed my lips. "When are you going to stop sneaking up on me?"

Gavon walked up beside me. "I announced my presence as magicals do. Perhaps you're the one not paying attention."

"Are you lecturing me again?" James once mentioned how tired he was of Gavon's lectures.

"More like checking up on you." Out of the corner of my

eye, I saw him give me the once over. "You should get Marie to heal you again. Or Nicole should brew more healing potions."

"I can brew my own potions, thank you."

We stood in silence for a moment, and as grateful as I was for Gavon finding my sisters, I couldn't be happy to see him.

"You should have let me kill him."

Gavon put his hands behind his back and stared into the darkness. "I should have killed him seventeen years ago. Please, place the burden where it is due."

"Well, you screwed up and can't, so you should've let me do it."

"Have you killed anyone before?" He finally turned to me, his piercing brown eyes making me uncomfortable. "Have you ever ended a life? It is no laughing matter, and not something you should take lightly."

He'd had this same conversation with James, and James had looked so haunted. Was that conversation a lie, too? "He deserves to die."

"But not by your hand."

"Well can you get on with it?" I snapped. "I'm tired of having to deal with him every few years." But the unspoken truth hung between us. James was the one who'd betrayed me this time. Cyrus might have pushed him, but...he'd confessed to the crime.

"I don't think you'll have to worry about him, or the Guild," Gavon said. "You terrified them, you know. Everyone knew you would have obliterated Cyrus had I not intervened. And you were still standing after. They would be foolish to try again."

"They were foolish already."

"James was foolish," he replied softly, and the bitterness was unmistakable. "I don't know…I have no idea what he was thinking. Or whether he was working with Cyrus, or on his own or…"

"So you had no idea."

"None. In fact, I was under the assumption the two of you were getting along well. He did not roll his eyes in disgust when I asked about you these past few weeks." The ghost of a smile lit his face, but it was tinged by sadness. "I only suppose that was a ruse for my benefit so I wouldn't suspect."

Something ached in the bottom of my chest as loss came roaring over me. This was different than when Jeanie had died. For her, I'd felt gratitude, familial love, and the loss had been one of a limb. A constant presence in my life. But with James, it was like losing a piece of my soul. My love for him was built on what I'd thought was a rock-solid foundation of friendship. I hadn't just lost my boyfriend, I'd lost my best friend. My only friend.

"James will no longer be a problem, but the rest of the Guild…I would prefer to have a more permanent solution." He procured a piece of parchment.

"What's that?" I said, trying not to look interested.

"A distance pact between your clan and my guild," Gavon said.

"M-my clan?" I said, blinking at him. "But you know I'm not—"

"You and your sisters," Gavon clarified. "Now I thought I'd leave it up to you to decide the distance. Does five miles sound like enough?"

"I don't understand," I said.

"We're signing a distance pact," Gavon said, looking up at me. "I assume you remember what a pact is? I'm afraid that my compendium on the subject seemed to have walked away earlier in the year."

I swallowed nervously and was reminded, painfully, of James. "You can have the book back."

"Oh, I don't need it." Gavon smiled. "I have too many books anyway."

"This pact, once I sign it…everyone in your Guild will be kept a minimum of five miles away from me and my family?" I asked.

Gavon nodded, transforming the parchment into a golden vortex. He procured a small knife out of thin air and pricked his index finger, a small drop of blood falling into the center.

I watched it glow and procured my own knife, looking at the vortex for a moment.

"Everyone in your Guild?" I asked, looking up at him with wide eyes.

He nodded.

"Forever?"

He nodded again, smiling slightly.

I clenched my jaw and pricked my finger, watching the blood ooze out. Closing my eyes, I reached out my finger, letting the blood drop. This was the last moment I might ever see Gavon, but I couldn't look at him. Couldn't bear to know that I'd permanently severed any relationship with the man who—

"I didn't take you for much of a hemophobe."

Twenty-Eight

My eyes shot open. Gavon was still standing in front of me, although his expression was much brighter than it had been.

"You're still here?" I said, more breathlessly than I meant to.

Gavon smiled at me warmly. "Yes, you see....there was a little fine print in the pact."

My eyes widened, terrified that I'd, yet again, just made a grave mistake.

"The pact only applies to anyone with the intent to harm members of your Clan," Gavon said. "I tossed that in there, with the rationale that if we ever wanted to renegotiate, we would need to be able to be in the same room. Standard practice in treaties, you know."

I opened and closed my mouth, processing the wording of the pact. I looked up at him, brow furrowed. "So...you're not included?"

"Doesn't appear as though I have any intent to harm you," Gavon said, looking around the quiet park with a smug smile on his face.

My mouth fell open. "B…but you…"

He procured the very document we'd just agreed to, and I snatched it from his hand. There it was, the fine print I'd missed. He was telling the truth. A rush of relief poured through me, as well as a thousand questions. There was so much I needed to talk with him about—almost three years' worth of questions that needed answers.

"Why did you make the deal with Nicole?" I blurted, before I could stop myself.

"Deal?" Gavon said, thinking for a moment.

"You gave her money and agreed to keep your distance."

"Ah, that deal." Gavon looked at the ground. "You found out about that, did you?"

I nodded.

"Well, in life, there are choices we must weigh," Gavon said. "You girls needed help, and Irene wasn't going to give it. I couldn't, in good conscience, let Nicole take on the burden by herself. So I offered my assistance, no strings attached." He chuckled, although there was sadness in it. "As you might expect, she was reluctant to accept it. But she made it very clear that she wanted me out of your lives. So I told her if she let me pay her a sum every month to cover living expenses, I wouldn't as much as check on your grades. I kept my word, up until this year. James was more than I could handle, and I needed to put him somewhere he could be humbled. The best place for that was with you, at your school." His eyes grew sad. "I thought he'd changed."

So had I. But I didn't want to think about James anymore.

"I'm sorry, for what it's worth," Gavon said. "I never meant for…well, I'm sorry. For a lot of things. The last thing I ever wanted was to hurt you, Alexis."

"Why do you call me that?" I asked quietly. "Did you name me after your mother?"

Gavon actually smiled. "Your mother *hated* the name Alexandra. Alexis was our compromise. She fought so hard for it, it feels wrong to call you anything else."

"But why did you name me after your mom?" I said, looking at my hands.

"A few reasons," Gavon said, looking away. "Some of which aren't the most reasonable. It was a little revenge against Cyrus for being the Warrior my mother trained. He might've had her attention, but I was able to pass her magic on to you."

"Cyrus killed her after they wanted you to be Guildmaster, didn't he?" I said, and Gavon nodded. "But…I don't understand why you told them about me? If you had this whole other life that you'd kept a secret from them, what prompted you to suddenly screw everything up?"

"Another selfish, ill-thought out decision," Gavon said with a shake of his head. "I wanted to tell my mother about you. I'd wanted her to keep it in confidence, mother-to-son, but all she saw was the potential benefit to the Guild. And I couldn't stop her from spreading the word and setting off the chain of events that led to so much devastation."

I frowned. "But why me? You didn't want to tell her about Nicole and Marie?"

"Of course I did," Gavon said quickly. "But she wouldn't have understood. She still held the same prejudices against healers and potion-makers as everyone else in New Salem. It would have killed me for her to know about them and not...not love them." He sighed. "I supposed I should've known better than to tell her anything. But I have an unfortunate habit of thinking the best of people."

So that's where I get it from, I thought sadly.

"She told them everything. And when they began talking about making me Guildmaster—after all, I'd been living in this world for twelve years—"

"*Twelve*!" I said with a gasp. "But Nicole was only four when —?"

Gavon chuckled. "Mora and I wanted to have a few adventures before we settled down."

I made a face, that horrific magical memory returning with a vengeance. I needed to change the subject. "So if your mom had prejudices, how come you didn't when it came to Nicole and Marie?"

"I did," Gavon said pensively. "But I guess I knew what it was to be the other. Cyrus had received all the accolades when we were younger, and I'll admit it made me jealous at times— especially to see him with Alexandra. But it also taught me humility and empathy. Your mother, too, helped open my eyes to how much can be accomplished without magic. Her family has a very Puritan ideology about magic—it should only be used when all other options are exhausted." He chuckled. "Besides, my entire worldview changed the first moment I saw Nicole. I knew I had to do everything in my power to keep her safe, to help her make the most of her gift. And in learning about potion-makers, I realized they had incredible powers. If she'd let herself, Nicole could do more than even me."

A smile formed on my face. "She's so damned stubborn."

"A trait I found hopelessly endearing in your mother," Gavon said. "My biggest regret is that you never got to meet her. It's incredible how much you favor her in so many ways."

I swallowed. "I sometimes get magical memories about her. Well, you and her…fighting…sparring, I mean."

Gavon's eyes widened. "You mentioned something, but I didn't understand… Are you telling me you remember your mother and I sparring?"

"Yes," I said, unable to look at him. "And I have a pretty vivid recollection of the night she died, too."

Gavon sucked in a breath and for the first time, I saw pure regret on his face. "Oh, Alexis. That's what you meant when… Oh, I'm so sorry."

"At first, it really bothered me," I said, returning my gaze to my hands. "But now, it's like…it's kind of like my own memories of her. I got to hear her voice, to feel what she felt. And that's why I was so good at sparring. It wasn't an innate thing, it was because you trained her using my magic."

He nodded pensively. "I knew your mother had your magic when she was pregnant, but I had no idea you retained a magical memory of it. The same thing happened with your sisters, too. I wonder if they remember any of it."

"I think I'm the only one. I mean, I don't think anything traumatic happened to them." I stared at the space in front of me. "Why didn't you save her?"

"I didn't know," he replied. "I had no idea Cyrus had even found the tear, let alone crossed it. I was stupid for not taking more precautions. I returned home to find it in shambles. I found your mother at the hospital but by the time I got there she was..." He released a shaky breath. "I didn't even get to say goodbye."

The younger man from my magical memory returned—the one who'd flirted and smiled and loved my mother. There was no denying it. Gavon had been as crazy about my mother as she'd been about him. He'd carried the guilt of her death with him all this time.

"I wanted to end my life," he said, shocking me. "I couldn't really see a reason I should continue. My girls had lost their mother because I was too stupid to realize..."

He closed his eyes and the pause stretched between us, filled with almost two decades of self-hate and regret.

He turned to me, and a ghost of a smile appeared on his face. "And then, something very interesting happened. A nurse saw me in the room with Mora. I remembered nothing of what she said until I found myself holding this tiny little girl with a head full of brown hair. My Alexis."

A tear slipped down my face as he looked at me.

"I couldn't believe you'd survived, but there you were. Healthy and pink and perfect. Seven pounds, twelve ounces. Already powerful, and just so..." He brushed a strand of hair out of my face. "It was like the cloud lifted, and I knew what I had to do. To protect my girls, I would take over the Guildmaster, but only until I could close the tear."

I furrowed my brow. "But...it's still open?"

"It has been excessively difficult to find information on something so unique," Gavon said sadly. "I've looked in hundreds of libraries and read thousands of books. Luckily for me, the Guild had no interest in Nicole or Marie, and I was able to delay them for fifteen years by promising you would be our next Guildmaster. Irene helped me a great deal when she placed you under the containment spell until your fifteenth birthday. Since you were bound by their rules, I told the Guild I couldn't touch you."

I eyed him. "But…that wasn't exactly true, was it?"

He shrugged, a little mischievous glint in his eye. "They're rather unstudied in the particulars of magical law." His face darkened. "But in order to keep Cyrus from causing trouble, I still had to keep my distance. I had to let my girls grow up thinking I was a monster." He shook his head. "Marie, of course, never believed it. But I fear my relationship with my Nicole is gone forever."

"So why show up on my fifteenth birthday?" I asked.

"I knew Jeanie would be telling you about magic, and I wanted to be nearby just…" He looked at his hands. "I liked to check in on you three. Talk to your teachers, make sure things were going well. I'd slip them a memory charm afterward so they wouldn't remember. But when I saw the look on your face, I couldn't not help you." His gaze lifted to the skies. "And, if I'm being completely honest, I just wanted to have a conversation with my little girl. Even if she couldn't know she was talking to her father."

A dull ache echoed in my chest.

"I didn't mean for us to become so close. It was supposed to be one conversation and set you on your way. Then you showed up the second night, and the third. And you told me about

Irene's disinterest." His gaze hardened. "I had wanted her to take over your training, but—"

"But she's afraid of me," I said. "She thinks I'm going to take over her clan or something."

"She's always been a proud woman," Gavon said. "But if she'd seen past her own pride and helped you, I would've been able to leave you alone, and none of this would've happened."

I swallowed. "So you never would've told me?"

"I…" He sighed. "Maybe once I'd closed the tear. Once the threat of danger was gone. But Cyrus had been looking for any weakness, and just talking with you had put me on thin ice as it was." He sighed. "And when you collapsed and I had to bring you to New Salem…that was when he found out we'd been sparring. It gave him the opening to inform the rest of the Council, and well, the rest is history."

I remembered the warm day Cyrus had first appeared outside. He'd certainly looked like his birthday had come early.

"You have to know, I never intended for you to learn to fight, to be introduced or inducted into the Guild. James was…" Gavon sighed. "James was supposed to be the answer."

James was supposed to be a lot of things. My friend, possibly my boyfriend. Definitely my first love, my first kiss, my first… well, I doubted I'd tell Gavon that James and I had slept together. There were just some things a girl didn't discuss with her…paternal figure.

"But now we have a pact, and the Guild won't be bothering you anymore," Gavon said, producing a large envelope. "And I don't want you to suffer because of decisions I made ever again. So here."

I took the envelope from him and cautiously opened it. Before I even pulled out the first document, I saw the Georgetown seal. "Gavon, I can't afford Georgetown."

"I can," Gavon said with a bright smile. "Your tuition bill has been prepaid for the next four years."

I stared at him, because he couldn't possibly have said what I thought he said. "What?"

"I've paid your tuition in full," he repeated. "As well as your housing and food costs. I've also arranged for a small monthly stipend to be deposited into a bank account for books and other incidentals. Just please try to not spend it all at once, okay?"

A nervous laughter bubbled out of my lips. "You're fucking kidding me."

He cast a stern glance in my direction, but I didn't even care. *"You paid for my college?"*

"Yes," Gavon said with a small laugh. "As well as—"

"Oh my God," I whimpered, collapsing into my hands. My emotions were fried, and I had nothing left to keep them at bay. So relief, glorious, beautiful relief and excitement, and happiness and gratitude, and a thousand other emotions rocked my body. I sobbed into my hands for a few moments, unable to believe that after so much had gone wrong, something could go so damned right.

"I'm glad you're pleased," Gavon said, patting my back.

I lifted my head, furiously wiping away tears. "How did you…what did you… What do you want in return?"

"As and Bs?"

I sniffed. "I'm serious. This is so much money…"

"But you're worth it," Gavon said. "All I've ever wanted is

for you and your sisters to be happy. And for you to know how proud I am of all you've accomplished—magically and otherwise." He paused for a moment. "To know how much I love you."

The remnants of my emotional barriers blew away and bubbled forth in whimpered sobs. "You've never...you've never..."

"Oh, Lexie," he said, pulling me against him in the kind of embrace I'd wanted since I met him. He pressed his cheek to my forehead and let me cry like a little child into his chest. "I've loved you since before you were born, and I'll love you even after I die."

I quieted my hysterics and pushed away from him. "And Marie and Nicole?"

"Of course," he said with a shake of his head. "Even though Nicole refuses to speak to me and Marie is a pain in the ass." He brushed a tear off my cheek. "I'm sorry I didn't know she wasn't with you, or I would have found her sooner."

I smiled. "Why didn't you tell me where she was?"

"She didn't want to be found," Gavon replied with a sad shake of his head. "She was very angry with me, and with you and Nicole. I had to make a deal with her that if you sought her out, she'd listen."

"And in return, she got that swanky apartment?" I asked with a laugh.

"I think she genuinely wanted to make amends, but her pride wouldn't let her," Gavon said with a wink. "So I gave her an easy excuse."

"I don't care how it happened, I'm just glad she and Nicole

and me are all on speaking terms again." A nasty thought popped into my head. "You aren't going to stop paying for Nicole's apartment are you? Give her the money you gave me. I don't need to go to Georgetown—"

"I've got plenty of money to go around. Though I know I can trust you not to spend it all at once. With Marie, we've had to work out a stipend system." He chuckled. "And with Nicole, she'll receive the money whether she wants to or not."

I look down at the papers again. "She doesn't want me to leave, you know. I think she's going to be really lonely."

"You're just a transport away," Gavon said, echoing what I'd said to Nicole earlier. "And besides, if that boy I saw her with is any indication, she might be a little more amenable to some privacy."

I gasped. "*Gavon!* What do you know about that?"

"A few weeks ago, I became aware that Nicole was spending a *lot* of money at a mechanic and I popped in to have a chat with the man. When I realized there was nothing truly wrong with her car, I might've suggested that he return the money or suffer consequences." He cleared his throat. "I had no idea it was some elaborate ploy to ask for her number."

"Well, please stay out of it," I said, wiping the rest of my tears from my face. "She's skittish enough as it is."

"I plan to," Gavon said, growing somber. "Now more than ever, it's important that I find a way to close the tear. That's the only way this ends without any more bloodshed."

"Didn't creating it take a hundred magicals?" I asked.

"To create the world, and leave enough magic in there to sustain itself, yes. But closing the tear should be much less taxing. I just haven't been able to figure out the magic for it."

"I could help you," I offered. "I mean, help you look?"

"I don't want to—"

"Gavon, I want that tear closed," I said. Then, hesitantly, I added, "But I'd like you on this side of it when it happens."

He tilted his head. "I don't deserve to be in your life."

"I want you in my life. And I want to help."

He stared at me for a long time before nodding. "As long as it doesn't interfere with your schoolwork."

"It won't," I said with a grin. "I've got all summer, too."

"Fine, Alexis—"

"But you'll call me Lexie," I said, and then, heart pounding, I added, "And I'll call you Dad. And no more secrets between us. Deal?"

His breath hitched, and he stared wordlessly at me for a moment. Then, clearing his throat, he smiled. "Deal. No magical pact required."

To be Continued...

In the next book, go back to the beginning

dawn &devilry

Available now

Acknowledgements

As always, thanks first go to you, the reader, for picking up my magical book and reading it to the end. If you've got a spare minute, I'd appreciate it if you'd leave a review on Amazon, Goodreads, or your favorite eBook store. Even a short review is incredibly helpful to an indie author like me!

Thanks go to my bevy of brilliant beta readers. Brooke, Emilys L. and G, and Kristin.

Dani, as usual, you're the best. One of these days, I might write a manuscript with no typos. But until that day comes, I'm so grateful for your careful eye.

Thanks also go to my typo checkers, Lisa, MC, Amanda, and Mom.

I'd also like to thank the members of the S. Usher Evans Street team: Chelsea, MC, and Emily, for being the mod-god amongst mortals, as well as superstars Elizabeth, Alan, Julie R., Rebecca S., Theresa, and everyone else who helps spread the good Sush word.

DEMON SPRING TRILOGY

Three years ago, Jack Grenard's wife was brutally murdered by demons. Now, along with his partner Cam Macarro, he's trying to rebuild his life in Atlanta. But on a routine investigation, they find a demon who saves instead of kills. They must discover who she is before Demon Spring, the quadrennial breach between the human world and demon realm, when all hell—literally—breaks loose.

The Demon Spring Trilogy is the first urban fantasy from S. Usher Evans and will be released in 2018 in eBook, Paperback, and Hardcover.

The Razia Series

Lyssa Peate is living a double life as a planet discovering scientist and a space pirate bounty hunter. Unfortunately, neither life is going very well. She's the least wanted pirate in the universe and her brand new scientist intern is spying on her. Things get worse when her intern is mistaken for her hostage by the Universal Police.

The Razia Series is a four-book space opera series and is available now for eBook, Audiobook. Paperback, and Hardcover.

THE MADION WAR TRILOGY

He's a prince, she's a pilot, they're at war. But when they are marooned on a deserted island hundreds of miles from either nation, they must set aside their differences and work together if they want to survive.

The Madion War Trilogy is a fantasy romance available now in eBook, Paperback, and Hardcover.

empath

Lauren Dailey is in break-up hell, but if you ask her she's doing just great. She hears a mysterious voice promising an easy escape from her problems and finds herself in a brand new world where she has the power to feel what others are feeling. Just one problem—there's a dragon in the mountains that happens to eat Empaths. And it might be the source of the mysterious voice tempting her deeper into her own darkness.

Empath is a stand-alone fantasy that is available now in eBook, Paperback, and Hardcover.

About the Author

S. Usher Evans was born and raised in Pensacola, Florida. After a decade of fighting bureaucratic battles as an IT consultant in Washington, DC, she suffered a massive quarter-life-crisis. She decided fighting dragons was more fun than writing policy, so she moved back to Pensacola to write books full-time. She currently resides with her two dogs, Zoe and Mr. Biscuit, and frequently can be found plotting on the beach.

Visit S. Usher Evans online at:
http://www.susherevans.com/

Twitter: www.twitter.com/susherevans
Facebook: www.facebook.com/susherevans
Instagram: www.instagram.com/susherevans

9 781945 438097